To Justin Richards

CHAPTER ONE

'You're doing it again, Professor.'

The Doctor didn't answer. He hadn't answered all morning, though Ace had asked him at least half a dozen times to please *stop it*. He wasn't being rude. Not exactly. He was just in one of those moods, well, states of mind, really, where he didn't know she was there. Probably didn't know *he* was there, she thought, watching him at the TARDIS control board. Had he been staring at that same screen all morning? She'd sneaked up behind him to have a look over his shoulder at what was so fascinating, but all she'd seen was a jumble of numbers.

It wouldn't be so bad if he'd just *stop humming*.

'Professor!'

No reaction.

'You know what they used to call that? On Earth? A tune stuck in your head was called a "soundworm". Nasty, huh?'

The Doctor turned slowly towards her and blinked. 'Hello, Ace. Have you been there long?'

'Only all morning.'

'Is it still morning?'

Ace wasn't going to get drawn into another fruitless discussion about what time of day it was in the floating-in-the-timeless-vortex TARDIS. 'And you've been humming.'

'Humming?' He looked more surprised than the information warranted. 'Humming what?'

'I don't know. I didn't recognise it.'

He paused delicately, trying to think, she knew, of a polite way

5

to point out that her knowledge of music was limited to about ten years in the late twentieth century.

'It wasn't even a tune,' she protested.

'Can you hum it back to me?'

'No, 'cos it wasn't a tune. It was just sort of a drone, only with bits of melody in.'

'Hm.' He lost interest and turned back to the control board.

'What's going on, then?'

'Oh nothing, really. The TARDIS is acting up a bit.'

'Oh?' Ace said hopefully. She knew she ought to be worried, but the TARDIS's acting up generally meant they were in for an interesting trip, not some visit to a green-skied planet containing nothing but weird-looking orange groves. Or that naff marmot planet. Of course the Doctor had defended the marmots. Said they were "humble".

'What's it doing then?'

'Well, that's what I've been trying to work out. She's been veering subtly off course, and I've been stopping her to see what she does next. We go on as usual for a bit, then she starts veering again.'

'Same direction?'

'Not exactly. That's what's odd. I think,' he mused, 'I'll simply let her veer.'

'We were just *here*, Professor.'

'Not exactly,' said the Doctor. 'We *will* be here.'

'When?'

He checked his pocket watch. 'Eighteen minutes.'

Ace shifted from foot to foot, looking around. She and the Doctor were in an alley ending at a pair of sagging, chained-together junkyard gates bearing the weathered letters "I M Forman". The Doctor went to the gates and peered between them.

'Same as it ever was,' she said. 'If we're coming in 18 minutes, that means that there are already Daleks here. So we ought to go.'

He remained at the gate. 'There aren't any Daleks *here*,' he said. 'In this alley at this moment, and there won't be for a few hours.'

'Yeah, well, we don't want to meet ourselves, do we? Doesn't that mess everything up?' He didn't answer. 'What's so interesting in there, anyway?'

'Nothing.' The Doctor sighed and stepped back. 'I'm just indulging in nostalgia.'

'For *this* place?'

Again, he didn't answer. He was reading the letters on the gates, frowning. He read them again. 'That's not right.' he muttered. 'Ace – was the name like this before?'

She shrugged. 'I suppose so.'

'Well, try to remember. It's important.'

She slouched over to join him. 'Why?'

'Try, please.'

Boring. Ace ran her eyes over the gates. 'Yeah, it was like this.'

'Not "Foreman", with an "e".'

'No. I remember 'cos when I looked at it, it was like it read "I am for man".'

He tapped his chin with the handle of his umbrella. 'That's wrong.'

'No, it isn't. I remember –'

'Not "you're wrong". The sign's wrong.'

He wasn't making sense. Again. 'You mean it's not the right name? How could –'

'It's the right name, but it's spelled incorrectly.'

'How do you know?'

'I know,' the Doctor said softly. His eyes remained on the letters. 'Ace, did you ever hear the saying that all the things you do in life are a mirror – that when you look at them, you see your face.'

She smiled. 'You must be well beautiful then – all the times you've helped people. Not to mention saving the universe.'

He gazed for another minute at the sign, then he spun and took Ace's arm. 'Come along, then. Back to the TARDIS. As you said, we mustn't run into ourselves.'

* * *

A man lay unconscious in a gutter. Though it was only early autumn, the night was cold, and the fog occasionally thickened into hard little bits of ice. The man was about forty. He had somehow retained his hat, and still clutched a fine malacca cane. A half a block away, drinkers staggered in and out of a noisy, well-lit tavern. But the streetlamp near the man had burned low and he lay unnoticed. Being in either a stupor or a coma, he didn't hear a groaning, grinding two-note bray, like a police siren gone hoarse, nor did he see a small man of indeterminate age, with sharp blue eyes and dark hair gone to tuft, step out of an alley, followed by a teenaged girl in a leather jacket. The girl started forward.

'No, Ace!' The Doctor held his arm in front of her.

'But he's sick.'

'He's dying,' said the Doctor. 'Stay here.'

'You mean this has already happened? Why'd you bring us to something terrible that we can't do anything about?'

'I didn't. The TARDIS did.'

She looked helplessly at the man. 'How do you know this has happened before? You can't be sure. We could get help and –'

'That's Edgar Allan Poe,' said the Doctor. 'And this is 3 October, 1849. We're in Baltimore on election night, and, as was the practice, a group of poll-workers have got Poe drunk and dragged him from voting place to voting place in an effort to highjack the election. In a little while Joseph Walker, a printer, will find him, and he'll be taken to the Washington Medical College hospital. He'll die three days from now, after calling one name over and over.'

'What name?'

'"Reynolds".'

'Who –'

'Ssh.' He pushed her gently back into the shadows. 'Here comes Mr Walker.'

A man in a frock coat and well-brushed top hat came along the pavement. At the sight of the figure in the gutter, he slowed down, looking concerned, then hurried to him. He checked the man's pulse, wiped his damp face. 'Good God, sir! What – You there!' he cried to a young black boy holding a horse outside the tavern. 'Fetch your master! This man is dying!'

'Master!' said Ace in disgust.

'Yes, Ace. Nineteenth-century America, remember? The Civil War isn't for another fifteen –'

The Doctor stopped. Suddenly, smoothly, the scene in front of them had shifted, as if a wave swelled beneath its surface, and now Poe was once more alone in the gutter.

The Doctor said something terse in a language Ace didn't understand. She knew why. He never liked it when time went wobbly.

'Is it going to happen again?' she whispered. 'Are we in a loop?'

'Look.' He pointed. 'The boy holding the horse is gone.'

'Then things are different. But –'

'Wait,' he ordered.

They waited. Ace shivered slightly. It was the damp, she thought, seeping through her jacket. Leather wasn't really that good against the cold. What the man in the gutter was feeling she didn't want to imagine. At least he was unconscious. Or was he this time? She peered across the cobblestoned street but couldn't tell.

'Professor, we can't just –'

'Yes,' he said. 'We can.'

Ace knew he was right, she always trusted him to be right, but she was still upset. She walked away from him a few steps down the alley. It was filthy and stank like a loo, so she stopped and went back. The Doctor hadn't moved. He was watching Poe as if he were afraid that looking away would make him vanish. She shoved her hands deep in her jacket pockets and hunched her shoulders. She didn't think she could stand here and watch Poe dying over and over and over. She tried to recall what of his she'd read in school; he was one of the few writers she'd enjoyed. Oh yeah, 'The Tell-Tale Heart'. And that well weird one about the house. And the raven poem: 'Once upon a midnight dreary'. Like it was now.

The Doctor's head turned abruptly, like a dog's at a scent. Ace looked over his shoulder. A drunk had stumbled from the tavern and was reeling happily down the street. He'll see Poe, she thought with relief, and the next minute the drunk tripped over him. After some cursing and confusion, he realised what he was lying on and, considerably sobered, jumped up and raced back to the tavern for help. Ace was momentarily elated, then her heart sank.

'That's not how it happened, is it?' she whispered. 'Not how it's ever going to happen.'

'Except that now it has happened,' said the Doctor. He sounded worried.

'Maybe it's one of those blips you've told me about that are so small they don't mess up time.'

'Poe isn't a small blip. He was a writer of enormous influence. If he'd lived and written another twenty years, the whole history of American and European literature would be different.'

'But it's not anything really important, like a vaccine or something. It's just books.'

'Literature is an integral part of Earth culture,' he said tightly. 'I'm not going to argue with you now about the place of art in –'

He cut off. Once again, the wave swelled the surface of reality, and Poe was back in the gutter.

'I don't like watching this,' Ace said in a small voice.

'I know,' he said gently. 'Just once more.'

But she didn't look this time. She stared down at her feet. A thin, watery crust of ice was forming on her shoes and she felt droplets melting lightly in her hair. Why hadn't the Doctor brought his silly umbrella? She stomped, knocking the ice away. 'Is it getting colder?'

'Perhaps,' he said. 'As the night goes on.' He leaned forward, squinting. Ace couldn't see anything different. As far as she

could tell Poe hadn't moved. At all. She took a deep breath.
'Professor –'

But he was already hurrying across the street. Ace glanced
nervously toward the tavern, but there was no one outside to
see them. She ran to join him. The Doctor knelt on the dirty, wet
cobblestones, a hand on Poe's wrist and another pressed to his
forehead.

'Is he –'

'Yes. He's dead.' The Doctor got to his feet and looked down
at the body. Ace did too. Poe had a high forehead and a dark
moustache. Even aside from his death pallor, he didn't look as if
he'd been healthy for a long, long time. '"The fever called living
is conquered at last",' the Doctor said softly.

'But this isn't the way it happened either,' she said. 'Not really.
Only...'

'Yes,' said the Doctor.

'...only now it has.'

'Yes.'

'But then... which one is real?'

'Exactly the problem,' said the Doctor.

'Who was Reynolds?' said Ace. She was sitting curled up in
an armchair, warming her hands with the cup of hot chocolate
the Doctor had brought her. The two of them were in one
of the many TARDIS rooms she had never seen (and for all she
knew had never existed until a few minutes ago), a small cosy
den with a fireplace. The Doctor had finished his chocolate
and slumped back, the chair nearly engulfing him. Ace supposed
it had originally been a seat for one of his earlier, larger selves.
He was watching the fire, which bronzed his odd little face
and made his eyes glitter. Another line from Poe had come into
Ace's mind: *And his eyes have all the seeming/Of a demon's
that is dreaming*. She must have really liked that poem, she
thought; she remembered parts of it as well as song lyrics. 'Poe's
best friend or something?'

'No. Reynolds was the author of a book on polar exploration that Poe used as research for his story "The Narrative of A. Gordon Pym".'

'What did he die of exactly?' She was still disturbed and saddened by the wretched figure in the gutter.

'No one is quite sure. Probably exposure – he was frail at the end. Some historians thought it might have been rabies.'

'You could find out, couldn't you?'

'Well yes, if I wanted to spend months following Poe around waiting to see whether a rat bit him.' He smiled his sudden, surprising, crooked smile at her and she felt better.

Before she went to bed, she found a collection of Poe's stories in the library (and, of course, though the library was enormous and chaotic, she located the book she wanted immediately) and read 'A. Gordon Pym'. It was heavy going, not nearly as good as his scary stuff, and racist too, and she started to skip ahead and finally just turned to the end, which she had to admit was freaky:

And now we rushed into the embraces of the cataract, where a chasm threw itself open to receive us. But there arose in our pathway a shrouded human figure, very far larger in its proportions than any dweller among men. And the hue of the skin of the figure was of the perfect whiteness of the snow.

Something out of a right nightmare, she thought, and sure enough, she dreamed about the figure, but in such a deep sleep that when she woke the next morning she had forgotten it.

Once he was certain Ace was asleep, the Doctor returned to the console room. Sure enough, the TARDIS had landed again. The viewing screen showed a barren icy landscape. The Doctor sighed. For a moment he hesitated, then he threw the door lever and stepped outside. After crunching a few yards across the ice, he looked back at his ship, apparently, as always, a metropolitan police call box circa 1963. He'd seen it in many stranger places, but never looking quite so dramatic, its dark blue exterior the only colour in the vast bleakness.

An ice storm was raging; the Doctor held onto his hat. He walked on for a bit, then stopped when he saw the tent. He was neither worried about being seen nor happy about what he was going to see. He waited. In just a little while, a muffled-up man emerged from the tent and started walking, weakly but purposefully, into the storm. The Doctor quietly followed. Soon the man fell to his knees. He crawled forward a few steps and fell over. The Doctor watched, but he never moved again.

'You may be some time, Captain Oates,' the Doctor said softly. 'Or perhaps not. No,' he murmured as the icy waste swelled and snapped back, 'perhaps not.'

The man still lay as he had fallen. He didn't move. But in the distance there was a shout, 'Oates! Oates! You can't do this, old man!' Two muffled figures were staggering towards the fallen man. The Doctor watched as, incredibly, they managed to lift and drag him back to the tent.

Oates would die soon, of course, as they all would. But not alone and in the frozen cold. A happy ending of sorts. Just not the right one.

Patrick Unwin helped himself to a Scotch from Brett's drinks cabinet then sat down in a Chippendale armchair and looked around the room. He wanted to find it obscenely, vulgarly rich, but Brett – or probably, he thought snidely, Brett's late father – had excellent taste. That was a Stubbs on the oak-panelled walls; he'd checked earlier. And next to it a minor Rembrandt. Probably a fake by one of Rembrandt's pupils – a lot of them were. And frankly, the El Greco was a bit... lurid. He was overrated, El Greco.

Brett came calmly into the room. Unwin watched him enviously. Brett was always calm. Sometimes Unwin hated him for that. But then, there were so many things to hate about Brett. First on the list being the fact that he didn't appreciate Unwin's genius, didn't realise that all of this was *owing* to Unwin, not to Brett, who couldn't even handle simple logarithms.

'Why so jumpy, young Pat?'

That was another thing Unwin resented. Brett was hardly three years his senior. But he held his tongue.

'It's your theory, after all,' Brett continued dryly. 'You should have perfect confidence.'

'Something can always go wrong,' Unwin muttered.

'Well, that's the sort of thing we're going to fix, isn't it?' Brett smiled, as he always did, at nothing in particular, as if his facial muscles had just decided to twitch that way. It was more like a spasm than a smile. 'You certainly have the means, what with all that fancy equipment I bought for you.'

'Well, you have the money,' Unwin said ungraciously.

'And all honestly inherited by the sweat of my brow.' Brett said casually. He had an aristocratic languor as well as an aristocrat's natural sense of power and entitlement, though Unwin knew his great-great-grandfather had made his money in commercial boilers. Still, he looked the part, with his clean-cut features and high, arrogant forehead. Even his rather small eyes, a disagreeable burnt coffee colour, couldn't ruin the effect. Unwin himself was slender, almost weakly so, with thin lips and thinner hair.

Well, let him pose and condescend, Unwin thought resentfully. He couldn't have done it without me! *I'm* the brilliant one. In a cold little hollow of his heart some other truth quivered, but he didn't want to think about that. So they had accepted a little outside help. So what? Unwin's was still the primary work, the *important* work. And it had all been his idea to begin with, the stunning and revolutionary idea that randomness *could be eliminated*. That was why computers were ultimately superior. None of that science-fiction silliness about AI. They were superior because they were *incapable* of true randomness.

'Have another drink, young Pat,' said Brett. 'Nothing to worry about.' And he smiled.

In the console room the Doctor watched as, on the viewing screen, Vesuvius erupted and its lethal ash descended to destroy

Pompeii. Then, for half an hour, he watched the mountain shudder, releasing sporadic spurts of lava. The scene shimmered, and once again the volcano erupted, but mildly. There was little ash. Two or three streams of brilliant lava flowed down at such a leisurely pace that the city's populace were able to take to their boats and evacuate.

The Doctor turned off the screen. He didn't need to see any more.

He made a cup of tea, then took it to the console room and sat in the room's one armchair. But he didn't drink, only rested the saucer on his leg and stared absently ahead of him, thinking.

After a while, tea still untouched, he left the cup on the floor and went to the console. He set the controls and waited while the TARDIS groaned and wheezed – like a car with a motor on its last legs, he thought, though of course the comparison wasn't really apt. When the last groan had faded, he opened the viewscreen. It showed the same London alley he and Ace had just visited – though clearly, from the condition of the buildings on either side, some years earlier than they had been there. He read the name on the gates:

I M FOREMAN

The Doctor made his way through the TARDIS corridors to a small room walled with glass charts. A computer sat between two of them, and he fiddled around on this for about half an hour before pressing a button and turning to look at the charts. Each showed a green line bisecting its illuminated grid: one climbed steeply in a straight line, several were parabolas of varying curvature, and one had a pattern on it that a human being, though able to take it in through the eye, could not have processed into an image. He fed the coordinates of each graph into the computer, pressed a few lighted areas on the control panel and studied the equations that came up on the screen. He ran these through a series of functions, then pressed another button.

The charts on one wall shifted configuration and became a set of monitors showing several views of a shabby London street crowded mostly with immigrants – Africans, newly arrived Pakistanis, a few Koreans – and some down-at-heels natives. The Doctor zoomed in on one of these: a slight, intense young man in a threadbare jacket and scarf, hurrying through the cold.

The Doctor frowned, checked the numbers and ran them again. The images on the screen remained the same. He enlarged the view of the man's face: bony, dark-eyed, wire-rim glasses. In need of a haircut. The Doctor folded his arms and studied this unlikely looking centre of the time disruptions, and wondered what to do.

CHAPTER TWO

When Ethan Amberglass walked into his flat and found an odd little man sitting there, he didn't think anything of it; he presumed he was hallucinating again. The medication had really worn out quickly this time; probably he was on his way to another breakdown. Nothing to be done. He crossed to the linoleum-topped table – which, when new and bright yellow, had graced some long-gone kitchen – and turned on the computer to check his email. It was all from the office. When he had deleted most of it and stood up to go to the kitchen, the man was still there, hands folded on the red handle of an umbrella, watching him with bright blue eyes. He wore a loosely cut, cream-coloured suit of lightweight wool and a handsome burgundy waistcoat, but the elegant effect was spoiled by his small-brimmed flat hat and the fact that the umbrella handle was shaped like a question mark.

Ethan saw that he'd hallucinated another figure as well – a sturdy, handsome girl in her late teens. That was a pleasant change. He wasn't crazy about her shoes, though.

In the kitchen, he went over his limited stock of food. Health Puffs? No, no sugar rush. Canned macaroni and cheese? Hm. Perhaps. Marmite? No. He checked the refrigerator. Success. Three slices of leftover pizza. He tried to remember how long they'd been in there. Well, what difference did it make – it was basically just cheese and bread. To be on the safe side, he peeled off the pepperoni and threw it in the bin.

Pizza in the oven, he returned to what in someone else's flat might have been called the sitting room. Aside from the computer table, it contained a piano nearly buried beneath journals and papers. To Ethan's disappointment, the little man was still there, sitting quietly in the same pose. The girl was still there too, looking bored and twisting a strand of her long ponytail. If he was going to hallucinate a woman, he would have thought he could manage someone less disdainful.

The man raised his hat and gave him a gap-toothed, sweetly childlike smile. 'Hello. I'm the Doctor, and this is my friend Ace.'

So they could talk. Ethan preferred it when they couldn't, but he was stuck with the situation. He said, 'Ace isn't a proper name.'

'It's *my* name,' the girl said warningly.

From exactly what part of his unconscious had these people come? And how could he get rid of them? He went to the kitchen and downed a couple of pills. That should do it. They'd vanish shortly.

'Don't you want to know why we're here?' Ace had come to the kitchen door.

'I know why you're here,' he said, irritably pushing past her.

'Yeah? Why then?'

'I made you up.'

'Ah,' said the man, the Doctor. 'That explains it.'

'What are you talking about?' Ethan asked. This was really beginning to get on his nerves.

'There's something burning in the oven,' called the girl. 'Ugh. It's all black. Why'd you heat it on gas mark 9?'

'I was distracted,' Ethan snapped. 'I don't know how I feel about someone called Doctor,' he said to the man. 'I've had some dodgy experiences with doctors.'

'Yes,' said the man sadly. 'They've never really helped you, have they? It must be hard.'

From the kitchen, the girl announced, 'I think I've saved bits of it. Mostly cheese.'

She entered with a plate of scraped cheese and handed it to him.

'Thanks,' he said. He stared at the melted cheese. It looked real enough. But hallucinations couldn't move actual physical objects. Had he made up putting the pizza in the oven? He went back and opened the fridge. No pizza. Perhaps he'd eaten it another time and forgotten.

'You could offer us a cuppa,' said Ace. She was back in the doorway.

'I'm not feeding you. I draw the line at that.'

'What line?'

'The line between me and psychosis.' He pushed past her again.

'It's only a cup of tea.'

'The first step on the slippery slope. Next it would be sandwiches. And before you know it you'd be – Do you mind? That's private.'

The Doctor was at the computer, bending forward to examine the screen. 'Ah – the Riemann hypothesis. Very interesting. I see you're approaching the proof sideways – the way Fermat's Last Theorem was finally solved.'

'It never was solved the way Fermat indicated it could be.' Ethan looked at the Doctor suspiciously. 'I'd be impressed if I didn't know you were a figment of my imagination.'

'I'm not, actually. Tell me, have you noticed anything out of the ordinary recently?'

'You. Now go away. Fade into nothingness.'

'How about your clocks?'

'What?'

'Your clocks. Do they work?'

'As far as I know,' Ethan said bewilderedly.

'Do they ever get out of sync?'

'No more than usual.'

'Have you been experiencing events more than once?'

'You mean like *déjà vu*?'

'More extended.'

'No.'

The Doctor frowned. He got up and began to pace. Ethan looked for Ace. She was leaning against the wall, finishing off the cheese he hadn't touched.

'There must be something,' the Doctor muttered. 'Your work with prime numbers – anything other than Riemann?'

'Quite a bit of code-building.'

'Hm. I doubt that's it.' He stopped and looked at Ethan with those piercing eyes. 'Ever study time?'

'I'm not a physicist.'

'There is a mathematical element.'

'Einstein took care of that.'

'Not entirely,' said the Doctor incomprehensibly. 'Have you ever –'

Ethan smelled something burning. The pizza. Damn! He ran into the kitchen and slammed open the oven door. Smoke came out. He looked for something to extract the pizza with. Where was the tea towel? What the hell had he done with the tea towel? He squinted into the oven. The pizza was black. Not worth saving. He slammed the door on it and returned furiously to the sitting room. The expression on the faces of his unwelcome visitors brought him up short – both were staring at him in something like shock. For a moment they all just looked at one another, then Ace said, a bit shakily, 'Why'd you put the oven on gas mark 9?'

'I was distracted,' he snapped. He looked angrily at the Doctor. 'I don't have much use for doctors.'

'No,' said the little man, studying him intently. 'They never helped you much, did they?'

'Got any tea?' said Ace, as if she were an actor trying to remember lines.

'If I want you to go, I'm not going to bloody feed you, am I? Use your head. Or my head,' he muttered, shutting his eyes.

'I see you're working with prime numbers,' said the Doctor. 'The Riemann hypothesis.'

Ethan opened his eyes. The Doctor was peering at the computer screen. Ethan strode over and shut the machine off. Very quietly, he said, 'I'm going out to get something to eat. Do not follow me.' Then he grabbed his jacket off a chair and was gone.

Ace and the Doctor looked at each other.

'It happened again, didn't it?' she said. He nodded. 'But why?'

'I'm afraid we may have caused it. He's at an axis of time disruption, and our coming into it was a tipping point.'

'But nothing changed for us.'

'No, we're time stable. There *has* to be some explanation for all this.' The Doctor switched the computer on again. 'Go after him, Ace. See if you can bring him back.'

'What if I make things shift again?'

'I think I'm the main problem there.'

'But then if I bring him back here where you are –'

'Just go, Ace! Before he freezes in that jacket.'

'Right!' she said shortly. It got on her wick when he ordered her around. She banged down the stairs and out into the cold street. Which way had he – okay, there. She spotted his back heading towards Earl's Court Road and ran after him, dodging people in hats and scarves. On the chilly air, she smelled curry and Middle Eastern spices. She could use a proper meal after all that machine-generated stuff in the TARDIS. 'Oi,' she yelled. 'Hang on! Ethan!'

He looked over his shoulder and froze, as if she were a car rushing toward him that it was too late to dodge. She slowed down, panting, and stopped a few feet from him. He watched her rigidly.

'It's all right,' she said. 'It really is. We're not hallucinations, the Doctor and me. Honest.'

'You all say that,' he said between his teeth.

'That's not my fault.' The Doctor had been right – his corduroy jacket was too thin for this weather. He was so small, almost as small as the Doctor and almost as intense, but all nerves where the Doctor was all stillness. He couldn't be that much older than she was. 'What d'you expect me to say if I'm real, that I'm not?

And all those ones trying to fool you, well of course they'd say they were real too. So that's just how it's going to be.'

He considered this. 'Good point.'

'That's right,' she said cheerfully. 'I'm hungry. Let's find a café.'

He pulled his shoulders up reluctantly. 'I don't want to sit in public talking to myself.'

Ace just stopped herself from rolling her eyes. 'Right. I'll get some take-away and we'll go back to your flat.'

'Not the flat.'

She resisted the impulse to shake him. If he wouldn't sit in a café and wouldn't return to his flat, where were they going to eat? On a park bench in the cold? Oh give it up! she thought, but she knew the Doctor wouldn't want her to. She took his arm firmly. 'Come on, then. We'll get some food and work out where to go.'

The Doctor sat in front of Ethan's computer, legs crossed under him, hands on his knees. There must be something here somewhere that would explain why the TARDIS sensors had picked out Ethan Amberglass at the centre of the disturbances, the break in the mirror from which all the cracks ran. Of course, given the temporal unsteadiness, it was possible that he and Ace were early, that Ethan was yet to become a problem.

The Doctor went through the files. They all had to do with aspects of the Riemann hypothesis. He checked the email. Business-related exchanges about various projects. Only one was interesting: 'Have you considered U's notes?', and Ethan's terse reply, 'Waste of time.' The Doctor searched for other references to these notes but didn't find anything. Well, he'd just dig a little deeper.

'So what's this Riemann hypothesis?' said Ace, munching on her samosa.

'You really want to know?' His tone was sceptical.

Actually, Ace didn't want to know, but anything was preferable to watching the movie. They were in an art cinema showing a festival of prize-winning Latvian films, and the only other patron was an elderly woman who seemed to be asleep. On the screen, a man stared mournfully into a black pond. Reeds waved sinuously in the dark water, and a woman could be heard sobbing, apparently in the man's memory as he periodically shut his eyes in anguish.

'Yeah, I really do,' she said earnestly.

Ethan considered for a moment, obviously trying to work out a simple explanation. 'You know what prime numbers are.' It was a statement, but he glanced at her for affirmation.

'Well...'

He sighed. 'A prime number is divisible only by itself and one. No one knows whether there's any pattern to their occurrence in the number line. The Riemann hypothesis suggests that there is a pattern and that a way can be found to prove this.'

'That's it?'

'That's it.'

'And no one's found the answer? How long have they been working on it?'

'One hundred and forty years.'

'One hundred and forty years! What for?'

He grimaced and turned back to the movie. 'Never mind.'

'No, really. That's bonkers. What does it matter if they have a pattern?'

'I am bloody well *sick* of this!' His rage was so sudden she flinched back. He had actually stood up, and now he was leaning over yelling at her. Across the cinema, the elderly woman jerked awake. 'It has no purpose! It *is,* and it's beautiful. There's mystery at its centre, and we approach and approach forever, but we never get there. And you ask me if it matters, you idiot!'

Ace almost punched him but she tried not to hit people wearing glasses. What would the Doctor do? she thought, forcing herself to stop seething. What would he do in that calm, always-in-control way of his? 'Considering I'm an illusion,' she spat, 'I've got you well pissed off.'

He stood back, puzzlement replacing anger. Ace felt a smug satisfaction. Not bad. There might be something to this reasoning stuff.

'That's right,' he said, aloud but to himself. 'I couldn't project someone so stupid.'

Now she stood up. 'Listen, mate. You're one tick away from getting it, glasses or not.'

'Oh that's impressive.' He was unruffled. 'I knew you'd been the playground bully.'

'What?' she shouted, enraged.

'Beat up anyone who got in your way.'

'They beat *me* up, you –'

'There they are!' cried a wavering voice from the back of the cinema. While they'd been shouting at each other, the elderly woman had crept cautiously up the aisle to complain to the management. She stood now with an usher in the lobby door-way, waving a trembling arm at them. 'There...' she quavered. 'There...'

'I'm afraid I must ask you to leave,' said the usher. He was a reedy young man who looked to Ace like a film student. Probably a cabal of them ran the place.

'Rotten movie anyway,' she said as they went past. The old lady tried to swat Ethan with her handbag but missed.

'That was exciting,' he said dryly. 'Do you always make scenes in public?'

'You started it.'

'*You* started it, being so thick.'

'Screw you, you snotty little genius.'

They walked on in sullen silence. Ace took in deep breaths – she'd heard it calmed you down, though it had never worked for her yet. Left on her own, she'd just have stomped off, but that would be letting the Doctor down. She shot a sulky glance at Ethan. He was walking with his hands jammed in his pockets, shivering. He wasn't half bad looking, really, in a beaky sort of way.

'You're so smart, only you're too daft to have a proper coat.' But she spoke less angrily. He had struck her suddenly as forlorn, even vulnerable. 'You ought to have had an older brother,' she said, 'to look after you in the playground.'

'So ought you.' He too sounded less angry.

'Just one of me.'

'I had a younger brother. I wasn't much use protecting him.'

'Where is he now?'

'Accountant in Scarborough.'

'So maths runs in the family.'

'Accounting isn't exactly *mathematics*,' he snapped, then caught himself. 'I mean, it's not really the same as what I do. More arithmetic.'

'What's this Fermat's last theory? Why's it so special.'

'Theorem,' he corrected absently. 'It's not special in and of itself. But Fermat wrote in the margin of his notebook that he'd found a simple proof for the theorem, and no one has ever been able to come up with it.'

'I'll bet the Doctor knows.'

He stared at her. 'Why on earth do you say that?'

'Well...' she shrugged. 'I just wouldn't be surprised, that's all. He knows an awful lot of things.'

'Who is he, anyway? Who are you, for that matter? How did you get into my flat?'

'That's one of the things he knows.'

'He's a burglar?'

'No...! Well, sometimes. But only when it's necessary.' The look on Ethan's face implied that he'd found someone madder than he was. 'He helps people,' she said defensively.

'To do what?'

'Helps them when they're in trouble.'

'So he's brought me some new meds?'

'He's not that kind of doctor.'

'Then I don't see how he can help me.'

'You'll see,' she said, wishing the Doctor would tell her what was going on. He was too mysterious by half. Of course, things always came out right in the end, but did he have to keep her in the dark so much? And sometimes – she knew he didn't realise he was doing it – he was almost hateful. Like that time he'd pretended to Fenric he thought she was stupid and useless... She decided not to think about that.

'Listen,' she said. 'You ran out in the middle of a conversation. When we get back to the flat, he'll finish it, and you'll see he has a plan. He always has a plan.'

But when they got back to the flat, the Doctor wasn't there. A note on the table in his small, neat handwriting read, 'Gone out'. Beside it sat a chocolate pot and two mugs. Ace lifted the lid. 'Hot chocolate.'

'I didn't have any chocolate,' Ethan said. 'I didn't have a chocolate pot, either.'

'I guess he had one.'

'Where was it? In his pocket?'

She started to say something but didn't.

'Where's he gone?'

'Don't know.'

'When will he be back?'

'Didn't say, did he?' Ace poured herself some chocolate.

'But, this is insane.'

'Look who's talking.'

'Oh shut up!' He ran his hands frantically through his hair. 'Just shut up.' He went into the kitchen and took two more pills before he remembered that she wasn't a hallucination and the pills wouldn't help. 'Look.' He came back into the sitting room. 'You can't stay here.'

'Well, I'm not going to sit out on the doorstep, mate.'

'I have work to do!'

'You think I'm happy about this? Stuck in this grotty flat with a maths nerd? But here we are. Have some hot chocolate.'

'No.'

'Oh, stop being so childish. Here.' She filled the other mug and handed it to him. He stared at it as if he didn't know what it was. 'You look sort of nervy. Samosa go down wrong?'

'No.' He sat down heavily in the armchair. 'I'm just stuffed with anti-psychotics.'

Ace wasn't sure where to go with that. 'I was never into drugs, saw them mess up too many of my friends.' He leaned back in the armchair, eyes fixed on nothing. 'You've stopped blinking. Maybe you ought to blink.'

He shut his eyes. Maybe he ought to sleep, she thought. She looked into the bedroom. Like everything else the bed was buried under books and papers, as well as some clothes. Maybe he slept in the armchair. Which, she looked over her shoulder, he was doing now.

Ace plopped down in the computer chair and looked at him glumly. This was the bloody limit. She was stuck with this weirdo till the Doctor returned, whenever that might be. What was more, she couldn't sneak out because as soon as she was gone, the Doctor, with his uncanny sense of timing, would return and catch her letting him down. Not that she wanted to let him down anyway, of course, but this really was a right –

She suddenly focused on a background noise that had been humming since they'd returned to the flat. She turned to the computer – it was on! At least she could listen to music. She found headphones in a drawer, and happily fetched some CDs from her backpack. As she inserted one, it struck her that leaving his computer running was an odd thing for someone like Ethan to have done. It must have been the Doctor – he'd found something that made him dart out immediately, forgetting everything else. She wondered what it had been.

CHAPTER THREE

Earlier that day, Lethbridge-Stewart had stood at the edge of a field, hands behind his back, certain that a few drops of dew had found their way to his moustache and frozen there. He wanted to check, but the presence of his assistant, Sergeant Ramsey, stopped him. Even in retirement, he believed it was important to maintain standards in front of the men. Wouldn't do to be rubbing his face; set a bad example. He straightened a bit more and examined the field with what he hoped was a knowing expression. Actually, he couldn't see much of anything except some wheat stubble and a man and woman wandering around and occasionally stooping. The man had a camera; the woman was taking notes.

'Not our usual line, is it, sir?' said Ramsey. 'Hoaxes and all that.' His tone was curious rather than dismissive.

'Something odd about this one, they tell me. That's why they sent me out.'

From the corner of his eye, he saw Ramsey smile slightly. Lethbridge-Stewart was aware of his reputation. It was natural, people said, for UNIT to retain the Brigadier in an on-call/emeritus position; in his day he'd investigated so many of the 'odd ones' that in some circles it had been whispered that the old boy was a bit – well, the polite word was 'susceptible'. This pained Lethbridge-Stewart, who was responsible, intelligent and, as he would be the first to boast, almost entirely without imagination.

Light was beginning to seep into the grey morning. The woman waved at them to come over.

'Why did they start work in the dark, sir?' Ramsey asked as they crossed the field, the thin frost vanishing beneath their steps.

'Said parts of it would vanish when the sun comes up.'

'Vanish? That's hardly the usual thing.'

'As I said, this one's odd. The woman, by the way, is Jessica Tilbrook, from the local farm bureau. The man is Adrian Molecross and he really shouldn't be here.'

'Why not, sir?'

'Because he's a fool.'

The woman came forward to shake hands. She had short grey hair and a pink-cheeked, good-natured face. Molecross, plumpish and bearded, sported an incongruous safari hat.

Lethbridge-Stewart looked around. As far as he could see, they were standing in the centre of the usual sort of crop circle, although it was odd to find one among stubble rather than mature wheat.

'Look here,' said Tilbrook. Lethbridge-Stewart bent to examine what she was pointing at.

'Ice,' he said in surprise. He crouched and put his hand on it. 'Thick, too.'

'I've never seen anything like it,' said Molecross solemnly. He held out a hand to Lethbridge-Stewart. 'I'm from *Molecross's Miscellany* magazine.'

'Yes,' said Lethbridge-Stewart, ignoring the hand. He stood up and walked around the site. 'It seems to be everywhere.'

Tilbrook nodded. 'The whole pattern is laid over with ice about an inch thick.' She handed Lethbridge-Stewart some desiccated material. 'And this is what was underneath.'

The Brigadier realised that he was looking at brittle, shattered wheat stubble. 'Ice couldn't do this. Only a temperature well below zero could cause this sort of damage.'

'Interesting, isn't it? I must say, it makes a nice change from teaching people how to hack up thistles. They go organic, and then the first time they have to use a hoe instead of poison they fall apart.'

Lethbridge-Stewart handed the stubble to Ramsey, who crumbled a bit of it in his fingers. 'It almost looks burned.'

'In the sense that intense cold is said to burn, it is,' she said. 'The whole pattern was "burned" into the field.'

'This opens up a huge area of possibilities,' said Molecross 'It's a totally new method of communication.'

'I assure you,' said Lethbridge-Stewart, 'aliens do not communicate by means of crop circles. Especially as there are no aliens,' he added quickly.

'Why not? Why exactly not? The circles and spirals follow mathematical rules that are universal, at least in this galaxy. It's a common language between us.'

'That's the other anomaly,' said Tilbrook. 'This isn't a circle.'

'No?' Lethbridge-Stewart surveyed the surrounding area. The pattern was too big for him to get a sense of its shape.

'No, it's squares and rectangles and triangles. Much harder to make,' Tilbrook said. 'You can do circles with a bit of string and a peg, but a flat-edged figure is something else.'

'No one "does" circles,' Molecross snapped. 'Those two old farts who claimed –'

'Let's not get into that.' Lethbridge-Stewart paced out a few yards. The sun had come up, but the ice was still solid.

Ramsey joined him. 'Don't see how the ice could be done, sir,' he said.

'I daresay an ingenious person could work out something. Still...' Lethbridge-Stewart surveyed the field a final time. It glistened now under the first rays of the sun. 'Still, I think some aerial photographs would be in order.'

The photos were emailed to him later that afternoon. The Brigadier had Ramsey print them out – he had come late to computers, and looking at photographs on line gave him the uneasy feeling that he wasn't quite *seeing* them – then pinned them to a large corkboard in his office over a set of Ordinance Survey maps.

'Reminds me a bit of that maze near Winchester,' he said to Ramsey. 'What's the name of it?'

'The one on St. Catherine's Hill, sir?'

'That's right. Squared off instead of curving. Only one in the country. This is rather more complex, of course.'

Ramsey thought that was understating it. The photos showed at least ten straight-sided geometric shapes, including a dodecahedron, laid down almost haphazardly, some overlapping. 'Not very orderly,' he observed.

'No. Bit of a mess, really.'

'Possibly the hoaxers were drunk, sir.'

'If that were the case, I don't think the lines would be so straight: they look as if they were laid out with a ruler.'

'Hard to imagine anyone accomplishing this in one night.'

'We don't know that they did. The press is always going on about how astonishing it is that crop circles appear over night, but in fact we have no idea how long they've been there when people discover them. They're out in the middle of fields and not visible until you're in one.'

'How was this one found?'

'Usual sort of UFO sighting. Fellow up late, looks out his window, claims to have seen the stars blacked out. Calls the police and says he's going out to investigate. Damn foolish, if you ask me. Could have been anything. Police come, more to save him from himself really and discover what looks like vandalism.'

'Who contacted us?'

The Brigadier sighed. 'Molecross. He belongs to some Internet group that tracks crop-circle appearances. Ordinarily we'd ignore someone like that, but the presence of the ice was a new twist. I'm always on call for this sort of thing.'

Ramsey wondered what other examples of this-sort-of-thing might be. Fairies at the bottom of the garden? 'Yes sir,' he said.

'Molecross has taken it as one up for him. He's always pestering us, claiming we're covering up things that the public has the right to know about.'

'What kinds of things?'

'Oh, Yetis in the Underground. That sort of rubbish. Anyway, it won't be so easy to brush him off now. He'll insist on his right to cover the story along with the mainstream press. Speaking of which, please tell Lieutenant Fedder to prepare a briefing.'

'Right away, sir.'

When Ramsey had gone, the Brigadier remained where he was, eyes shifting from photograph to photograph. He did not consider himself an intuitive man – far from it – but something about this made him uneasy. He wondered whether the Doctor was anywhere on the planet.

Ramsey stepped back in.

'Fellow to see you, sir. Says he's a doctor.'

To Ramsey's surprise, the Brigadier laughed.

'Send him in, Mr Ramsey.'

'You say there was more ice?'

The Doctor was poking at the ground with his umbrella, humming tunelessly to himself. With the aerial photographs in hand, he had slowly paced the whole pattern, stopping now and then to look back along his route. The Brigadier didn't see the point in this personal reconnaissance, but he followed patiently. The Doctor had his own way of doing things.

As they walked, Lethbridge-Stewart examined his old friend. Even after several years, he wasn't yet quite used to this latest incarnation. The changes were always so extreme. This was the gravest of the personalities the Brigadier had known. Stern – the Highlands accent made Lethbridge-Stewart think of a Scots elder – and somehow troubled. He seemed tenser than usual this trip.

'Yes. It was originally about two inches thick.'

'Mm. Hasn't gone down much. Not under this sun.'

Lethbridge-Stewart nodded. The pale winter light held no heat.

'And the depth of the track itself has been measured?'

'Yes. It's consistent, oddly consistent in fact, except –'

'Except where the lines break off.'

They were standing at one of these dead ends now, where the earth was violently gouged. The gash was over a metre deep.

'Might almost have been done with a gigantic claw,' Lethbridge-Stewart observed.

'Nothing organic made this,' said the Doctor grimly. He rifled through the photographs again.

'The haphazardness of the patterns is confusing.'

'Not at all.' The Doctor handed him the pictures. 'Look closely. None of the shapes is completed. Almost there but not quite. As if someone tried several times and didn't get it right.'

There was a long pause. Then the Brigadier said slowly, 'You mean that...'

The Doctor nodded. 'Something was trying to come through.'

'Hello!' called a voice.

The two men turned to see a stocky figure running toward them. 'Damn,' said Lethbridge-Stewart.

'Who is it?'

'A journalist. More or less. Writes for one of those nonsense web magazines. Complete idiot.'

'Hm.' The Doctor tapped the handle of his umbrella against his chin, watching the man approach.

'Brigadier Lethbridge-Stewart,' Molecross panted as he came up. 'Just the man I wanted to see.' He nodded at the Doctor, who smiled and raised his hat. Lethbridge-Stewart did not make introductions.

'I'm busy at present, Molecross.'

'More investigating, I see. What have you found out?'

'Nothing new since this morning.' From the corner of his eye, the Brigadier saw that the Doctor had somehow concealed the photographs about his person. 'There will be a press announcement when we know more.'

'Oh yes,' Molecross said sarcastically. 'We all know how much to trust government press announcements.'

'Really, Molecross, you should be in the States. They have all sorts of phenomena there – UFOs, Bigfoot, some monster that eats goats. A whole area devoted to government cover-ups of alien visitations.'

'Well, I'm not in the States, am I? And neither is this crop pattern. Who are you,' Molecross said rudely to the Doctor. The Doctor only smiled.

'A scientific adviser,' said Lethbridge-Stewart stiffly. 'I don't have any more time for you, Molecross. And as of 1800 hours, this will be a restricted site.' He strode away. The Doctor, after tipping his hat again, followed him.

'So, Doctor,' the Brigadier said as they drove off, 'what did you want to see me about?'

Molecross stared after the departing car bitterly. Snob. Lethbridge-Stewart would give an interview to *The Times* quickly enough. Or some television journalist – they all loved to be on the telly. Just because Molecross ran a webzine, that was no reason to dismiss him. The Internet was the future. Look at that fellow in America who'd published those details about their president's sex life. Part of history now, that bloke. Someone from a marginal publication was more likely to find out the truth about this crop pattern than any mainstream reporter, because mainstream reporters had to have their imaginations surgically removed before they were even allowed to apply for their jobs. They weren't open to anything that didn't fit their prejudices. And that was true for the tabloids too. All *they* wanted was the sex lives of the royals. All right, he admitted it, he'd had a bit of a thing for Princess Di, even cried when she – But that wasn't the point!

The point was, he was in a position to find things out. And if Lethbridge-Stewart had only treated him with *common courtesy* Molecross would have told him that when he first arrived, before anyone else, with the morning only a breeze and some birdsong, he'd passed another car coming *from* the site. And not a farmer's car either, a Jaguar. He couldn't make out the driver, but he'd caught the number plate briefly in his headlights and memorised its number. Let Lethbridge-Stewart find that out in his own time. In the meantime, Molecross was doing some investigating on his own.

Ethan woke up. His tongue tasted as if a rubber eraser had decomposed on it, and he had a stabbing headache. Things didn't get any better when he opened his eyes and saw the little man perched on the piano stool, legs crossed, elbows on knees, chin in hands, watching him. Unnerved, Ethan looked around for Ace, but she was gone.

'Off at an INXS concert,' said the Doctor, 'and very relieved to be there, I imagine. Who is U?'

Ethan just gaped at him for a moment. Then he looked at the computer. 'You've been in my files!'

'I apologise; it was necessary. I didn't find anything personal. You don't seem to have much of a life.'

'What gives you the right to break into my computer!' Ethan yelled. He regretted it immediately, as a particularly vicious bolt of pain hit his skull. He put his face in his hands.

'Nothing,' said the Doctor. 'But I need your help. I need it very badly. Please tell me who U is.'

'He used to work for us, that's all. I never knew his name. Here!' Ethan looked up sharply. 'How'd you open it? I have so many passwords and blind alleys it takes *me* a full minute to get in there.'

The Doctor shrugged. 'I have a lot of experience. U's computations are interesting. He appears to have started out working on infinity.'

'Yeah, well, that in itself is a problem. People have gone around the twist working on infinity.'

'He does go off in some very odd directions.'

'It's rubbish,' said Ethan. 'He convinced himself there were equations that could solve entropy. Entropy! That's like something out of a comic book.'

'An end to disorder,' said the Doctor thoughtfully.

'That's it. And of course, that's why he was working on infinity.' Ethan leaned back and closed his eyes. 'Infinity and zero are twins: everything forever and nothing ever, the irrational poles of the sphere of mathematical order.'

'One can understand wanting to master it.'

'Yes,' said Ethan wearily. 'Like the poles of Earth. Do you know that there isn't even such a place as the north pole? There's no land there. The pole is a point on the latitude–longitude graph. How many poor bastards threw themselves into that vacuum?'

'Of course, now there are planes and helicopters.'

'Yes,' Ethan agreed dismissively. 'But to this day, no one has ever got to the pole and back by foot. It can't be done. It's what I was saying earlier about Fermat's Last Theorem – it was solved with the aid of computer computation speed, but it hasn't been solved the way Fermat indicated it could be.'

'Still, so long as it's solved...'

'Ah yes: practicality. Concern with the beauty of a solution is trivial romanticism.'

'Speaking of beauty, or lack thereof, I wonder whether you'd mind looking at these.'

Ethan opened his eyes. The Doctor was holding out a sheaf of photographs. Ethan took them and sorted rapidly through them. 'Crop circles? That is, crop other-things-than-circles?'

'Yes.'

'I've never heard of this sort of pattern.'

'I believe it's unique.' The Doctor retrieved the photographs and squinted at them, frowning. 'Something here is eluding me. Tell me, what's the first difference that strikes you between something like this and a circle.'

'Other than that it's harder to do?'

'Other than that.'

'Well, the circle contains irrationality and the straight-sided figures don't. Some do – the ones that fulfil the proportions of the Golden Ratio, for example – and these particular figures don't. The mathematical delineation of a circle includes pi, which so far as we know goes on in decimals forever, so it's one of the irrational numbers. But the –'

'Of course.' The Doctor sat up straight. 'Of course. That's it. Mr Amberglass, you've been invaluable.'

'Glad to help,' said Ethan, feeling rather like Watson when Holmes took one of his innocuous remarks and solved a complete case with it.

'Should have seen it myself,' the Doctor muttered, putting the photographs in his pocket. 'Is it migraine?'

'What?' Ethan felt even more like Watson.

'Is your headache migraine?'

'Oh. No. Well, perhaps. It's on one side of my head like migraine, but the doctors aren't really certain.'

'Look at me,' said the Doctor gently.

Without knowing exactly why, Ethan did. The blue of the Doctor's eyes was dark yet brilliant, like deep ocean under a high sun. Ethan stared into them in fascination. There was something wrong in there. No, not wrong exactly, but...

'How do you feel?' said the Doctor.

Ethan realised his head was clear. Also that he was afraid. 'What are you?'

'I'm a friend. It's U who's turned out to be the problem.' The Doctor got up and raised his hat. 'Thank you for your help. I won't be bothering you again.'

And he was out the door. Ethan heard him trot lightly down the stairs. 'Hang on!' he called. 'What –' But he stopped. He wasn't sure exactly what he wanted to ask. He looked around the room. The chocolate pot was no longer there. Somehow, he knew it wasn't in the kitchen either.

CHAPTER FOUR

'Amberglass,' said Clisby. 'Good man.'

After several polite routings, the Doctor had found himself in the office of a middle-aged man with large glasses and a receding hairline. Like everyone else the Doctor had met in the last hour, the man had a public-school accent

'Bit high-strung,' Clisby went on. 'Jewish, you know. Brilliant people, but sometimes overbalanced in the brains department. Can make them unstable. Need less imagination.'

The Doctor thought that Clisby certainly didn't have to worry about being overbalanced in the brains department. Or having too much imagination either. 'What exactly is his diagnosis?'

'Well,' Clisby consulted the files on his desk. 'Wandering, if you take my meaning. Some doctors say schizophrenic. Some say dissociative personality disorder. One chap thought migraine. They tell me it's not that unusual, not being able to pin these things down. Mind's a mystery, what?'

'Yes, indeed.'

Clisby paged through the files. 'Grammar school – a good one, though. Up to Cambridge at 17. I'm an Oxford man myself, but there's no denying they have an edge in maths and that sort of thing.' Clisby's tone was faintly condescending. Obviously a humanities man, the Doctor thought, wondering how he had ever got through Oxford.

'Anything unusual in his background?'

'Bland as porridge. Both parents deceased – cancer. Father was a solicitor. Brother in Scarborough, accountant. First breakdown at...' he thumbed through the papers. 'Ah, here it is. Yes, first breakdown at 19. Could have been academic pressure. Did you know Oxbridge leads the country in suicides per capita?'

The Doctor said no, he hadn't known.

'Came to work for us when he was 22. Most of them are that young. Burn out early, mathematicians. Had an "episode" – funny word for it – 18 months later. Hospitalised for three weeks. Then right as rain for two years. Some problems recently. Authorised him to work from home.'

'What sort of problems?'

'Report says headaches and hallucinations. Didn't handle it myself. Glad he's not American – probably come in with a howitzer.' Clisby chuckled. The Doctor gave a strained smile. 'Now, what was that other information you wanted? Oh yes.' He picked up another file. '"U" working on entropy. That must have been Pat Unwin. Not a strong character, our Pat.'

'Where did he study?'

'Warwick. Should have warned us. Still, a triple first at Oxford. He was a damn fine mathematician and we'd have kept him on if he hadn't gone alcoholic on us.'

'I understand you're generally tolerant of... that sort of thing.'

'Within reason. Very high-strung a lot of these chaps. Have to make allowances. But as soon as they become unusual, we ship them off to a doctor or a rest home with an AA program. Unwin wasn't having any of that. Took to reeling through the halls muttering. All right. Not the first one. We could deal with that. But when he started sneaking into people's offices and erasing their files it was a bit much. When we called him on it, he began ranting about how useless the work here was and how his ideas were going to change the world. We got in the lads in the white coats pronto, I can tell you.'

The Doctor nodded sympathetically. 'So he did go to a "rest home".'

'Should have thrown him in an institution. Drying-out place we have near Dover; he just walked away. We've been searching for him ever since. The things he has in his head. Classified, you know. Don't want them showing up in the hands of people who aren't our friends. Though for all I know, he might write them on the wall of a toilet, or publish them on that cyber place, space, what's it called?'

'The Internet.'

'That's it.'

'But so far he doesn't seem to have said anything. Exactly how long ago was this?'

'Hasn't been seen since 2 August. See here, UNIT aren't after him, are they? What's their interest?'

'I'm afraid I can't say. But I assure you, if he's found they'll turn him over to you immediately.'

'Don't like this poaching on the other fellow's territory.'

'They regard it as trying to help,' said the Doctor carefully; the last thing he wanted was bureaucratic infighting. 'Obviously, your department is considered the primary authority. They haven't your background on the situation, or your understanding of its particulars, and they know it.'

'Well,' said Clisby, somewhat mollified. 'As long as they know it. Still, I intend to meet with Lethbridge-Stewart on the matter.'

'He asked me to tell you he waits on your convenience.'

Clisby relaxed. He almost smiled. 'Good man, Lethbridge-Stewart.'

'The best, in my experience.'

'And you're their scientific adviser. Not on the staff, though.'

'No. I consult in a variety of places.'

'Hope you can keep secrets.'

'Oh yes,' said the Doctor, and he almost smiled.

Molecross lived in a little stone cottage left to him by his mother. It was picturesque but not very comfortable, having small windows, cramped rooms, and an added shower with beige plastic walls and no water pressure. Fortunately, Molecross had very little furniture – a computer desk and chair, a folding table for meals, a wardrobe, a bed – except for the bookshelves that covered every wall from floor to ceiling. The cottage was also crammed with filing cabinets, which, since they mustn't block the bookshelves, were set more or less in the middle of each room. Molecross had made little passages between them.

In spite of the eccentricity of the layout, the rooms were scrupulously neat and clean. The books were sorted carefully by subject and author, the files alphabetised and orderly. Molecross subscribed to a good many magazines. These sat in a pile beside the bed, and as soon as he finished one, he cut and clipped the articles he wanted, filed them and threw the remaining pages out. He had owned a cat until it knocked the magazines over and shredded one, and he'd given it away. This was just as well, as the smell in the little space had been getting him down.

His webzine – *Molecross's Miscellany of the Mysterious and Misunderstood* – had an impressive number of subscribers. This was because he could be counted on to get his details right. Most esoteric zines were sloppy; some could even be called hysterical. Molecross never leaped to conclusions. In investigating extra-real phenomena, adherence to fact was of supreme importance, simply because the material was so out-of-the-ordinary. Molecross knew that Borley Rectory was a hoax, and that no military pilots had vanished over the Bermuda Triangle – that mental spoon-bending was slight-of-hand and the moving coffins of Barbados were shifted by flood waters. He did not believe in ghosts because he did not believe in God. When he wrote up his report on this new and unusual crop pattern, he stuck strictly to what he had seen and heard. No speculation. Well, except for saying the military were obviously covering something up, and you couldn't really classify *that* as speculation, could you?

Contrary to what might be supposed, Molecross was not a materialist. He knew the yearning for the hidden that fills the mystic's soul. Whenever he encountered the truly inexplicable he felt a rush of joy. The narrow world expanded: out there, through that seemingly absurd door, lay the freedom of the transcendent *not knowing*. He never consciously tried to visualise this place of infinite possibility, but when occasionally an image crept into his mind it was of the sky at its palest blue, stretching away forever.

Molecross knew the pattern he had seen that morning was unique; he knew because he had on disk photographs of every known crop circle in the world. When he had walked the trail of the pattern, he had noticed what was later to strike the Doctor, the sense of an action interrupted.

They would be back.

Some hours later, shivering in the cold, he remained steadfast. Nothing came easily, and it was possible he would have to hold this vigil for many more nights. It would come when it was coming.

He stood in a fringe of trees on the edge of the field. He wasn't worried about the UNIT patrol. Irritated at this chilly, obviously useless duty – what pranksters would come out in temperatures like this? – they stood close together and smoked. So as not to take the slightest chance of his car engine alerting them, Molecross had parked a mile away and walked to the site. He and the soldiers kept their vigil together. He had thermal socks and underwear for just this sort of occasion and wasn't particularly uncomfortable. Still, he looked forward to morning. The night had a hard, heavy feel, as if, like a huge wall, it could fall slowly forward and crush him.

He looked at the sky. Clear as glass. He could pick out the constellations. Orion. Taurus and Gemini. There were, of course, really thirteen constellations in the zodiac – between Sagittarius and Scorpio intruded the foot of Ophiuchus, the serpent-holder, who was also Asclepius, the physician to the gods. That was the sort of thing you knew if you were a scrupulous researcher.

Molecross shifted his stance, sighed and inhaled deeply. A shock of freezing air hit his nostrils. His mouth tasted of steel.

He staggered and tripped, fell on his back. This was it. It was happening. It was *happening*. The terrible air filled his throat. He lay motionless with wonder, his harsh breath scraping the silence. It would come when it was coming. It would come when it was coming.

And then it came.

Lethbridge-Stewart didn't like interruptions in the first half hour of the morning, a period when he had a quiet cup of coffee and organised any work left over from the day before. He looked up in irritation when he heard a knock and held the expression as Ramsey came into the room. 'This had better be important.'

'I'm not sure, sir. But it seems to be something you should know about.'

'Well?'

'That journalist fellow is at the gates –'

'Which journ– not that idiot Molecross?'

'Yes sir.'

'Oh for God's sake, man! You came in to tell me that?'

'It's a bit –'

'The man is mentally unsound. He runs a magazine for people as unstable as he is. The secret of the crystal skulls. Egyptian hieroglyphics found on the walls of prehistoric caves. He's a joke.'

'Something's wrong with his hand, sir.'

'What?'

'Something's wrong with his hand. The men at the gate think you ought to see it.'

Molecross was weeping. Lethbridge-Stewart didn't blame him. His left hand was black, flopping like something wilted. The UNIT doctor examined it gently, his expression somewhere between disbelief and worry. 'I'm going to send in a nurse to give you some morphine, Mr Molecross.' Molecross nodded. His red, wet face was slack with shock. The doctor touched Lethbridge-Stewart's elbow and they went into the hall.

'What is it?'

The doctor shook his head. He was a middle-aged Pakistani, with a worn, seen-it-all face. Now he looked almost stunned.

'Have you encountered it before?'

'I have, yes. Years ago in Greenland. But in this climate, never.'

'What is it then? Some extreme form of frostbite?'

'You could say extreme. Almost the whole hand is necrotic. Don't ask me how it happened,' he added as the Brigadier started to speak. 'I don't know. And it's localised in the hand. I don't understand that either.'

'Can anything be done?'

'No. The hand will have to come off. For the present, it must be kept as cold as possible.'

'As *cold* as possible? Why?'

'Because,' the doctor said wearily, 'if it warms up, gangrene will set in.'

After some insistence, the Brigadier had persuaded the Doctor to accept a pager, though not a mobile phone. He couldn't work out the reason for this reluctance. It was hardly as if the Doctor were uncomfortable with advanced technology. Lethbridge-Stewart had concluded that he simply liked the freedom of no one knowing how to reach him or where he was, or what he was up to. If he didn't want to be found, he'd simply ignore any attempt to contact him.

But the Doctor showed up shortly after being paged, looking cheerful, as if pieces of this puzzle were falling into place. But he sobered when he heard about Molecross. 'Has he said what happened?'

'He was hysterical when he came in, and now he's heavily sedated.'

'Has anyone been to the site?'

'No.'

'Then let's go.'

As they drove, the Brigadier related what the men on duty

had told him, which was basically nothing. No one had heard anything, no one had seen anything, the temperature suddenly dropped noticeably, then just as suddenly shot back to where it had been. Presumably, Molecross had been knocked out too quickly to scream. The men had no idea anything had happened.

At the field, they found and followed the new pattern. Like walking a turf maze, Lethbridge-Stewart thought, only this one was of ice.

'It's laid down over the original pattern,' he observed, 'only slightly skewed.'

'Yes, that's peculiar, isn't it?' Hands on hips, the Doctor turned in a complete circle, taking in the expanse of icy trails. 'It's difficult to tell until we get aerial photographs, but it seems as if this second pattern is identical to the first.'

'As if they were meaning to hit the same place but missed.'

'Exactly. By just a few metres, but close only counts in horse-shoes. Now, if you were Molecross, where would you have stood?'

'The trees.'

'Yes. They're on the opposite side from the road, too. Shall we have a look?'

It took very little time to find what they were searching for. Right next to one of the ice tracks, a man-sized patch of stubble was crushed and broken.

'His hand seems to have been about here.' The Doctor got down on his hands and knees and peered closely at the ground. 'Ah ha.' From his pocket he took a pair of tweezers and poked carefully into the matted stubble. When he raised his hand, he had apparently caught hold of a bit of black thread. Lethbridge-Stewart shook his head unhappily.

'Molecross?'

'A shred of him.' The Doctor held up the scrap of tissue, squinting at it. 'His hand was black like this?'

'It was certainly black. Dr Kalen said it was destroyed by freezing.'

'In what I wonder? Liquid nitrogen?'

'Is that likely?'

'No.' The Doctor deposited the tissue in a glass vial into which he firmly pushed a cork. 'The damage would look different. But something as cold. Perhaps colder.'

When they returned to the UNIT hospital, Molecross had stabilised enough to be questioned. He was hooked up to a morphine drip and his eyes tended to drift away from his visitors.

'I don't want to tire you,' the Brigadier said, taking a chair, 'but I'd appreciate your telling me what you can.' Molecross nodded again. 'Can you describe what happened to you?'

'I was at the, the circle, the pattern,' Molecross said unsteadily. His voice was so faint Lethbridge-Stewart had to lean forward to hear him clearly. 'And it, they... they came back.'

'What did you see?'

'I didn't see anything. I didn't... hear anything. There was nothing.'

'Except the cold,' said the Doctor.

'Yes,' said Molecross wonderingly, as if he had forgotten that. 'The air... too cold to breathe. Tasted like metal.' His eyelids fluttered.

'One more question,' the Brigadier said quickly. 'Do you know what hit you?'

Molecross rolled his head heavily from side to side. Tears seeped from his closed eyes. 'I shouldn't... I was...'

'You weren't in the wrong place,' said the Doctor gently. 'They were off-target. That's why you were hit. It wasn't your mistake.'

There was no response, and the Doctor wasn't sure he'd even heard. But as he and Lethbridge-Stewart went to the door, Molecross stirred. He seemed to have momentarily come up from under the drug, and his tear-filled eyes were clear. He said something.

'What?' The Doctor bent over him. Unexpectedly, Molecross grabbed his wrist. 'It came to me,' he whispered. 'I felt it. I *knew* it.'

'What? What came to you?'

'The universe, its beautiful infinity... Do you understand?' His grip tightened. 'Do you *understand*? It was worth losing a hand.'

The Doctor went for a walk. UNIT HQ had been carefully built away from A roads, down in a dell. If not hidden, it was at least isolated. There was open land and bits of forest nearby. The Doctor climbed over a stile and made his way across a pasture. The grass was brown, the sheep droppings dried out and crumbling.

He hadn't witnessed any of those time rewrites since Ethan's flat, but that didn't mean they weren't happening elsewhere. When he'd called up the events again from the TARDIS files, the records had been interesting. None of the changes had in fact influenced the main timeline. Poe survived but never wrote again, so there were no later works to influence other writers. Oates' death had followed hard upon his rescue, and all that was missing from history was the story of his heroism. Pompeii had avoided destruction by volcano only to succumb to a plague; the survivors had left, and shortly thereafter Vesuvius had erupted and buried the city. Ethan's storming out hadn't made any difference since the photographs that he was to comment on so astutely hadn't even been printed yet. The bumps were very slight. So far. He could only hope they didn't get worse while he was trying to work out what was going on.

He had run the time sensors again, hoping to locate Patrick Unwin, but the focus remained on Ethan. Had the boy contributed something vital to Unwin's theories? No, they didn't even know each other, and Ethan had dismissed Unwin's work. The Doctor shook his head. There was nothing to do but keep an eye on Ethan and continue to search for Unwin. In the meantime, he'd work on this problem of Lethbridge-Stewart's, which was alarming enough in its own way.

He thought about Lethbridge-Stewart. He hadn't seen him

since telling him about the destruction of the Daleks – an event some forty years in the Brigadier's past. They had different attitudes about the matter. Obviously they were both glad that the threat was gone forever. But Lethbridge-Stewart was a soldier with a soldier's straightforward attitude: destroy the enemy. When that was accomplished, you had done your duty. The Doctor didn't know what his duty was. To time and the universe? To the individual ethical action? Long ago, in his fourth body, he had been given a chance to destroy the Daleks and hadn't. It was not his place to, as the Earth expression went, play God; he refused to destroy an entire race. And since then, how many billions had died for his virtue? So, given a second chance, he had turned the Daleks' planet into a fireball. And how many billions had died for his justice?

The Doctor came to another stile, but instead of climbing over he sat on the fence. His house in Allen Road was only an hour or so away; perhaps he should go over there. It might need a bit of sprucing up. Then again, another of his selves might have visited and done that already. Or he might have himself. Or some future self might be heavily into drugs and cutting-edge music – though he rather doubted it – and have torn up the place. It was very confusing.

He gazed at the landscape. The day was bleak, but the soft undulation of the Kentish weald was as beautiful as ever. How had he come to this? He had started out as an explorer, sick of his stultifying home, anxious for new experiences. And of course when he encountered people in trouble, he had helped them. He was good. His acts were good. When had he started playing on a larger board? Overturning social orders centuries old. Descending to a planet and 'fixing' things. The stage got larger, his actions became larger. He guarded the universe. He guarded Time itself.

He destroyed worlds.

The Doctor bowed his head. Sin was an alien concept on his home world. But he thought that now he understood what human beings meant when they spoke of it.

Never again, please never again, in all his future lives, let him exterminate an entire race.

CHAPTER FIVE

Ace was bored. Two nights of clubbing had been great, but she missed the Doctor. After being around him, other people seemed flat and dull – unless they were cute boys. She'd checked out a few of those, but nothing had clicked.

'Where've you been?' she'd asked the Doctor. 'And why can't I come?' And he'd replied that of course she was welcome to come if she wanted to spend all day at UNIT. Right. So she sulked around the TARDIS. Not that *it* was dull. It was amazing. But she spent most of her time there; she wanted a change.

'Oh God,' said Ethan when he opened the door.

Well, all right, she'd made a mistake. What had she been thinking? Get out quickly, she told herself. 'Just wanted to see how you were.'

'I *was* fine.'

Ace's temper flared. 'Listen, geek, you ought to be grateful someone even bothered.'

'Well I'm not.'

'Then why'd you even answer the door?'

'I have a headache. And you kept pounding and pounding.'

'The bell didn't work.'

'Of course not. I disconnected it.'

'You ought to live in one of those bubbles, mate. Or a sensory deprivation tank.'

'I tried it. It only gave me bad dreams.'

'I don't believe you even have dreams. You don't have any imagination. Only those stupid numbers.'

'Why are you standing here at my door insulting me?'

'Because you haven't asked me in.'

'What for?'

'For a cuppa, anyway. I came all this way.'

He sighed and turned away. But he left the door open. Ace followed him in. The mess looked exactly as it had on her first visit. Maybe it wasn't real mess but some kind of art instalment. Maybe he was a secret artist who pretended to be a maths nerd. Right. Why was she even here?

Because the Doctor said Ethan was the centre of it all. So maybe she'd find something out.

'If you want tea you'll have to make it,' he said sullenly, returning to the computer.

'You even have tea?'

'Of course I have tea.'

'Only I wondered. I thought you might not even know about tea.' She went into the kitchen. He did have tea. Typhoo. And a teapot standing on the counter. With, of course, yesterday's leaves and stale tea in it. Ace washed this and plugged in the kettle.

'Any sugar?' she called.

'In the fridge.'

'The fridge?'

'To keep it away from the mice,' he said impatiently. 'I'm not completely barmy, you know.'

'I'm suspending judgment there. At least you don't think I'm a hallucination.'

'I wish you were.'

'No you don't,' she said, amazed at her patience. She went into the sitting room. ''Cos then you'd be bonkers again. Has to be worse than having me here.' She sat in the armchair. 'This isn't your regular bed, is it? Guess not – it would smell.'

He put his head down on the keyboard. 'Can you say anything that isn't snide?'

'I didn't mean you don't bathe. Only upholstery absorbs

odours, you know. Like sheets do. I don't know how you'd use the bed. D'you just clear off the papers every night?'

'I don't sleep much,' he said, his attention back on the computer.

There was a silence. Ace tried again. 'The Doctor says this bloke you used to work with was trying to solve entropy and that was daft.'

'It is.'

'Why?'

'Why?' He turned and stared at her. 'Do you even know what entropy is?'

'Everything loses energy when it moves and finally the universe is all the same temperature.'

'Uh, right,' he said after a moment. 'Good enough. Entropy is a fundamental aspect of physical reality, the way energy *works*. The two are inseparable. If you changed the mechanics of energy... Well, it wouldn't be energy any more, it would be something else, and all the laws of physics would be different and probably we wouldn't exist. Make that certainly.'

'So we're all going to become this cold soup. Forever.' The Doctor hadn't told her that part. In fact, the Doctor hadn't explained it quite so clearly.

'Well... yes. The heat death of the universe. Obviously, everyone would rather that didn't happen. But it's built into physical reality. You can't "solve" entropy. Anyway, it's only a problem for us because we don't want to die. Entropy slots quite nicely into its place in physics, not a problem there at all.'

'Even if it was possible, I don't see how you could fix it with maths.'

'Exactly! God knows what U thought he was doing.'

'Well,' she said slowly, 'he was trying to find a way for all life not to die, wasn't he?'

Ethan blinked at her. There was another silence.

'What about the tea?' he said.

To Ace's surprise, she not only found two clean spoons but

two clean cups. No sugar bowl, though – she took the bag from the fridge and carried it into the sitting room. Ethan put four spoonfuls in his tea.

'Have some tea with your sugar,' Ace said.

'That's very original. No one's ever said that to me before.'

'The way you live, this place should be a dump. Who cleans up for you?'

'Someone comes in once a week.'

'Some poor Nigerian, I'll bet.'

'She'd be a lot poorer if I didn't give her work. Don't get holy on me. My great-great-grandparents were immigrants. The women scrubbed floors and worked in the weaving mills, and the men sold needles and nails. I'm grateful to the people who hired and bought from them. Not everyone would give work to Jews.'

Ace had no retort for that. 'What about your papers and mess?'

'What about them?'

'She clean around them?'

'Of course.'

Ace looked around. 'Then the whole job must take her ten minutes.'

'I don't know; I'm at the office.'

'You're not there now.'

'I work at home a lot.' Ethan got up and went into the bathroom. He returned with two large pills, which he took with his tea.

'What are those?'

'I can't keep the names straight. These are the blue ones. The blue ones are for headache.' Ace presumed this was a hint. She was just about to give up and leave, when he said, 'Your friend the Doctor is good with headaches.'

'He's good with a lot of things.'

He was looking at her narrowly. 'Is he really a doctor?'

'He's really *the* Doctor.'

'And what the hell does that mean? Why did you two come to see me in the first place?'

Ace wasn't sure what to say. She didn't think this was the moment for the travelling-through-time-and-space bit. 'He's working on a problem and he thought you could help.'

'He told me he'd thought *I* was the problem.'

'But he doesn't think so now, does he?' she said brightly. 'So it's all right.'

'And what about these crop circles or whatever they are?'

'Er?' said Ace, feeling caught out and stupid. Not to mention really, really angry at the Doctor. All that blather about going off to dull old UNIT and it turned out he was investigating crop circles and leaving her out. 'He hasn't said much about it. Only that they're well fascinating.'

'These are odd.'

'Er?' she said again.

'He showed me photographs. Haven't you seen them?'

'Yeah, of course I have. I don't know much about them though. Why are these odd?'

'Because they're not round. They're squares and triangles and other straight-edged patterns, which are much harder to fake.'

'Oh yeah?' she said, trying to sound very calm and unangry. 'You know, I've never seen one. Have you?'

'No.'

'Wonder where this one is.'

'Why?'

'Well, wouldn't you like to see one?'

'What for?'

'Because you never have! You're a right dormouse, aren't you?'

'It's *winter* out there,' he pointed out. 'Besides, we don't know where it is.'

Ace jumped up. 'But we can find out. Use your computer.'

'I don't see how listings for crop circles in general can help us find this particular one,' he objected, but he called up a search engine, entered 'crop circle sightings', and started going through the list. After eleven screens of sightings and dates, none of which was current, and a lot of rubbish, Ace began to think this wasn't going to work after all. Then she spotted a listing whose description included the phrase 'Updated Daily'.

'That one,' she pointed, and Ethan accessed the site for *Molecross's Miscellany of the Mysterious and Misunderstood*.

There was some difficulty about getting a car. Ethan, not at all to Ace's surprise, couldn't drive. And when they got to the Marble Arch rental office, Ace discovered that she'd mislaid the licence the Doctor had provided for her. Furious argument on her part while Ethan stood as far away as possible looking at the wall, resulted in nothing. She stormed out with him in tow.

'There's no problem,' she said. 'We'll take the train.'

'The train?' He sounded as if she had suggested swimming down the river to Greenwich.

'Don't tell me you've got train phobia?'

'That would be agoraphobia, and no I don't. Only I don't like being in crowds.'

'How d'you get to work then?'

'I walk. It's only two miles. And if I work late, the buses are emptier and I can take one home.'

Ace gritted her teeth and pulled him along the pavement.

'I sit upstairs,' he explained.

'I just bet you do,' she muttered, trying to remember which station they needed. 'Well, you'll just have to hold it together because – Here!' She stopped and stared at him. 'You've never been on a train have you?'

'I'm telling you,' he said earnestly, 'this is not a good idea.'

He turned out to be right, although Ace would rather have sat through a Barry Manilow concert than admit it. The train broke down, and after waiting for an hour they were put on a bus. She took the aisle seat while Ethan pressed himself against the window as if he'd like to ooze through it. The bus took them to another bus stop, where they sat in a dirty café and drank weak tea and took turns going outside to see whether the second bus was coming. They did this for two hours.

When the bus finally arrived, she sat on the aisle and Ethan did his thing with the window again. The driver somehow got lost and took them into a village with a roundabout too small for the bus to get round. Finally they reached the town nearest the crop-pattern site. Ace called a taxi.

By this time it was well after dark, and the taxi took its time. Ethan hadn't spoken for the last couple of hours; now he stood on the pavement with his arms crossed tight, head down, shivering. As the trip had progressed, she had begun to appreciate how hard it was on him. He never complained, just become more and more still. She had to give him credit.

He finally spoke, 'Are we going out to look at this crop circle in the *dark*?'

'There's a moon coming up. Look.' He didn't. 'Listen,' she said, 'I'm sorry. I really am. It's been an awful trip, I know. But honestly, now that we're here, don't you think we may as well go see the thing?'

He sighed. She waited. After a moment, he shrugged his shoulders. Ace grinned. 'It'll be fun, you'll see.'

He didn't respond.

The negotiations with the taxi driver were protracted. He couldn't understand why they wanted to go to an out-of-the-way field in the cold, and when Ace explained it was a star-gazing exploit he wondered where her telescope was. He complained that he was unlikely to pick up a return fare. Ace offered to pay him a double rate. This cheered him, and in a short while they were standing by the side of the road watching his tail-lights disappear.

'Well,' Ethan said. 'Here we are.'

'Not yet.' She took out a penlight and the map she'd printed out.

'You might have brought a torch.'

'I didn't know it was going to be dark when we got here.'

'British Rail. Might have guessed.'

He had her there. She ignored him and concentrated on the map. It was a section of an inch-to-the-mile Ordinance Survey map with an overlay of coordinates and a hand-drawn outline of the site. 'We just walk straight in and we'll hit it. We can't miss. Come on. It'll be a new experience.'

'It's already been a new experience.'

'That's the wrong attitude, mate.' She plucked at his sleeve and they started off. 'The Doctor always says a catastrophe looked at properly is an adventure.'

'He's quoting G. K. Chesterton, and I don't think the saying's particularly encouraging.'

They were crossing the field now. The rising moon reflected on something on the ground a few hundred feet ahead. As they came closer, they saw that it was a glimmering network of ice.

'Here we are!' she said.

Ethan tapped at the ice with his heel. It cracked slightly. 'I don't understand. The weather's certainly cold enough to freeze water, but why would water only be here?'

'It's a bit dug out – maybe water drained into it.'

'I don't think the land lies that way.' He walked off alongside the pale track. Amused, she followed.

'See, it *is* something new.'

'Yes,' he admitted. 'You win that one.' He stopped and looked over the dark field. Trails gleamed all around them. 'It's not much sense just following the lines. We can't get a decent impression of the pattern this close up, probably not even in the daylight.'

'What caused it, d'you think?'

'No idea.' He tapped at the ice with his heel again. 'But I can't see anyone faking this. It would be an enormous amount of work, even if all that was involved was mowing down the stubble. But to dig a trench...'

'And fill it with ice.'

'I honestly can't imagine how that was done.'

Though her experience of oddities both extraterrestrial and

earthly was, to say the least, expansive, Ace, couldn't imagine either. She found that slightly unsettling.

He said, 'This is really here, isn't it?'

'Yeah, unless we're both nuts.'

'Pass,' he murmured. 'I wonder whether –'

He stopped. She had grabbed his arm. 'Ssh! There's someone here.'

'What?' He looked around.

'Be quiet!' She pulled him to a crouch. 'Over there.'

He peered ahead. After a few seconds he spotted an inexplicable vertical shadow that might have been a person. It moved a few feet and he was sure. 'Man or woman?' he whispered.

'Can't tell. What're they doing, then?'

Ethan watched the figure's dim movements. 'I think they're... digging.'

'You're joking.' She squinted across the field. 'You mean it really is a hoax? And that's who did it?'

'So it appears.'

'Wicked!' Ace grabbed his arm again. 'We'll catch them in the act!'

He hung back. 'What are you talking about?'

'We'll catch the hoaxer!'

'What? What if he's armed?'

'We'll sneak up on him.'

'Sneak up – This isn't a movie!'

'It's all right,' she whispered reassuringly. 'I've got some explosives.'

'What!?'

'Ssh. Nitro Nine. It's –'

'Oh God!' He banged his head against the ground. 'Why me? What did I do in a past life –'

'Oh shut up!'

'I'm not coming. Explosives! God, let this be a hallucination.'

'Hard cheese,' she said shortly. 'We're all real. Now d'you want to do something useful or just lie here?'

'Lie here.'

'All right. Fine.' She stood up angrily. 'No wonder you don't have a life. You don't deserve one.'

The figure suddenly turned towards them. They froze.

'Ace?'

'Doctor?' she squeaked.

CHAPTER SIX

'What in heaven's name are you doing here?' The Doctor was
very angry. 'And who's that with you?

'Ethan. He –'

'Ethan? You brought *him* into this?'

'Into what? Professor, what are you doing?'

'Get out of here.' He strode toward them. 'As fast and as far
away as possible.'

'We can't.'

'We came in a taxi,' Ethan explained.

The Doctor spat something incomprehensible and grabbed
Ace's wrist. 'Hurry,' he snapped. 'Both of you.'

They ran back to where he had been digging. The Doctor
grabbed the hoe and frantically gouged out another foot or
so. Ace saw that he had closed a circle. 'I had the Brigadier send
the guards away and evacuate every dwelling within a mile. And
you show up.'

'I'm here to help you,' she said weakly.

'And how exactly,' he yelled, 'will you help me by being frozen
to a black husk?'

She was too cowed and bewildered to respond. The Doctor
hurried around his circle, checking for gaps.

'Perhaps you ought to tell us what's going on,' Ethan said. The
Doctor ignored him. 'Look... Doctor, Batgirl here may be used to
this kind of thing but I'm way out of my depth. I didn't ask you
people into my life. You brought me the damned photographs,
you involved me. So you can bloody well tell me what's
happening.'

The Doctor took off his hat and ran a hand through his hair. He looked at the sky. 'I don't know when it will happen,' he said. 'When it does, whatever you do, stay inside the circle.'

'What is "it"?' said Ethan.

'I don't know.'

'Are you always this gnomic?'

'Please be quiet,' the Doctor said. He had recovered his temper but sounded horribly tense. 'I don't know what is going to happen and I don't know when and I wish I were by myself. Just *stay in the circle*.'

'But what good's the circle?' Ace asked, a bit hesitantly. 'It's just a shallow ditch. Something could step right over –'

'Hang on,' said Ethan. 'Not a square or a trapezoid or a triangle, but a *circle*.' The Doctor nodded. 'No straight lines.'

'Very good. Yes. We should be immune.'

Ace sidled up to Ethan. 'What are you two talking about?' she whispered.

'Maths.'

'Great.'

'There was a man out here last night,' said the Doctor. 'Adrian Molecross.'

'Molecross?' said Ace. 'But that's the bloke who runs the website that got us here.'

'You may have noticed he hasn't posted anything today. He's in hospital at UNIT HQ.'

'Why? What happened to him?'

'He wasn't protected.'

Ace bit her lip. 'Is he a black husk?' she said in a small voice.

'Just his hand.'

'So,' Ethan said carefully, 'you're saying that this *circle* will protect us?'

'I think so.'

'Right. Good. Just so I have that clear.'

'We'll be all right,' Ace told him as the Doctor nervously checked his furrow again.

'What makes you say that?'

'He's the Doctor.'

'He's just drawn a circle in the dirt and told us that means we aren't going to die.'

'It does mean that,' she said fiercely. 'You don't understand.'

'Obviously not.'

'I think we should all stand at the centre,' said the Doctor. 'That puts us a good 15 feet from the perimeter.'

They huddled together in an uncomfortable little knot. The Doctor, Ethan noticed, was wearing neither coat nor gloves. And his breath didn't mist in the freezing air. I've got myself into something all right, he thought, a little dizzily. I hope it doesn't kill me. He looked at the moon, still shining peacefully, and the still and brilliant stars. This isn't going to happen. Whatever it is. We're just going to stand here, freezing, till dawn and then –

Blackness slammed across the sky. Ethan jerked, knocking into Ace, and fell down.

'Ethan?' Ace groped for him. She couldn't see anything, yet the darkness had an almost shining intensity, as if it were itself some form of light. She touched Ethan's back, searched for her penlight.

'No, Ace.' The Doctor's hand was on her shoulder.

'But I think he's hurt.'

'It's only one of his headaches. He'll be all right. No light.'

'Why? What's happening?'

'Something wants to come through.'

Ace realised that her teeth were clacking together violently. She was freezing. Or maybe it was terror. The Doctor's hand remained firmly on her shoulder, anchoring her to the memory of light and warmth. She rubbed inadequately at Ethan's back and tried to say, 'We're with you,' but nothing came out of her mouth. Around them the silence was violent. 'Professor,' she tried to whisper.

His hand suddenly left her shoulder. Immediately she twisted and grabbed at him, catching his left leg. 'Professor!' He was still, but she clung to him as if he were being ripped away from her. 'Answer me! Ethan, help! Help me.'

'What is it?' he gasped.

'The Doctor! Something's wrong!'

He staggered forward on his knees, fell into her. 'Where is he? What's –'

'Hold on to him!'

'Where the hell *is* he?' His voice broke with pain.

'Follow me!' she cried. The Doctor still hadn't moved, yet she somehow felt him slipping away. 'I've got his leg. Find something to hold on to.'

He scrambled awkwardly over her. 'I've got his jacket.'

'No! Something stronger.'

'He's not even moving. We don't need –'

'Oh shut up, shut up!' She was sobbing desperately. 'Get his other leg, get his arm, get his bloody finger! He's going, I tell you, I can feel him going!'

'But –'

'Just do it, do it!' she screamed. 'Do it now!'

She heard him scrambling again. 'Right. I've got his arm – Oh God!'

'Hang on!'

'Oh dear God! What is this?'

'Don't let him go!'

'He's going to take us with him!'

'No. He. Is. Not,' she said through gritted teeth. 'No he is bloody not!'

In spite of the unmoving leg she held, Ace sensed a terrifying motion in the Doctor, upward, spiralling, as if there were a whirlpool in the sky. Around them, the hard darkness was quiet, almost peaceful, which was so *wrong* it made her feel like screaming. The Doctor was so cold that it hurt where she hugged him to her. She wished he'd make a noise, even a groan. Was he unconscious? Trapped in a force so powerful it absorbed all sound?

Then it ended.

The Doctor fell in a heap, jerking Ace and Ethan down too. They lay half on top of him, panting for breath. The moon shone, the stars glittered and the night was noisy again – cars in the distance, light wind in the trees, the cry of an owl. Ace looked around her. Like some huge gameboard, fresh lines of ice lay across the field. She felt for the Doctor's pulse. It was firm. 'He's alive.'

'What was that?' Ethan whispered. 'What *was* it? He wasn't moving, but he was being... It was like something inside of him was being sucked out.'

'Yes.'

'But what –'

'I don't know. Stop asking me.' She got to her knees and rolled the Doctor over. His breathing was even but he was shivering violently. Ace pulled off her jacket and laid it over him.

'Is he all right?'

'He's terribly cold.' She hugged him to her. 'Terribly... terribly...'

The Doctor sat up.

'Professor?'

'I feel dreadful,' he said in a perfectly ordinary voice. 'Something tried to hoover me.'

'What?'

'Haven't the faintest.'

'Can you stand up?'

'Why would I want to stand up? It's quite comfortable sitting here. Except that I seem to be freezing.' He got up. 'Ah, not as bad as I feared.' He trotted off along one of the new tracks. Ace turned to Ethan. He'd rolled onto his back and was gulping in air. 'You all right?'

'No,' he snapped.

That was good enough for Ace. She grinned and gave him a reassuring pat on the shoulder, then ran after the Doctor.

'What happened to you? Are you all right?'

'I'm not sure and I seem to be.'

'Well, guess, then. We were clinging to you like you'd take off, but you weren't moving. Only you were. We could hardly hold you.'

He stopped, looking thoughtfully at the ground. She wished she could see him better. 'It's difficult to describe. Something essential, something fundamental was being... drawn out of me. Thank goodness you were here, Ace.'

'Too right. You should have *told* me.'

'Yes, I know. I'm sorry.'

Sorry? This was a historic moment. 'Well, all right then,' she said inadequately.

'Did you feel anything?'

'Only you.'

'Hm.'

'So whatever was trying to get through, didn't?'

'No.'

'You said this has happened before?'

'Twice.'

'Why doesn't it, they, make it?'

'I believe we had something to do with that this time.'

'You mean you? When it was getting at you?'

'That would be flattering myself.' He pointed with his umbrella and she saw that the lines running towards the circle turned sharply away as they came up to it.

'Your circle did that?'

'Mm.' He nodded, tapping his chin with the umbrella handle. 'Interesting, isn't it? I'm very angry with you, Ace,' he went on, his voice flat. 'You could have been killed.'

'So could you have been killed just now.'

'It's a professional liability.'

'For me too, Professor. You know it is.'

'Well it's not for Mr Amberglass,' he said sharply. 'You had no right to pull him into this.'

'That's not fair. If you keep me in the dark, I'm going to have to do the best I can with what I know.'

'Ace,' he sighed, 'you know very well that if I do tell you and then ask you to stay away, you won't do it. You don't give me a choice.'

'You might get hurt,' she said quietly. 'You could have been hurt tonight. And you would have been,' she added defiantly, 'except I *was* here.'

'Well, yes.' He smiled. 'You have me there.' He put his arm around her shoulders and they walked back to the circle.

Ethan was sitting with his palms pressed to his eyes. As they came up he lowered his hands and looked apprehensively around and up at the sky.

'Are you all right?' the Doctor asked.

'More or less.' Ethan's voice was unsteady.

'Professor!' said Ace. When he turned, she was pointing. The hoe had fallen so that its handle lay outside the circle on one of the lines of ice, black and withered as a dead branch.

'Mr Molecross?'

Molecross wasn't sleeping, just drifting in a druggy haze. He opened his eyes and stared drowsily at the odd little man.

'Do you feel well enough for a conversation?'

'Sure.'

The man sat down neatly on a chair beside the bed. All his movements were neat and self-contained; he made Molecross think of a domestic cat.

'I went out there.'

Molecross started to nod agreeably, then jerked a bit more awake. 'To the field?'

'Yes, to the field.'

'Did they come back?'

'They came back. But they didn't come through.'

Molecross licked his lips. 'Do you think,' he whispered, 'they're aliens?'

'Well, they're not human beings,' the little man said dryly.

'They might be some Earth-generated force we know nothing about. Are you aware that we know more about the bottom of the sea than the centre of the Earth?'

'You won't like what you find at the centre of the Earth,' the man said. 'I want to confirm what you told the Brigadier and myself.'

'Well...' Molecross grasped at his slippery thoughts. 'I didn't see anything. I didn't hear anything. I was very cold. Then my hand burned off.' He looked at the bandaged stump of his arm and began to cry. The man stood up to make a tactful withdrawal. 'I know who you are.'

'Hm?'

'You're him.'

'Him who?'

'You're the Doctor.'

The Doctor sat down again. 'I beg your pardon.'

'You've been sighted many times, in many different forms. But the information is sketchy. The accounts are all third hand. I thought you were a legend.'

'My name is John Smith.'

Molecross smiled and wagged his remaining forefinger at him. 'When I had your wrist,' he said smugly, 'I felt the double pulse.'

The Doctor said nothing, just regarded him thoughtfully.

'I can't believe it,' Molecross sighed happily. 'I can't believe I've been so lucky. Twice in two days!'

The Doctor glanced at the bandaged stump. Molecross must be very drugged indeed. 'I have no idea what you're talking about.'

'Your pulse...'

'You may have felt something anomalous – I have high blood pressure.'

Molecross swiped at his wrist, but the Doctor easily eluded him. 'Then let me feel it again.'

'I certainly will not. You have a lamentable lack of respect for other peoples' privacy.'

'I know it's you. I know. I'll tell.'

'You sound like a schoolboy snitch. Whom would you tell?'

'The world!'

'Through your webzine?'

'The media will hunt you down.'

'Really? Oh dear me, how worrisome.' The Doctor got up. 'I think it's best I leave now.'

'Oh please.' Molecross's voice was pitiful. 'At least give me an interview.'

'Now that's just silly. Why would anyone believe you'd actually talked to this Doctor person? Everyone will think you made it up.'

'I have a reputation for integrity.'

'Not after that you wouldn't.'

'Don't go away,' Molecross pleaded. He was crying again. 'Don't leave me. You're a miracle.'

'You made me up, Mr Molecross. I'm only a dream.'

The Doctor slipped out the door.

'You'd better tell Molecross I don't exist,' the Doctor said to Lethbridge-Stewart.

'Well, officially you don't.'

They were in the Brigadier's office having tea.

'I need not to exist for him. If he persists, persuade him Dr Smith is real.'

'Whatever you want. We took some new aerial photos and one of our specialists made a diagram.' He turned his computer around so that the Doctor could see the pattern, neatly rendered in green lines.

'How were these lines laid over the earlier ones?'

'Almost exactly on top of the first pattern. They didn't miss this time. It was your circle that threw the spanner in.'

The Doctor could see that. Lines were interrupted by the circle, broken. 'Amberglass was right.'

'Hm?'

'He said the straight-edged patterns were all rational. The

circle isn't. That's what blocked them.'

'Mm, yes, of course.' The Brigadier put his cup down. 'You plan to keep using this chap Amberglass? He'll need clearance.'

'He already has some, because of his job. But no, I'd rather not involve him further. He shouldn't have been there last night. That was Ace's idea.'

'Impulsive girl, I seem to recall.'

'That's one word for it. Is he doing all right?'

'Yes. Seems to be. We have him under observation, but I don't think there's any real need. He said he often gets these sorts of headaches.'

'Yes, I'm afraid he does.'

'More tea?'

'No, thank you.' The Doctor set his half-full cup on the tea tray.

'So, what do you propose to do next?'

The Doctor put his hands behind his head and leaned back, gazing at the ceiling. His hat stayed on. 'I'm not sure. I think the circle will hold off whatever it is needs holding off.'

'What if they choose a different site?'

'Why wouldn't they have done that the first time they failed? No, there's something special about that place. Some thinness between universes, perhaps.'

'And that little circle is stopping them?'

'You don't smash through universe walls. The area of possible entry is invariably quite small, in terms of both space and time. It takes very delicate handling. I've known cases where a mote of dust scuttled the whole thing. We don't know whether it's a "them", by the way. It might be an impersonal force of some sort. Molecross thinks it's some heretofore-undiscovered power from the centre of the Earth.'

'Molecross! What are we going to do about him?'

'Nothing. Let him go home when he's able. Any claims he makes will sound ridiculous, if not outright mad. He can't do any harm.'

The Brigadier smiled and sipped his tea. 'You're right there.'

The Brigadier said, 'More tea?'

The Doctor looked down. There was a cup in his hand. It was empty.

Oh no.

'Er, no, thank you,' he said, carefully placing the cup on the tea tray.

'So,' Lethbridge-Stewart said as he poured, 'what next?'

'I don't know,' the Doctor said hastily. 'I think that circle will hold things off for now, but obviously we need to find out exactly what's going on. In fact, I think I'd better return to the TARDIS and get to work.'

'I'll order you a car.'

They had to be happening everywhere, these glitches, the Doctor thought as he hurried down the hall. Like bubbles that popped up in the time stream then broke and were gone, leaving the stream itself unchanged. So far, no actual harm had been done. But what if matters escalated?

'You were right,' said Ace. 'I was wrong. I'm sorry.'

'So that was an adventure,' said Ethan. He was propped up in the medical-ward bed, still looking slightly shell-shocked.

'Well, yeah, it was.'

'Not a catastrophe.'

'Oh no. Catastrophes end badly.'

'Like, say, if I'd lost my hand.'

'Like that, yeah.'

Ethan thought for a minute. 'You know that thing you said about my not having a life.'

'Yeah,' she said, embarrassed.

'I don't think I want a life.'

At the moment, Ace had no argument for this. 'You sure you're all right, then?'

'You keep asking me that. And I keep telling you, it was just one of my headaches.'

'It looked bad.'

'They are bad.'

The Doctor poked his head in the door. Ethan eyed him warily.

'How are you doing?'

'I'm dying,' Ethan said shortly. 'I'm already dead. This conversation is a post-death experience.'

The Doctor smiled cheerfully. 'Sarcasm is always a sign of recovery.'

'Seen a lot of recoveries, have you?'

'Yes,' the Doctor sighed. He took the chair beside Ace. 'We're going to get out of your life, Mr Amberglass.'

'Forgive my scepticism.'

'All right. We intend to get out of your life.'

'But first...?'

'Just a couple of questions.'

'Right,' Ethan said tiredly. He folded his arms. 'Fire away.'

'During the experience last night, when your headache came on, was it only a headache?'

'As opposed to what?'

'You didn't hear anything?'

'You mean voices? Like when I'm nuts?'

'No, no.' The Doctor was apologetic. 'Not at all. I mean, as if someone were trying to communicate with you.'

'Like ESP?'

'A bit.'

Ethan shook his head.

'Hm.' The Doctor tapped his chin with the handle of his umbrella.

'Did you?'

'Receive any communication? No.'

'Look,' said Ethan, 'I really think I deserve to know. What's happening? Is it aliens?'

'Something like that.'

'But I don't believe in aliens,' Ethan protested, almost plaintively.

'Would you find it easier to believe that what happened last night was an *earthly* phenomenon?'

Ethan looked alarmed. 'I'd prefer not to.'

'Then what's the alternative?'

There was a long pause.

'You *are* going to get out of my life, aren't you?' Ethan said at last.

The Doctor stood up. 'Now, as a matter of fact.' He shook Ethan's hand. Ethan was surprised at how cold his hand was. 'Thank you for all your help. I'm sorry it got a bit nasty.'

'Yeah,' said Ace, 'me too.'

'Oh,' said the Doctor, just as they got to the door. 'I should warn you. There's a fellow down the hall who runs a webzine of weirdness. He might want to interview you. I'd avoid him.'

'What does he look like?'

'Oh you'll know him. He's missing a hand.'

As he and Ace left, the subject of this comment peered through his cracked door, watching them. Who else had the Doctor been visiting? But when Molecross started down the hall to investigate, an orderly intercepted him and returned him firmly to bed. And when he was able to sneak out again a few hours later, the room was empty.

In the TARDIS the Doctor ran himself through a number of medical scans. He found nothing out of the ordinary. Again, he sat with a cup of tea in the console room armchair, thinking. What exactly had happened to him? He'd had a feeling of awful, terrifying *loss* – if he were human, he'd have said his soul was being pulled out of him. Except... He shut his eyes for a moment. Except that wasn't quite all. They had reached out to him, and something in him had *responded*. He'd *wanted* –

He shook his head briskly. Absurd. He had many quirks, but a death wish was not among them. No sense speculating on exactly what had gone on till he had more data. There were other puzzles to consider.

For instance, why, after the first failure, had they – or it – attempted to come through in the same spot? The boundaries between universes must be particularly permeable there. But that could hardly be the only place on the planet with thin walls. No, they particularly wanted to enter at this point, which implied... what? That there was something special they could only get here. Some object? Something from UNIT? It was possible, even likely. And the third alternative was some*one*. An ally on this side.

Which would mean they needed help getting through. But it was clear from the experience he'd just been through that the others were so alien that they couldn't even manifest to human senses. How could they communicate?

He sat up straight. A cold little rivulet ran down his spine.

Through the universal language, of course.

Through mathematics.

CHAPTER SEVEN

'It's not working, young Pat.'

'I know that,' Unwin snarled. 'You don't have to tell me that.' He stared at his glass. Was this his third drink or his fourth? Quite a luxury getting drunk on Cognac. He tilted what remained down his throat.

'Not working at all.' Brett strolled to the window and looked out at the comfortable view. Field and forest. Very *Wind in the Willows*, very Merrie Old England. Burn it all. Burn this house – he ran his eyes over the seventeenth-century oak panelling and the tapestries and stained glass, and Unwin slouched in a leather club chair. This decaying, shameful country, lost with its empire. Destroy and replace it. Let Jerusalem be builded here. 'You're supposed to be the genius.'

'I am the genius!' Unwin's consonants were a little muddy, but he wasn't really drunk. He wished he were. He wanted badly to be drunk. 'The computations are... You can't imagine. You can't imagine the complexity. You think you've had a good day if you balance your chequebook.'

'My business manager does that for me,' Brett said languidly. 'Our friends on the other side seem displeased. I can't say I blame them.'

'To hell with them.'

'We're letting down our side.'

'It's not my fault!' Unwin banged his glass down on the table. 'It's not my fault if the equations are so bloody... Unnatural. That's what they are.'

'Well, what do you expect?'

Unwin put his face in his hands and began to weep hysterically. Brett grimaced. Histrionics annoyed him. But he had to comfort this spineless bastard, get him back on his feet. He gave Unwin a reassuring, manly pat on the shoulder and sat down opposite him. 'Now, my lad,' he said, lighting a cigarette, 'you mustn't let it get to you. Naturally it's frustrating. Nothing like this has ever been done. I don't mean something equivalent has never been done, I mean *nothing*. Ever. Since this little speck was spawned.'

'Exactly,' Unwin sniffled. 'Why not give me credit for the extraordinarily difficult things I've accomplished? All this nagging.'

'You feel unappreciated.'

'I *am* bloody unappreciated.' Unwin rubbed his sleeve across his eyes. The drinks had suddenly made themselves felt. 'And I'm drunk. Oh God I'm drunk. I didn't know I was drunk.'

'Cognac sneaks up on you,' said Brett, although he knew this wasn't exactly true. Four Cognacs bolted down couldn't be said, in any sense of the word, to sneak.

'I'm not getting enough help.'

'It's *your* help that's needed,' Brett said supportively. 'It can't be done without *you*. Where would *I* be without you, old man. I'm ashamed to admit it, but when I'm nasty it's out of envy. I barely scraped a third, you know. I'm dependent on you. Makes me feel useless, say things I shouldn't.'

Unwin took out his handkerchief and blew his nose. 'How did you get your position then, with only a third?' He sounded somewhat appeased.

'Family connections, obviously. Really, Unwin, you know how the system works. But you got your position,' he continued admiringly, 'on brains.'

'My family is not exactly unimportant.'

'No, no, certainly not. Not what I meant at all.'

'I may not have your lineage, but through my mother's second cousin we go back to the Plantagenets.'

'Yes indeed,' said Brett, wondering how long he was going to have to keep this up.

'That damned circle. Who made it?'

'I'd like to know that,' Brett said slowly. 'I'd like to know that very much. However, even without that interference, I don't believe they'd have made it through. The pattern breaks off like it did before.'

'How did you get those papers that let us onto the site?'

'I have my sources. I have my little ways.'

Unwin slid down in the chair, his head back. Brett presumed he'd passed out and was about to shake him and get him to bed when Unwin said, 'Some of the computations they want don't make any sense.'

'I thought none of it made any sense.'

'This is different. They don't match the others. It's as if I'm working on two different problems. Prime numbers. I explained primes to you.'

'Many times.'

'But this second problem, these primes equations, are similar to code-breaking.'

'Well, you're good at that, aren't you?'

'But why two problems? They're quite different sets of equations.'

Brett sensed an abstruse lecture coming. He stood up. 'You're done in, old boy. Why don't you go to bed?'

'My mind won't stop. It runs round and round like a hamster.'

'Then you should definitely go to –'

'A hamster in a wheel, I mean. Not a hamster running to and fro. A hamster doing that *gets* somewhere. Did you ever own a hamster? I did. It went to live in the sofa.'

'Where I dare say it was very happy.'

'I think it starved to death. But we never found the body.'

Brett leaned over him, one hand on the chair back. 'You're not going off on me, Pat old man?' he said in a dreadfully soft voice. 'Not going off on me, eh?'

Unwin's eyes snapped open. He stared into Brett's face for a second, then looked away. 'No. No, of course not.'

'There's a lad.' Brett smiled and patted his arm. 'Now, off to bed.'

On the first storey Brett had refurbished a room, formerly a small parlour, to serve as Unwin's work station. It contained no fewer than three computers, as well as shelves of books and journals. Brett rarely entered it, preferring to leave that sort of thing to Unwin, who knew how it worked. He himself was just barely computer literate. But he had some grasp of the basics, and after leaving Unwin collapsed fully clothed on his bed – to hell with him if he woke up sick – Brett went down to the workroom and seated himself at the middle computer.

He examined the keyboard for a few minutes, trying to remember exactly what he had seen Unwin do to call up the program he wanted. Usually he'd just read over Unwin's shoulder, but a few times he'd watched him key in the codes. After a couple of false starts, he found the correct site and clicked on the Contact icon.

Originally, Unwin had communicated in equations and sets of numbers that Brett found incomprehensible, but after a few weeks their correspondent had worked out enough English to make this unnecessary. With one finger – there was no reason he should ever have learned to type – Brett typed the word 'Contact'. Nothing happened. He watched the screen tensely as if by looking away he might miss something. Minutes passed. At last, he decided he didn't know what he was doing after all and was about to hit Exit when a word materialised letter by letter:

HERE

Quickly he typed:

THIS IS BRETT

YES

I AM UNWIN'S PARTNER

YES

WE HAVE BEEN DISCUSSING THE FAILURE

YES

ASIDE FROM THE INCOMPLETE CALCULATIONS HERE, IS THERE ANY PROBLEM ON YOUR SIDE?

YES

Loquacious bastard, Brett thought.

WOULD YOU DESCRIBE IT TO ME?

NO

'Oh for Christ's sake,' Brett said aloud.

WHY NOT?

IT IS TOO TECHNICAL FOR YOU TO UNDERSTAND.

TRY TO COMMUNICATE ON MY LEVEL

WHAT?

Brett took a deep breath, then, lips tight, typed:

TRY TO EXPLAIN IT TO ME IN A WAY I MIGHT UNDERSTAND

Several minutes passed. Brett waited impatiently.

THERE IS A PROBLEM WITH LACK OF POWER

YOU DO NOT HAVE AN ADEQUATE POWER SOURCE?

YES

YOU THOUGHT THAT YOU DID BUT DISCOVERED YOU DID NOT.

NOT ENOUGH POWER TO COME THROUGH YOU MUST SUPPLY MORE COMPLETE CALCULATIONS THEN WE WILL NOT NEED AS MUCH POWER

IS THERE ANY WAY TO SUPPLY YOU WITH POWER FROM THIS SIDE?

Another pause.

THERE MAY BE

WHAT?

THE MAN WHO DREW THE CIRCLE THAT PREVENTED US

EXPLAIN

IRRATIONALITY

EXPLAIN FURTHER

IRRATIONALITY

'Jesus,' Brett muttered.

STOP HIM

WHO IS HE?

WE DO NOT KNOW
HOW WOULD I KNOW HIM WHAT DOES HE LOOK LIKE?
THE QUESTION IS MEANINGLESS.
IS THERE ANYTHING UNUSUAL ABOUT HIM?
HIS ENERGY IS DIFFERENT
HOW?
DIFFERENT
It was like questioning a bloody Ouija board.
IF I MET HIM WOULD I SENSE THIS ENERGY?
NO
BUT HE DREW THE CIRCLE HE WAS IN THE FIELD
YES
BUT I CANNOT FIND HIM?
WE HAVE BEEN FINDING
FINDING HIM?
POWER
IS HIS ENERGY THE POWER?
PERHAPS WE ARE TRYING UNWIN IS HELPING
HELPING HOW?
HE UNDERSTANDS THE NUMBERS
WHICH NUMBERS?
THE PRIME NUMBERS
The bloody prime numbers. Brett supposed he'd have to get
Pat to explain them again and listen this time. He typed:
END CONTACT
STOP HIM
THE MAN WHO DREW THE CIRCLE?
YES. STOP HIM.
HOW?
HE IS DANGEROUS STOP HIM
HOW?
END CONTACT
'Come back you bastard!'
But the screen had gone dark, and an instant later the
computer itself shut down.

CHAPTER EIGHT

Molecross insisted, against all advice, on leaving the medical ward. Before they reluctantly released him, he went through one last round of questioning. He didn't find this a problem, he simply told them the truth: that he had neither seen nor heard anything. What he did not, could not, reveal was the ecstasy that filled him. He wept as they interrogated him, and they thought it was the pain, but it was from joy. Wonder quenched his dry soul.

When he got home, he took a handful of painkillers and collapsed on the carpet between two filing cabinets. He lay suspended. No food passed his lips, no waste passed from his body. The thin pile beneath him was a couch of feathers. Time was only a murmur at the edge of his consciousness. He knew things now, knew them powerfully. Oh rapturous secrets. Truly, he was one of the blessed.

Then the snake entered his sweet Eden.

Curiosity. He wanted to know the cause of his vision.

No, he thought desperately, but it was no use. Human nature claimed him and he fell back into his self, a husk dry as nutshell. In rage and anguish he pounded the carpet. He shoved furiously at the filing cabinets like Samson at the pillars of Gaza and strained his back.

Molecross spent the next several minutes sitting on the floor of the shower with his neck beneath the dribbling spray and his bandaged stump stuck outside the curtain, until the hot water ran out. Then he huddled in a blanket next to the space heater and thought. When he returned to himself just now, had he really descended *that* low? After all, he was a journalist, one of the world's highest callings. He pursued truth. Not just transcendent truth, but the ordinary, small, earthly sort too. Such as: what exactly had happened that night?

Whatever it was, the Doctor was interested in it too. He knew the little man was the Doctor, even though he looked like none of the few descriptions Molecross had come across. The descriptions didn't look like one another either; perhaps he changed shapes. This was a wonder too. Molecross's heart beat faster. Another of the Great Secrets. A mystery only he could uncover. It would be the headline of every paper in the world, in 72-point type. Let them sneer then.

But what about the other problem? What had frozen the ground and taken his hand?

Sobering now, he realised that it was likely he had been the victim of some super-secret government weapon rather than an alien force. That was so much more probable. In Molecross's experience truth favoured probability, and he was committed to the truth. For a moment walls pressed in on him and he breathed the stale air of reality, glimpsed how very small, what a poor thing, the world was. Then he shoved the revelation away. The government had mutilated him. That would be a front-page story too.

His stump was beginning to throb beneath its bandages. He stumbled to the medicine cabinet and took some more pain pills. Damned things didn't really work. He could still feel the pain, dulled, like it was buried beneath a layer of rugs, but still there. How long would he hurt? He was supposed to return to the UNIT medical facility in two days to be checked.

God, what day was it? In panic he staggered into the kitchen to read the clock on the microwave.

He had only been home three hours.

Ace was frustrated. She had been well chuffed when the Doctor finally gave her something to do: i.e. sneak into Molecross's house while he was in hospital to see if she found anything interesting. The Doctor persuaded UNIT to send a car for her, so she didn't have to take another boring train and bus journey. From UNIT HQ, she cycled to Molecross's cottage, careful to stop about a hundred yards away and hide the bike in a spinney before she approached. The cottage was a pretty little place, like something out of a fairy tale, but Ace suspected it was not much fun to live in. She crept up to the tiny front window and peered inside. The interior was dim and for a minute she couldn't work out what she was seeing, then she realised it was a mass of filing cabinets. 'Like a bloody office supply shop,' she muttered and was just about to go round the back to break in when she spotted something on the floor next to one of the cabinets. Shoes. And with feet in.

Ace jumped back. Bollocks! Why wasn't he at the medical ward? Presuming it was Molecross. She carefully peeked in again. The shoes weren't moving, and there was no way to tell who they belonged to, except it was clearly someone with big feet. Hands in pockets, she looked around, squinting against the bright morning sun. Cycling out she had begun to sweat and had undone her jacket. Now she was cold again. She wasn't going to wait around here freezing. She'd go back to UNIT and try to get in touch with the Doctor. A sudden bump and bang came from inside the cottage, and when she looked through the window again, the feet were gone.

Ace retreated to the spinney, where she refastened her jacket and settled in to wait. Molecross's cottage was isolated behind a hedgerow with a few red holly berries among its twistings of blackberry thorns, and backed up to spindly woods. She wondered how much of the land actually belonged to the house – he'd wake up one morning and find them bulldozing to build a shopping centre. Now, however, it was quiet except for the occasional car passing on the other side of the hedgerow.

Curious about Molecross's own form of transportation, she moved softly through the trees till she could see the back of the cottage. A beat-up, purplish Mini, at least ten years old, sat among the weeds. She supposed he had to have a car to travel around investigating. Ace was of two minds as to whether Molecross was a total loony. She'd seen enough outrageous things in her time to reserve judgment on reports of strange happenings. On the other hand, she'd had mates in Perivale who were into all this paranormal stuff and it had always struck her as soft. Even after her mind-opening travels with the Doctor, she was still inclined to think it was rubbish.

It was odd, she thought, for the Doctor to be taking someone like Molecross even half seriously. But he always had his reasons, and they were always good reasons, just like he was good. He was going to stop these aliens and fix this time mess, and like always she'd watch his back. And commit a little b-and-e when necessary. Ace grinned. She quite enjoyed breaking and entering, actually, and it was nice to have an excuse to do it in the cause of right.

Whenever she finally got the opportunity. Molecross could be in there all – hang on. Ace stepped farther back into the trees. Molecross came weaving out the back door towards his car. It must be an automatic, or how could he drive? She hoped he was returning to the medical ward; he looked well ill. All white and wobbly. Probably shouldn't even be driving. Maybe it would be better to stop him and explore the house later – but as she hesitated, he drove the Mini, its exhaust spitting fitfully, through a gap in the hedgerow and was gone.

Ace sighed, put Molecross out of her mind, and went to the door. Unlocked. Disappointed, she pushed it open and entered a tiny, extremely clean kitchen, the neatest kitchen, in fact, she'd ever been in. She looked in amazement at the spotless stove and shining lino and was unable to resist peeking into the refrigerator. Equally neat.

The Doctor hadn't been worried about Molecross's computer, into which he could easily hack. He had asked her to look through his papers instead, particularly any notes he might have made. Well, hard cheese for the Doctor, she thought, examining the well-polished computer desk. Empty and shiny as a new-washed plate. She opened the drawers, but they were all filled with disks. Responsibly, if grudgingly, she went through each of these, reading the labels: Animal Mutilations, UFO sightings, UFO sightings America, UFO sightings Asia and Europe, Raptures – the last puzzled her and she brought it up on the computer. Something to do with people standing around in their kitchens or wherever and suddenly vanishing. Called to God, some Americans claimed. Ace snorted. She'd seen a lot of that sort of thing, and it never involved anything as pleasant as being called to God.

The rest of the disks were more of the same. Dubiously, she eyed the filing cabinets. How long would it take her to check everything in them? She went up and down the little passages between them – all very orderly. The journey brought her to one of the walls of shelves. Surely they'd be quicker to get through than the files. Cocking her head, Ace began to walk slowly along, as if she were searching for a book in a library. The folders were carefully labelled and appeared to contain articles torn from newspapers and magazines. She went meticulously from wall to wall. The folders were replaced by books: *Crop Circles: Why Not Now?*, *It's All Lies: the Truth About Mass Media*, *Velcro of the Gods*...

Ha! In its own little niche lay a blue folder labelled 'Pending'. If this wasn't it, nothing was. Ace leafed through the meagre contents. Bills, bills, more bills – jackpot! A leaf torn from a pad with a short series of numbers and letters. She was pretty certain they were from a number plate. She copied them, musing on the title 'Pending'. Was Molecross planning to find the car's owner? She couldn't think of any other reason to have a plate number.

This small find turned out to be her last one. Ace went over the room again and searched the bedroom wardrobe and the kitchen cabinets. She opened each filing cabinet drawer and checked the labels of the files. These appeared to be the same as for the folders on the shelves, only holding clippings from earlier years. The Doctor ought to hire Molecross to organise the TARDIS library.

Other than going through every one of the folders and files, which would take at least a couple of days, there wasn't much else she could do. And anyway, since Molecross was so organised, it was unlikely there was anything stuck randomly among his carefully labelled records. Mindful of his orderliness, she tried to put everything back exactly as she found it, and as she left she wiped up the small traces of dirt she'd tracked in.

Molecross returned to the UNIT hospital ward, but he was far from defeated. He had a plan. And anyway, his arm appeared to need attention; there were foul-smelling yellow crusts on his bandages. With a serendipity that he assumed blessed his purpose, the nurse at the desk was one who had attended him on his first visit. He made certain to stop and thank her for her previous kindness, and she smiled like a person not used to appreciation. All to the good, he thought as he proceeded to his room. He was impressed with his own wiliness.

There was indeed some infection. Molecross sat patiently through the scolding by the doctor, occasionally giving the proper apologetic responses. He was prescribed antibiotics and hooked up to an IV. He was given painkillers. But in spite of his new confidence, he faltered at the idea of actually seeing his injury; when his stump was being cleaned and disinfected, he looked away.

The painkillers set him peacefully afloat but he sternly applied his will and retained some clearheadedness. It was important that he make his move before the nurse went off duty, and he wanted to be coherent. He had no idea when her shift ended, and this made him anxious, which further cut the drugs' calming qualities. In a short while, he was actively nervous and, ignoring the muffled but persistent pain of his wound, he got out of bed and travelled with his IV into the hall.

The nurse was still there, thank heaven. She looked at him with professional alarm, but he waved and smiled reassuringly. 'Only wanted to say ta again.'

'That's very sweet of you, Mr Molecross.' She smiled briefly as she came around the counter. 'But you must return to bed now.'

'You're so nice,' he said sincerely, and her smile was warmer as she escorted him back to his room. After she settled him in bed and was checking the IV, he said, as if he had just thought of it, 'Oh, you know, there was another fellow in here with me the second day. Friend of the Doctor like me. We chatted a bit and made plans to get together, but you know,' he looked properly embarrassed, 'I was so, erm, cloudy that I've forgotten his name.'

'Oh that would be Mr Amberglass,' she said. 'He went home that day.'

'Amberglass. Of course. Jerry, wasn't it?'

She shot him an amused glance. 'Ethan.'

'Yes, yes, yes. Ethan. Where was my brain? How is he doing?'

'Quite well, apparently. Hasn't had to come back here at any rate.'

Molecross smiled. 'Lucky him.'

'Oh not to worry,' she said comfortingly. 'We'll have you out of here in a couple of days.'

But Molecross left that night.

Ethan stiffened when, at the beginning of the second movement, a late patron took the seat behind him. He had deliberately purchased a ticket for high in the gallery, where he would be isolated, and now some idiot had come and, in spite of the empty seats all around, sat right next to him. He was considering moving when the newcomer spoke:

'Bach is one of my favourites too.'

Ethan's head snapped around.

'These particular cello pieces aren't among his most popular, but I think they may be his most profound. I'm sure you share my opinion.'

'You gave me your bloody word!' Ethan hissed.

'Erm,' said the Doctor. 'Not exactly.'

Ethan started to get up but the Doctor caught his arm. 'I did come for the music.' His eyes were innocent and sincere. 'Stay and enjoy it. We'll talk later.'

At the interval, Ethan made straight for the bar. 'I'm bloody sick of turning around and finding you there.'

'I wanted to hear the performance. She's a genius in her way, don't you think?'

Ethan swore and ordered a large whiskey and soda.

'Hard day at work?' said the Doctor sympathetically. Ethan didn't answer. 'I noticed the piano in your flat. Do you play yourself? Mathematical and musical ability are often linked.' Ethan's drink arrived, and he gulped down a couple of pills. 'You know, particularly with alcohol, I'm not at all sure those are good for you.'

'That's a laugh coming from you.'

'You're not seeing me at my best.'

'I'm afraid I am,' said Ethan. He was livid and his dark eyes looked black. 'I'm afraid this is what you bloody do. Stand out in fields in the middle of the night and summon strange powers –'

'I didn't –'

'Materialise in peoples' flats.'

'I used the door –'

'Confer with mysterious government officials. Operate under an alias.'

'Doctor is not an alias –'

'Who are you!' said Ethan furiously. 'Tell me now!'

'Don't you want to hear the second half?'

'As if I could concentrate. Tell me.'

'If I do, will you promise to go back in?'

Ethan drained his glass and slammed it on the bar. 'Yes, god-damnit. All right. Yes I will bloody go back in. Now who are you?'

'I'm an alien from another planet. I'm here to save the Earth. It's what I do.' The Doctor checked his programme. 'Hm, Mendelssohn. A bit frivolous after the Bach, don't you think? Perhaps we should go after all.'

In the pub, the Doctor ordered an orange juice and Ethan got another whiskey and soda in spite of the fact that the first one had gone right to his head. He was glad he was foggy. More fogginess was bound to be better. Even as they left the concert hall, he had begun trying to persuade himself that he had heard the Doctor wrong, or perhaps simply made the remark up. Unfortunately he hadn't made up the Doctor himself, who was sitting across from him primly sipping his orange juice. Why did he wear that hat? It looked as if it had been run over.

'I need your help.'

'Oh go away,' Ethan groaned. 'We keep having this conversation. You come, I tell you to go, you stay, and things get crazy.'

'I think you're exaggerating. That trip to the field was Ace's idea. All I've done is ask you a few questions.'

Ethan finished his second drink. 'And tell me you're from outer space.' He slumped against the bench back. 'Are you from outer space?'

'I think the phrase is rather vulgar, but yes, I am.'

'You're not green.'

'The Edreki are. And many, many other races. You humans are so homocentric.'

'I thought you only appeared to Americans. In the desert.'

'That's a silly thing to say. I'm afraid you've had too much to drink.'

Ethan was afraid he hadn't had enough: the conversation was still making sense to him. On the other hand, he didn't seem to be able to focus enough to ask for another whiskey. He stared glassily at the Doctor, who waited politely, a helpful expression on his face. 'Look,' he said, enunciating carefully, 'if you're from outer space, or wherever –'

'I prefer to say from another galaxy. It's more precise.'

'Whatever. If you're from there, then to get here you had to have a very advanced... a very advanced... A thing that could travel between galaxies. Right?'

'That's right.'

'So your culture would be very sophisticated in terms of physics. And stuff.'

The Doctor nodded gravely. 'Stuff as well, yes.'

'So why the hell would you need help from a... an earthl– from me? You're bound to be mathematically so far ahead of us I couldn't begin to comprehend it.'

'An excellent question.' The Doctor looked very pleased. Ethan half expected him to add 'Top marks.' 'It's exactly your limitations that I need. I want to know how far a brilliant human mathematician could get working on certain equations.'

'What equations?'

'Your friend U's.'

'Oh no, no, no.' Ethan shook his head and then regretted it. 'We've been through this. That's all rot. You said so yourself.'

'I think I should take another look.'

'It's crap I tell you. Anyway, I think I've erased it.'

'Oh that won't be a problem.'

'No, of course not. I forgot for a minute. You're from outer bloody space.'

The Doctor pursed his lips. 'There's no reason to be impolite.'

'Want to bet? You know what I think? I think you're as nuts as I am. I think you're a chap who thinks he's an alien. You're barmy. Around the twist. Barking.'

'You know barking as a synonym for crazy hasn't anything to do with dogs. It was the name of a nineteenth-century insane asylum.'

'You've slipped your leash and gone out for a stroll.'

'No,' the Doctor said mildly.

'The furniture in your head is all nailed to the ceiling.'

'Now that may be true.'

Ethan leaned his elbow on the table, head in hand, and gaped stupidly at his beer mat. The Doctor waited.

'Can you prove you're really a spaceman?'

'I prefer the term "alien".'

'You're not green.'

'We've been through this, Mr Amberglass.'

'Aliens are green. Or grey.'

'Shall we compromise on "extraterrestrial"?'

'I've made you up,' Ethan whispered. 'I've made up the whole last few days. Please tell me I have.'

His face was suddenly so raw with pain that the Doctor glanced away.

'But I don't want to be mad again either,' Ethan went on, his voice quiet and flat. 'It's not good, you know. It's like being dragged over gravel for a long, long time. Every now and then you knock your head hard and go unconscious. Then you're just being dragged again. Do you know what I mean?'

'No,' said the Doctor gently. 'And it's a good thing for the universe I don't. Here,' he extended his arm across the table, 'feel my pulse.' Ethan stared at the arm uncomprehendingly. 'My pulse. Feel it.'

Ethan clumsily took his wrist. For a minute he sat completely still, head down, as if listening as well as feeling. Then he let go. 'Does Ace know?'

'Of course,' said the Doctor, surprised by the question. 'She travels with me.'

'In your spaceship?'

'TARDIS. Short for Time And Relative –'

'So she's your daughter?'

'Ace? Goodness no.'

'Are the two of you...?'

The Doctor blinked, confused, then said quickly, 'No, no. We're friends.'

'She cares a lot for you, you know.'

'I know,' the Doctor said quietly.

'You should have seen her in that field. Nearly out of her mind with worry.'

The Doctor said nothing. Sobering, Ethan studied him. 'So, you know, I think she doesn't know about you. Not really.' The Doctor remained silent. 'Because she loves you, she doesn't see it.'

'See it?'

'You remind me of my great-uncle David. There was this look about him. He'd seen bad action in the war. He never talked about it, and when I was older, after he was dead, I realised that was because, to survive, he'd done things no one should ever have to do. You don't talk about it either, do you? Especially not to her.'

In the dim light, the Doctor's eyes were brighter than they ought to have been, as if they contained their own light. He still didn't say anything. Ethan dropped his own eyes, poked a finger at his soaked beer mat. 'I lied to you.'

The Doctor shifted slightly and crossed his arms. 'Yes?'

'I did see something that night.'

'Really?' The Doctor's tone was neutral. 'You were the only one.'

'I gathered that. That's why I didn't tell you. I thought probably I was hallucinating.'

'Tell me now.'

Ethan hesitated. 'It's difficult to describe. It's as if there were lights – no, that's wrong. It was dark. Pitch dark. Is that how it was for you?' The Doctor nodded. 'Absolutely black. But I saw... well, I suppose lines is the best description. I don't know how I could see them. They must have been white. They...' he thought for a few seconds '...gleamed.'

'Like moonlight?'

'No. Harder, if that makes any sense. Like the darkness was harder. Do you know what I mean?'

'Yes.'

'Then, when it was over, they were gone.'

'And you haven't seen them since?'

'No. But I haven't had a headache since either. They might have been a migraine symptom.'

'But your headaches haven't caused anything like this before.'

'No.'

The Doctor chewed thoughtfully on his lip.

'Was it... them?' said Ethan. 'Did I see them trying to come through?'

'Yes, I think so. Or at least you saw what the human eye could make of them.'

'Why didn't anyone else see anything?'

'Mm.' The Doctor chewed his lip some more. 'Tell me, do you ever have odd visual experiences? Not seeing things. Distortions.'

'Yes,' said Ethan puzzledly. 'How did you know?'

'What are they like?'

'Well, it's really only one thing. Sometimes what I'm looking at sort of smears, like a rapid pan-shot in a movie where the scene goes out of focus. Then it snaps back. Only if I'm watching something that's moving it's as if I,' again he searched for the right words, 'skipped a beat. Missed out a split second.'

'What do your doctors say?'

'That it might be epilepsy. Only you can't test the brain for epilepsy unless the person is actually having a fit. Which doesn't coincide very often with being in the examination room. There's no other evidence, though. I don't have grand mal, I don't fall down or anything like that.'

'And you don't "miss time"?'

'Only that split second.'

'Does this happen often?'

'Fairly regularly.'

'And it's not caused by the headaches.'

'It happens without them.'

The Doctor regarded him speculatively, as if making a decision. Finally he said, 'I'm not clear on whether I can tell you this – I can't remember exactly when it was worked out on Earth – but I don't think there's any harm. The human eye, which mine also essentially is, doesn't take in information continuously.'

'What?' said Ethan, still back with the when-worked-out-on-Earth part of the sentence.

'The eye –'

'No, hang on. That part about you couldn't remember whether we've discovered this eye thing yet.'

'Oh yes, that would be confusing. I travel through time as well as space.'

'Oh really?'

'That's why it's *Time* and Relative Dimensions In –'

'Let's just get back to the eye, all right?'

'As you wish. The eye doesn't take in information continuously but in discrete frames, rather like a movie camera. A film has to run at 24 frames a second for motion to look smooth. Our eyes receive from 19 to 25 "frames" – that is to say, snapshots of what we're observing – per second. The question is,' he leaned forward, '*what's in the gaps between the frames?*'

Ethan wasn't sure how much more bizarre information he could process. The Doctor was looking at him as if he expected an answer. 'Aliens?' he said faintly.

'Apparently so.'

'I see *aliens*? I mean, aside from you.'

'Not all the time.'

'I *know* not all the time.'

'What I mean to say is, only when they're attempting to come through out of sync with our vision – in our visual gaps, so to speak.'

'But that can't work, surely. Not everyone sees the same frames at the same exact moment. It's not possible.'

'You're right,' the Doctor agreed. 'But think about this. How many frames could you possibly divide any visual field into? It would be like dividing a line forever: you quickly find yourself in the territory my culture calls reductive infinity – the infinity of smaller and smaller as opposed to larger and larger. And for every two discrete frames there must be a gap where the frames aren't. That's a lot of room. There will always be gaps that no one on earth *ever* sees. That *no one* in the universe who has this particular eye structure ever sees.'

'Then why do I?'

'There are always exceptions. Some peoples' film – to extend the analogy – occasionally snags. Images appear to move a bit too slowly, blurring, or there's a leap forward that elides a split second. When you receive more frames per second than the standard, you're also receiving that many more gaps.'

'But why does it happen?'

The Doctor rested his cheek on his hand. His eyes were sad. Ethan shifted nervously under his gaze. 'What is it?'

For a moment the Doctor didn't answer. Then he said, 'Though it's not concurrent with them, it probably has something to do with your headaches.'

Ethan tried to get hold of this, but his mind was starting to slow down. He had a feeling there was a discrepancy somewhere. His headaches, though organically real, had a psychological cause, whereas his vision... It was no good, he couldn't work it out.

The Doctor was talking again. 'These equations of U's. I know his goal in and of itself is nonsense. But I'm interested in the paths he took trying to get there. He's Patrick Unwin, by the way. Did you know him?' Ethan shook his head. 'Never mind. Will you help me?'

'I don't see what I can do.'

'I want you to go over his equations, see what he was attempting, see if you can carry his computations any further.'

'Even though they lead towards rubbish?'

The Doctor shrugged. 'One man's rubbish, as they say.'

'I don't know whether I can get the time off from work.'

'Leave that to me.'

'Oh right,' Ethan said dryly. 'I forgot. You're an all-powerful spaceman.'

The Doctor smiled. 'Extraterrestrial,' he corrected gently.

CHAPTER NINE

When he got back to his flat, Ethan pushed papers off the bed, fell onto it fully clothed, and passed out. Some time later he woke up with a gluey tongue and a huge thirst. As he moved unsteadily to the kitchen, he realised that a specific noise had woken him. Someone was pounding on his door.

Muttering obscenities, Ethan got a glass of water and drank it down. Then another. He looked in the refrigerator – what he really needed was something carbonated, or with lemon in it. All he saw was an old carton of orange juice. This made him feel slightly ill and he shut the door.

The pounding was still going on. Screw him, Ethan thought, drinking another glass of water. Screw the Doctor and his weird tales and his requests. Then it occurred to him that if his visitor were the Doctor he wouldn't be knocking, he'd only come in his usual way, whatever that was.

He cracked the door open. A tall pudgy man with a bandaged stump where his hand should have been beamed at him. 'Oh it's you,' Ethan said. 'No journalists. Go away.'

He started to close the door, but the man stuck his foot in the way. Ethan stomped on it. The foot withdrew, but the handless arm shoved in. Ethan couldn't bring himself to slam the door on this. He stepped back and Molecross pushed into the room.

'Mr Amberglass? I'm Adrian Molecross. Can we have some light?' He flipped the switch, then paused, surveying the room. 'You're not very neat.'

'And you're missing a hand. Let's not harp on each other's deficiencies.'

'I lost this hand in the line of duty,' said Molecross stiffly. 'At the circle.'

'Yes, I know,' said Ethan, ashamed of his quip.

'You were there too.'

'Yeah. Only it wasn't so...' Ethan trailed off. He thought of the withered hoe handle. 'How did... Why...?'

'Apparently I fell with my hand actually on one of the lines,' Molecross said matter-of-factly. 'Otherwise I was unharmed.'

In spite of himself, Ethan felt bad for Molecross. He didn't quite know what to do. 'Tea?'

'Seriously,' Molecross said when they were seated, he in the armchair and Ethan at the computer table, 'how do you find anything in this mess?'

'I manage.'

Molecross peered around, stopped at the piano. 'You're a musician?'

'Mathematician.'

'Ah.' Molecross daintily sipped his tea. 'So tell me, how do you know the Doctor?'

'I was in hospital,' Ethan said, surprised at his own quick thinking.

'Not that doctor. *The* Doctor.'

'Who?'

'He visited you,' said Molecross impatiently. 'I saw him there.'

'I was drugged out. I don't recall any visitors.'

Molecross eyed him suspiciously. Ethan finally remembered exactly who he was. 'You're the chap with the webzine.'

'*Molecross's Miscellany of the Mysterious and Misunderstood*. Who,' Molecross looked even more suspicious, 'told you I was a journalist?'

'No one. I remembered your website.'

'Really?' Molecross was childishly pleased. 'You read me?'

'Yeah, I read about the crop circle, and so I went out to see what it was about.'

'And did you?'

'No. It was kind of like something fell on my head.'

'Hm,' Molecross mused. 'Perhaps the Doctor was just checking on everyone who'd been in the circle.'

'This circle's a big story then?' Ethan said casually.

'The biggest. But I can't give any details.'

'No, no, of course not. But was it really worth knocking me up in the middle of the night for?'

'The press never sleeps,' Molecross said solemnly. 'Even as we talk, the mystery might be unfolding further.'

'The circle mystery?'

'Strictly speaking, it's not a circle. There! I've said too much! It's me who should be asking the questions.'

'Well,' Ethan said, 'I didn't see anything and I didn't hear anything and I didn't feel anything.' Molecross sighed, then frowned, thinking. His presence was beginning to make Ethan jumpy. 'Well, you've got your story. Sorry I wasn't more help.'

Molecross ignored this, still frowning. 'Can I confide in you?'

'No,' said Ethan. 'Everyone keeps thinking I don't have a life and barging in here to give me one but I do have a life or at least as much of one as I want, so just leave.'

'I think there's a government conspiracy and that the Doctor is helping. His involvement with Earth affairs goes back decades, you know.'

'Yeah?' Maybe there was some use to be got from this idiot yet. 'I didn't know.'

'Oh yes. He's not of this Earth, you know.'

'A spaceman?'

'I prefer "extraterrestrial". Also, he travels through time, not just space.'

'What's he look like?'

'Not like the clichés at all. He looks human. Only he *changes*.'

'Changes how?'

'Changes his body. He's not always the same person.'

'Mm hm.' said Ethan. They were definitely playing with the pixies now.

'He has a reputation for being an intergalactic do-gooder,' Molecross went on. 'But I've always thought there was something suspicious about his ties to the establishment. What if he's helping Them deceive Us?'

'About what?'

'Everything that suits them. This experiment that mutilated me, for instance. They don't want us to know.'

'But you know.'

Molecross nodded grimly. 'And they keep constant tabs on me.'

'Why haven't they just killed you?'

'It would arouse suspicion.'

'Among whom? Nobody else knows anything.'

'But they would if I were killed.'

'Not if they hid your body and destroyed your records. I don't see how it matters whether you're killed or not.'

'Well it does,' said Molecross sullenly.

'No it doesn't.'

Molecross's eyes narrowed. 'I understand. *You* must work for the government yourself.'

Ethan had been waiting his whole career for the opportunity to use his cover story, though he hadn't anticipated its being under these sorts of circumstances. 'I suppose you could say that. I design computer programs for the Inland Waterways Association.'

'An excellent cover.'

Ethan shrugged. 'Go to our website.'

'I might do that. I might just do that. I see I'm dealing with a contaminated source here.'

'If you say so.'

'Oh I do, I definitely do. You're not fooling me into putting any of your views into my story.' Molecross suddenly looked exhausted. He slumped. 'Do you mind if I spend the night here?'

'Of course I mind! Are you out of –'

Ethan jumped up, but he was too late. Molecross had slid to the floor and into sleep, and no amount of shaking or thumping stirred him.

When the Doctor arrived in the morning with Ace, he showed more courtesy than usual by knocking. After a moment, the door cracked open and Ethan peered out warily. He was pale, and the area below his eyes was shadowed and puffy. The Doctor raised his hat politely.

'Good morning. Were you expecting someone else?'

'You never know,' Ethan muttered.

'You look knackered, mate,' said Ace. He eased the door open and she popped in. 'Good luck for you, I've brought some coffee.' She stopped, frowning at the sleeping Molecross. 'Who's this then?'

'Dear me,' said the Doctor from behind her. 'It's Mr Molecross.'

'Yeah,' said Ethan.

Ace bent and examined Molecross curiously. 'What's he doing here?'

'Having a nap,' Ethan said dryly. 'Before that we had an in-depth interview in which I turned out not to know anything useful.'

'Mm.' The Doctor closed the door quickly. 'You didn't mention me, did you?'

'Don't be daft,' Ethan snapped. 'But he mentioned you. He thinks you're part of a government plot.'

'Ah.'

'Are you?'

'Sometimes yes and sometimes no. In this case no.' The Doctor tapped his chin with the handle of his umbrella. 'We really should remove him.'

'I thought of putting him in the hall, but it seemed not on, somehow.'

'Oh, but he'll be quite safe in the hall, don't you think?' said the Doctor brightly. 'No pickpockets coming in and out or anything of that sort.'

'Who knows? The front door lock's been broken for weeks. Don't do that!' After searching in vain for a clear flat surface, Ace had put the coffee containers on the computer table. Ethan snatched them off and set them on the floor.

'Sorry,' Ace said sarcastically. The Doctor handed her his umbrella.

'I'll attend to Mr Molecross. Just open the door, will you, Ace?' With surprisingly little effort considering his small size, he lifted Molecross under the armpits and started dragging him across the carpet. Molecross jerked and opened his eyes. 'Oops.' The Doctor dropped him and sprang back for the door but collided with Ace stepping forward to help. Molecross rolled over and gaped at them.

'It's you.'

'No, no, no,' said the Doctor hastily, snatching his umbrella from Ace. 'It's only someone who looks like me.'

Molecross pointed accusingly at Ethan. 'You lied!'

'I've never seen this man before,' said Ethan stoutly. 'I thought he'd come for you.'

Molecross swivelled to face the Doctor, forefinger still extended. 'So – you were going to abduct me.'

'Nothing of the sort.'

'You're the Doctor!'

'Oh bollocks,' said Ace. 'What are you on about? This is my uncle John. He's not a doctor, he sells cheese.'

Even as she spoke, this struck her as not the best occupation to have chosen, but the Doctor picked up smoothly:'English cheeses a specialty: Stilton, of course, and cheddar. Wensleydale. Cheshire.'

'You're not a cheese merchant!' Molecross staggered angrily to his feet. 'You're an otherworldly tool of the government!'

'Oh, I say,' the Doctor objected. Ace stepped in front of Molecross.

'Let's just turn down the gas, mate,' she said coolly.

Molecross dodged around her to seize the Doctor's arm, feeling for his wrist. The Doctor slipped from his grasp and

Molecross, thwarted and outnumbered, ran out the door. No one pursued him.

'Very convincing,' said Ethan.

'Yes,' sighed the Doctor. 'We didn't handle that very well, did we?'

'Not very well? It was like something out of Wodehouse, only not funny.' Ethan gloomily flopped into the armchair. 'What am I supposed to do when he publishes my address for all and sundry to visit?'

'Oh,' the Doctor said casually, 'I'll just have to sabotage his publication. Send in a worm so he can't send anything out. Erase his mailing list. Delete certain files.'

Ethan was impressed. 'How long will that take?'

'If I use the TARDIS computers, about ten minutes.' The Doctor raised his hat and was gone.

'Hang on –' Ethan called, but the only response was the sound of the downstairs door closing.

'Ah,' said Ace. 'Well.'

'When will he be back?'

She shut the door. 'Hard to say, really.'

'Look. He told me he was an alien. All right? You don't have to pretend any longer.'

'I wasn't pretending!' she said defensively. 'I only left some things out.'

'That's a pretty big leave-out, someone being extraterrestrial.'

'I knew he'd tell you when he felt like it.'

'Oh he did. He happened to feel like it during the interval of a concert, in the bar.'

'Kind of odd, that, since he doesn't drink.'

'Well, what *does* he do? Skip about the universe performing good deeds like some boy scout?'

'Yeah. And he's been more use than you'll ever be, so you can shut up.'

'What about harm? Does he ever do harm? Or is he some sort of angel?'

'Only by accident,' she said sullenly. 'Everyone does *some* harm. Except maybe,' she added nastily, 'people who hide in their flats all the time.'

'Right. Let's go back to the circle tonight. Maybe this time I'll get to lose a hand.'

'You're a snotty little loser, aren't you?'

He was on his feet. 'If this Doctor of yours is such a genius, why does he travel with a stupid girl like you?'

'Get stuffed!!'

'Screw you!'

'Creep!'

'Idiot!!'

'Wanker!'

'Bitch!'

And then they were in each other's arms, rolling on the floor, jerking at their clothes. For a few minutes things were clumsy and bumpy, then, all at once, they became deliciously slow. Well, Ace thought in happy surprise, who'd have guessed?

CHAPTER TEN

When, forty minutes later, the Doctor trotted up the stairs and knocked on the door, there was a scrambling inside. 'Hang on a minute,' Ace called. Humming quietly to himself, the Doctor hung on considerably more than a minute until Ethan opened the door. He was flushed and damp and his shirt was buttoned crookedly. 'Dear me,' the Doctor thought. He considered a number of remarks – 'Am I interrupting?' 'Your shirt isn't buttoned properly.' 'How's Ace?' – but none of them seemed quite appropriate.

'All done,' he said cheerfully, then realised that wasn't exactly appropriate either. 'Mr Molecross has been hobbled,' he went on quickly. 'Nothing will be revealed. About you. That is, about your address.'

'Oh. Thanks.'

There was a pause.

'Ace still here?'

'Oh. Yeah. Of course. Come in.'

The Doctor did, pretending not to notice the overturned coffee cups and other evidence of energetic activity. Ace came into the room, smiling awkwardly, her face red from a quick scrubbing. 'Hello, Professor.'

'Hello, Ace.'

Another pause.

'Erm,' Ace felt around in her pocket, 'I've got this for you.' She gave him the paper with the copied numbers and letters on it. 'You weren't around last night, and you were in such a hurry this morning, and then what with the Molecross stuff –'

'Yes, yes,' said the Doctor, glancing at the paper. 'Hm. Definitely a number plate. I don't see how it connects with anything in which we're interested, but it's worth investigating. Later, however.' He handed it back to her. 'I'd like to get you started first, Mr Amberglass.'

'Right,' said Ethan brightly.

Musing over the last few hours as he drove along the A20, Molecross wasn't best pleased with his behaviour. Research, not human interaction, was his strong point. He'd been far too impulsive when he ought to have thought things through. That he had actually seen the Doctor – the Doctor! – three times and got nothing from it was unforgivable. He should at least have waited till morning to visit Amberglass, taken things slowly, begun with their common experiences in the field. Then when, amazingly, the Doctor arrived, he'd have been in a position to approach him. And even if the Doctor hadn't come by, Amberglass would be a future contact. Now they'd never have anything to do with him. He'd really blown it.

He'd seen *the Doctor* – a walking mystery, a wonder – and behaved as if he were only the odd little man he looked like. And he'd been greedy. The miraculous could not be captured, grabbed at like a runaway dog. You had to be humble and quiet, and let it come to you.

On the other hand, the Doctor was in league with the government – the same government that had created the weapon that took his hand. So he needed to be stopped. Molecross frowned: as far as he could remember from the available information, the Doctor couldn't be stopped. That was how he managed to keep saving the universe. He was slippery; he embodied the unexpected. He wore a stupid hat, encouraging you to think he was an idiot.

Well, all right. Perhaps he couldn't be stopped. But his plan could be exposed. That was Molecross's duty as a journalist. There might not be higher truths than the truths he sought, but there were higher needs. The need of the public to be protected from the nefarious. The only secrets the establishment kept were evil secrets – otherwise, why not reveal them?

His damaged arm ached horribly, and its dried seepage smelled. He'd better stop by UNIT again to have it treated and rebandaged. Maybe he'd get an artificial hand, an articulated metal one like Schwarzenegger in *Terminator II*. Well, actually, Schwarzenegger's whole skeleton had been metal, but for a lot of the movie you only saw the stripped hand or the cool black leather glove covering it. That wouldn't be bad. Maybe he could get UNIT to pay for it. No. Taking a favour from the people he was investigating would compromise him.

Molecross's eyes filled with tears. The shabbiness of compromise, of concession and petty lies and half-truths. He so longed for the transcendent. For a few hours he thought he'd found it. He had fooled himself. A cold draft of doubt whispered across his mind – perhaps he'd been fooling himself all along, perhaps –

The Doctor. The Doctor existed. The door to transcendence cracked open again. All would be well, and all would be well, and every manner of thing would be well.

Brett was not a clubbable man, nor, with his arrogant, aristocratic features, did he look like a clubbable man. Nor, frankly, had he any desire to be one. This made him the wrong person, he knew, to drop into a pub for some information but he could hardly ask Pat to do it. The fool would just get pie-eyed.

Brett dressed down as well as he could – he realised he could only get away with a certain amount of common-man attire – in a second-rate suit with a cuff that needed reweaving. He chose a pub only a mile down the road from the crop-pattern field. As he crossed the small car park, he noticed that the pub sign was one of those 'cute' ones: a cuddly cartoon dragon holding a daisy. He averted his eyes and pushed open the door. Cigarette smoke and the odour of stale beer – exactly what he'd expected. His suit would stink for days. Probably he should just give it away.

Arranging his features into a suitably pleasant expression, he went to the bar, pleased to see that two other men were there. He ordered a pint of porter, nodded companionably at the bartender, a spotty boy who looked too young for the job, and in the act of surveying the room took in his two neighbours. One was a portly, handsome man in a business suit, possibly a solicitor; the other, sinewy and smaller, looked like a farmer. They were discussing the recent American outbreak of mad cow disease with a certain amount of satisfaction. When they had finished this happy indulgence in *Schadenfreude* and returned their attention to their drinks, Brett spoke up.

'Can anyone tell me what those soldiers down the road are guarding?'

'Damned if I know,' said the farmer into his beer. 'Lot of bother over a prank.'

'Prank?'

'One of those crop circles,' said the solicitor without much interest.

'But what an extraordinarily minor thing for which to call out the army.'

''s not the army,' said the bartender. 'It's UNIT, like. They handle all the weird stuff. UFOs and that. You know.'

'Complete rubbish,' said the solicitor irritably. '*This* is what I pay back-breaking taxes for.'

'It's a government plot,' said the farmer, 'like that damned dome. They use money for daft projects and then haven't any for the countryside. Bring in agribusiness, that's what they want. Hire Yanks as managers. Course, the Yanks have got their own farm problems now.' He and the solicitor chuckled. The bartender apparently had no quarrel with America and went on quietly polishing glasses. Brett laid some coins beside his glass and took his leave. That had been easier than he expected. Yokels.

'Prat,' said the farmer as the door shut.

He and the solicitor and the bartender snickered.

The rest of Brett's day wasn't as fortuitous. He roused Unwin and put him to work breaking into various files until he turned up a list of UNIT personnel and, after some more work, their biographies. Brett read through all of these carefully. He couldn't for the life of him see anything out of the ordinary about any of them: mostly British, some Indians and Pakistanis and Islanders, same sorts of educational backgrounds, same areas of expertise. These were in some cases a bit unusual, but what would you expect from a department of UFO spotters? He was in the right place, no doubt about that. But the right man wasn't there.

'What's all this about anyway?' said Unwin irritably. He was extremely hung-over and in no mood to be working out ways through firewalls.

'I think our man may be connected with UNIT.'

'What? The circle chap?'

Brett nodded, eyes still on the screen. 'Perhaps he's classified top secret. Push on a bit farther.'

Unwin groaned and kept going. After a number of false starts, stops and reroutings, opening what seemed to him like a hundred files that were of no use at all, he pulled up one that was peculiarly short. 'Two kilobytes,' he said curiously. 'It's practically empty.'

'But not entirely empty. Open it.'

Unwin did. He and Brett stared at the following information.

The Doctor
Birth date: n/a
Nationality: n/a
Personal statistics: variable
Education: unknown
Employment history: unknown
Address: n/a
Contact: none

There were no photographs.

Unwin stared, his jaw slack. 'But this is mad. What do they mean, *variable* personal statistics? Is he immaterial?'

'He's something,' Brett said grimly. 'But I don't yet know what.'

A noise shrilled up the stairs, startling them both.

'The phone.' Unwin looked at Brett in alarm. 'Who can it be?'

'Any number of people,' snapped Brett. 'Fools wanting to sell magazines, pleaders for charitable donations, the newspaper asking me to subscribe again.' He hurried down to the landing, and picked up the receiver. 'Yes?'

'Mr Brett? Mr Sheridan Brett?'

'To whom am I speaking?'

'It's about the crop pattern.'

Brett's eyes flicked to Unwin at the top of the stairs. 'What are you talking about?'

'The crop pattern. I saw your car there.'

'What? Who are you, please?'

'Oh. Yes. Sorry. My name is Adrian Molecross. I'm a journalist.'

'Oh really? A journalist.'

Unwin's eyes widened in panic, but Brett motioned to him to stay calm.

'Yes.'

'For which publication?'

'*Molecross's Miscellany of the Mysterious and Misunderstood*.'

'I don't believe I know it.'

'Well, it doesn't have a large circulation. It's esoteric.'

'Ah.'

'I'm investigating that crop pattern.'

'I wish you'd explain what you're talking about.'

'You know – in the field.'

'In the field?'

'The field. I saw your car leaving there.'

'When?'

'Four days ago, about an hour before dawn.'

'I was leaving a *field*?'

'That's right.'

'With a – what? A crop matter?'

'Pattern.'

'Pattern. I see.'

'Laid out in the field,' Molecross said earnestly. 'In ice.'

'Ice, did you say?'

'Ice.'

'Ah,' said Brett wonderingly. 'So *that's* what that was.'

'You saw it?'

'I noticed it. I certainly had no idea it was some sort of pattern.'

'Why were you there if you didn't know what it was?'

'If you insist on knowing, I was returning from a very late party in London and I needed relief.'

'Rel– Oh. Of course. Yes.'

'I noticed some lines of ice. I thought they were extremely odd. But as it was also extremely cold, I didn't investigate. You say they were part of a pattern?'

'Geometric shapes. They covered the field.'

'But how extraordinary. Some kind of hoax, I presume.'

Molecross lowered his voice. 'I don't think so.'

'No? But what else could it be?'

'It's a government plot.'

Brett rolled his eyes at Unwin. 'Really?'

'There are strange forces there. I've experienced them myself. And there were witnesses.'

'Oh yes?' Brett had been leaning languidly against the wall, but now he straightened up. 'Reliable?'

'Very establishment. Ethan Amberglass, who's a mathematician for the government – you see how it all adds up.'

'Indeed. And the other witness?'

'The Doctor. But I don't know about him. He's an alien.'

Brett stiffened. 'I'm sorry?'

'An alien. He's legendary. I thought maybe he didn't exist, but he does.'

'A legendary alien.'

'Yes,' Molecross said a bit defensively.

'I see. I don't suppose you have his address?'

'No,' said Molecross, a bit stung at the perceived mockery. 'I don't know that. I've only seen him at Amberglass's. But he exists.'

'I'm sure. Well, this has all been very interesting, Mr Molecross. I'm glad you explained those puzzling ice lines to me. But I honestly don't see how I can help you any further, and other matters are pressing.'

Molecross started to protest that he wasn't a crank, but it occurred to him that he might have said too much already. Particularly to someone who had no idea what was going on. What if he became curious?

'Yes, of course, Mr Brett. Thank you.'

'Thank *you*,' said Brett courteously and rang off.

'What was that?' Unwin jabbered. 'Some reporter who *knows* something?'

'He's an idiot,' said Brett dismissively, coming back up the stairs. 'But he did say something interesting. Did you ever work with a chap named Amberglass?'

'Ethan Amberglass.'

'That's right.' Brett's eyes brightened. 'You knew him?'

'No, I never met him. They liked to keep us separated. But he had quite a reputation – boy genius sort of thing.'

'Oh, really?' Brett took Unwin's elbow and led him down the hall. 'Let's look into him, shall we?'

'Why? Do you think *he* knows something?'

'Well, he knows the mysterious Doctor.'

'What?'

'And he was at the circle and witnessed a force of some sort. It's a bit of a coincidence that another mathematician should be there, don't you think?'

'But I understand he was practically a recluse.'

'All the stranger then. Let's get to know him better.'

* * *

Back at his cottage, Molecross reflected that he had handled this one better. Been professional, got the chap's confidence. Courteous fellow too. Posh accent. Nice life, partying all night in London and driving home in your Jaguar. Well, when this story hit the front pages... Molecross turned his abbreviated notes into complete words, then brought up his file on the story. Or at least tried to. Half an hour later, when the full extent of the damage was clear, he pounded his fists on the desk, which, one of his fists not being there, turned out to be a mistake. The stitches on the end of his arm broke open and he had to return to the UNIT medical ward.

'Dear God,' said Unwin when he had finally slipped past Ethan's home computer defences.

'What?' said Brett impatiently.

'This is incredible. Do you know what he's been working on most recently?'

'No, young Pat, I don't. So why don't you cease the rhetorical questions and tell me.'

'My equations.'

'I beg your pardon?'

'The work I was doing at the agency. He's been building on it.' Unwin scanned the figures. 'And very well too,' he said slowly. 'This is... He's done some intriguing things.'

'Isn't that nice?' Brett said softly. 'All the more reason to make his acquaintance.'

CHAPTER ELEVEN

Whatever else the Doctor might be, Ethan had to concede that he was a genius. He had leaned over Ethan's shoulder as he started in on Unwin's calculations and pointed out a few errors that he assured Ethan a human being would have caught sooner or later, though 'later' might be several years from now. The solutions had the elegant beauty that had lured Ethan into mathematics in the first place and he examined them with something like awe.

'"A wild surmise",' said the Doctor.

Ethan removed his attention from the screen. 'I'm sorry?'

'Nothing,' said the Doctor. 'References, see under Obvious.'

'They're another world,' Ethan murmured, turning again to the equations, 'different from ours but complete in itself, in a state of perfection.'

'Which is also stasis.'

'Perhaps not. An alphabet is static until it forms words, and the words refer to concepts, and the concepts move in the mind and become speech, and speech forms the world.'

'The French linguists would disagree strongly, but I think you have a point.' The Doctor straightened. 'There's enough there to keep you busy for days. I'll just pop off then.'

'What will you be doing?'

'Oh, things,' said the Doctor vaguely. He paused at the door. 'I suppose Ace will be dropping by to see how you're progressing and whether you need to consult with me.' His expression was neutral and courteous. Ethan swallowed.

'Right,' he said.

The Doctor smiled and left.

* * *

The Doctor had indeed been doing things, Ace discovered as she walked through the TARDIS. She kept finding various little constructions of wire and metal and glass, some with gears or antennae. These tended to appear whenever the Doctor was concentrating hard on a problem. She didn't know whether they served to distract and amuse him or whether they really were the prototypes of fantastic machines. For a long time she hadn't been certain they were actually the work of the Doctor – perhaps the TARDIS created them for its own mysterious purpose. When she'd finally got up the nerve to ask about them, he had said yes, they were his. But he didn't elaborate.

Ace had a nice long bath. Somewhere, the Doctor had found a frowning rubber duck with horns on its head, and presented it to her. Now she floated it on the soapy water, occasionally kicking at it moodily. She didn't understand this thing with Ethan. She really didn't. He wasn't her type at all. They didn't have anything in common, except – she surprised herself by colouring slightly – for what they, well, had in common, which she had to admit was fantastic. In fact, some of the best – she broke off the thought by submerging her head. He was naff, totally and completely and embarrassingly naff. Except in –

She surfaced violently, splashing water everywhere and turning the duck upside down.

And what was the Doctor going to say? she wondered nervously, rinsing herself off. She'd been asking herself that since this morning, waiting for him to mention it. But the Doctor had been cheerful and noncommittal, as if nothing had happened. Maybe things would just go on like that – though in a funny way she wanted to confide in him, or at least in someone. Why didn't she have a mother figure as well as a father figure? Or at least a girlfriend.

She found the Doctor, as usual, bent over the TARDIS console. He was frowning slightly.

'Hi,' she said hesitantly.

'I don't understand this, Ace,' he said without looking at her.

'No? Well –'

'It's complicated in all the wrong ways. Nothing quite comes together.'

The last sentence could hardly describe her and Ethan; Ace relaxed. 'What d'you mean?'

'I've been assuming that this crop-pattern business and the time anomalies and Unwin's work on entropy are connected.'

'Stands to reason.'

'A bit *post hoc propter hoc* though. They *could* be unrelated. Coincidences do happen.'

'Yeah, but –'

'These time shifts, for example. I've been to look at a number of important events – natural disasters, assassinations, medical discoveries – and sometimes there are various realities shuffling in and out, but in the huge majority of cases there aren't. Which is all to the good, of course, but I can't find any pattern in the anomalies that do occur. If they're random, it's difficult to believe they have a direct cause.'

'Such as these aliens making them happen for some reason.'

'Precisely. Have you experienced any more time shifts?'

'No. You?'

He shook his head. He was still concentrating on the control panel.

'So why do you think the other two are connected? This entropy stuff and the aliens.'

'It's a hunch,' he said unhappily. 'It *feels* as if they ought to be connected. Entropy is about perfect disorder, so to speak, and the invaders appear to depend on perfect order to come through. At least, their attempts to come through can be thwarted simply by introducing irrational numbers into their pattern.'

'Uh huh. You know...'

'What?'

'Nothing, really. Only, Molecross's place was incredibly orderly.'

'Not likely there's a connection.'

'He's well weird, isn't he?'

'And extremely active. It's bumblers like that who cause nine-tenths of the trouble. Fortunately, I think we've discouraged him temporarily. It should take him weeks to get his programs straightened out.'

'How long will it take Ethan to do whatever it is with those equations?'

'As the equations don't actually lead to anything, it's hard to say. There's a certain amount of help I can legitimately give him that will speed up the process. In the meantime, we just have to wait.'

'That's what gets you, isn't it? Nothing to do.'

'Yes,' he sighed.

She thought for a moment. 'I don't understand why it's so important to run those entropy numbers as far as they can go, since in the end they can't go anywhere.'

'Not anywhere in our universe.'

'What do you mean?' she said apprehensively.

'Well,' he didn't look up from the console, 'what if Unwin's calculations are just building our half of a bridge?'

Ethan ignored the phone. This was easy for him to do; he'd found that his answering machine was sufficient for 95 per cent of his messages. On the slender chance that any given call might fall within the other 5 per cent, he kept the volume turned half up. So the rings of the phone, the click of the machine, the silence while his outgoing message ran, and the beginning of the message passed by him like distant traffic noise, while he stared at the numbers and symbols on the screen, as if they might suddenly shift and regroup like an anagram and give him an answer.

'... really don't know me...' the voice on the machine droned.

Was it the function that was the problem, or another element of the equation? Or was he on the wrong track altogether? Perhaps he should start again.

'... greatly appreciate your...'

But from where? He didn't know exactly how far back he'd gone wrong – if indeed he had – and if he began again either too early or too late, it was hours, possibly days, wasted. If only –

'... rick Unwin. I'll try you again, then, in –'

'What?' Ethan almost knocked the answering machine to the floor but just caught it. 'I'm here!' he yelled into the receiver.

'I beg your pardon,' said the voice uncertainly. 'Perhaps I have the wrong number. I was attempting to reach Ethan Amberglass.'

'That's me.'

'Oh? Oh, well, that's wonderful. I was hoping –'

'Did you say you were Unwin?'

'Why, yes, I –'

'Pat Unwin, who went missing?'

'Erm,' the voice grew cautious. 'I really don't want to... I can't get into... Perhaps I should just...'

'No, hang on, I don't care. But you're the same one, right? Why are you calling?'

'I, uh, know we've never met.' The voice remained cautious. 'But I was aware of your reputation, of course. And, after a... nervous episode, I'm trying to get to work again, and I was wondering if you and I might meet. I think if I were able to discuss a few of my ideas with an equally apt colleague that it would help me a great deal.'

'What are you working on?' Ethan asked, glancing at the computations on his screen.

'Does that matter?'

'Is it the entropy stuff? I've been going over it. It's me who could use your help.' Ethan wished he knew how to get hold of the Doctor. This was about as good a piece of luck as could be hoped for. 'Perhaps we could meet tomorrow morning.'

'Er, well, actually, I'm here now.'

'Here where?'

'On the street, at the corner. I'm on my mobile.'

'At the corner? Why didn't you just come up?'

Unwin's voice lowered. 'You can't be too careful. They might be watching.'

Oh good, Ethan thought. A paranoid. He'd met a lot of them in the institution – very difficult to talk to. 'But it's freezing out there.'

'Perhaps we could meet somewhere? A restaurant?'

'There's nothing around here but kebab shops and fish and chips. Look, it's all right to come up. No one's watching the flat.'

'That's what you *say*,' Unwin whispered. 'But how can you be certain?'

Ethan pinched the bridge of his nose. It was no good trying to talk sense – they'd just go in circles forever.

'All right,' he said reluctantly, 'I'll come down. There's a pub a couple of blocks over.'

'I'm by the chemist's.'

Ethan had not only never met Unwin, he'd never even seen a photograph, so he examined him curiously as he came up to the corner. Unwin was standing right up against the dark chemist's window, a medium-sized man with thinning hair and a weak mouth. Though dressed in an expensive-looking coat, he was shivering. He smiled at Ethan inquiringly, the smile coming and going nervously.

'That you, Amberglass?'

'Yes. Hello.' They shook hands. 'Good to meet you after all this time.'

'Yes indeed. Isn't it strange, after working side by side not knowing each other, that we should turn out to be kindred spirits?' Unwin locked his arm in Ethan's in an overly familiar fashion, and they started along the pavement.

'I'm only building on your work.'

'But whyever did you start, old boy? Everyone thought I was barmy.'

'Not exactly,' said Ethan, treading carefully. 'They asked me to look over your stuff. At first I thought it was daft, but then it began to intrigue me.'

'I'm flattered. Or perhaps you should be, since your being intrigued shows you're brilliant enough to understand me.'

'I don't know. I haven't got far. Could turn out we're both mental.'

Unwin tittered. 'Oh I don't think so, do you?'

Ethan smiled weakly. He had been dreading a conversation in a crowded, noisy pub, but he was beginning to find that idea preferable to being out in the cold with a fellow whose mind seemed to have slipped a bit sideways. He tried subtly to disengage his arm but Unwin was hugging it as if it were a beloved toy. 'I think entropy is *the* problem, don't you? I mean, what's the point of all the rest of it if we're only going to end up cold toast?'

'Erm,' said Ethan.

'Nothing *matters*, does it, so long as that end hangs over us. "The paths of glory lead but to the grave." Not our petty individual graves, the grave of the entire universe. A cemetery for the time when all that will be has become all that was.'

'Yes indeed,' said Ethan, relieved they were approaching the pub. 'It's right up he–'

'Pat, you old bastard!' The back door of a large car parked at the kerb had swung open. 'Long time no see!'

Unwin stopped, peered into the back seat. 'Sherry! Is that you?'

'In the flesh, old boy.'

Ethan tried again to slip loose his arm. He really wasn't interested in attending a public schoolboys' reunion. But Unwin enthusiastically pulled him forward. 'This is my old friend Sheridan Brett. We were at university together. Sherry, this is Ethan Amberglass, a fellow agency mathematician.'

'Mr Amberglass.' Brett, who was seated on the far side of the car, leaned forward and took Ethan's hand. At the same moment, Unwin gripped the back of his neck and shoved. Ethan fell across the seat and, as the door slammed, Brett rolled him onto the floor and pinned him, one foot on his stomach and the other on his throat. Ethan's breath slammed out of him. He heard a match rasp and smelled cigarette smoke, then Brett leaned over him, smiling.

'Good to meet you.'

Unwin gripped the steering wheel with both hands, ignoring any sounds from behind him. Brett had given him Ethan's keys and made him go up to the flat and erase his message from the answering machine. He'd been terrified the whole time that he'd be seen. He felt like hell. He was afraid he was going to throw up.

This was a mad idea. Mad! Kidnapping! And there'd be murder at the end of it if he knew Brett, and he knew Brett. Knew him better and better every day and wished he didn't. Had he been this way at Oxford? He'd been aloof and self-contained, arrogant, but no one had dared rag him. That could only have been because something about him frightened them. Maybe Unwin himself had been frightened, even then. But it was nothing compared to now.

'Couldn't I just talk to him?' he had asked Brett. 'You know, old colleagues, what have you been up to, oh really that sounds interesting?'

'It's not merely a matter of gaining information,' Brett had replied coolly. 'He has to be stopped.'

Stopped. Unwin shivered. But surely not until they had got all they could from him. They needed his help. Brett understood that. Amberglass was alive as long as the project continued. And well as long as he cooperated. Unwin hoped to God he cooperated. He didn't want to think about what Brett would do if he didn't.

Tears of self-pity stung Unwin's eyes. What had he got himself into? He was only an idealist. A genius who had needed support and recognition and had got neither. Whose fault was that? He felt sick again. He mustn't think about any of this. He'd think... He'd think about the way Amberglass had built on his work. Wonderful stuff. Indicated all sorts of new possibilities...

When he reached the house and got out of the car, the night

was a clear, almost tangible cold. Unwin shivered in earnest. He opened the car's back door and saw that during the trip Brett had cuffed Ethan's wrists behind him and tied a rag in his mouth and another over his eyes.

'Is he all right?'

'He's fine,' Brett said shortly. 'Give me some help here.'

Between them, they half-walked, half-dragged Ethan through a side door. 'Cellar,' said Brett.

'Oh really,' Unwin objected. 'You must have half a dozen bedrooms. We could lock him in –'

'Cellar,' Brett repeated, and Unwin helped him manoeuvre Ethan down the steps. He stumbled and wavered, pulling against their grip, but Unwin thought this was less a struggle than the result of stiffness from being held immobile in the car. Poor bastard was too weakened to fight. He was so small. Unwin was suddenly badly afraid for him.

'Sherry,' he said weakly, 'is this really –'

'Yes,' said Brett. 'Shut up.'

Light from the upstairs hall fell narrowly down the steps, striking gleams in the shadows from the glossy wood of discarded furniture. Brett pushed Ethan into an overcarved chair, then ripped some ragged fabric from a sofa and secured him. He took Unwin's arm and marched him firmly up the steps.

'I need a drink, don't you?'

'What are you doing?' Unwin tried to keep the quaver out of his voice. 'You can't leave him tied up in the cellar.'

'Of course I can,' said Brett, striding toward the sitting room. 'I have.'

'But it's cold down there. And if he's tied for hours he'll be in awful pain.'

'Exactly.' Brett poured himself some Scotch. 'Something for you? This is a nice single malt from Skye. Ten years old.'

'He could never get out if we locked him in one of the upper bedrooms. What's the point of leaving him like that?'

Brett inhaled the aroma of the Scotch appreciatively. 'I want to give him time to think things over.' He smiled his rictus smile. 'Time to become afraid.'

Well, the Doctor thought, Ethan was up and out early. Gone for a fry-up, no doubt, to get the day started. The Doctor looked over the work from the day before. Nice, very nice. Bright lad. More than bright. The Doctor's eyes darkened unhappily.

He looked around the room. Something seemed not quite right. What was – Ah. The phone machine was sitting on a little table, atop a pile of journals. Hadn't it been next to the computer? The Doctor crossed to it curiously.

When Ace came by a few minutes later with coffee, she found the Doctor in the armchair, head leaning on fist, humming tonelessly under his breath. He looked grim.

'Where's Ethan then? In the loo?'

'No. He's not here.'

'The hermit is out?' Ace set down the coffee. 'Well unbelievable. Where's he gone, then?'

'He wasn't here when I arrived.'

Something in his tone caught at her. 'What's happened to him?' she said in a small voice.

The Doctor looked up, mouth tight. 'I'm not sure, but I don't like what I know. Someone erased his last message. Fortunately, on some of these machines, erasure just stores messages for a final delete. So I found it. These are the last words.' He pressed a button and a nervous voice said, 'Oh, ah, yes, I haven't said who I am, have I? This is Patrick Unwin. I'll try you again, then, in –' The machine clicked off as Ethan picked up.

'Unwin?' said Ace, confused. 'He's gone to meet Unwin?'

'The message is from last night. He might have gone this morning. Only it's an early breakfast.'

'Perhaps they're only talking naff maths talk. You know, two nerds together...' She trailed off. She didn't believe it herself. 'What are we going to do, Professor?'

'I think we had better find him as quickly as possible.'

CHAPTER TWELVE

Carrying a glass of orange juice, Brett descended the steps. Daylight now filled the hall above, and the cellar was much easier to see. Ethan was still in the chair; as he hadn't slumped forward, Brett presumed he was conscious. After much urging and talk of hypothermia from Unwin, Brett had allowed his partner to come down and wrap a blanket around their prisoner. He shoved this to the floor and pulled the gag from Ethan's mouth, then held the orange juice to his lips. 'Drink this.' Ethan drank. Juice spilled over his chin and ran down his neck.

Brett removed the cuffs and blindfold and untied the strips of upholstery. He gave Ethan a small push, and he slid to the floor, gasping. Brett poked him lightly with his foot. 'You're still with us, aren't you? Haven't done a mental slide? I know you're unstable.'

Ethan didn't say anything. He lay sprawled as he had fallen, eyes blankly open. Brett sat and leaned forward, elbows on knees.

'Now, listen. I tied you fairly loosely last night, and after an hour or so you'll be able to walk normally. But if I tie you up tonight, I'll make it tight, and probably you'll be crippled.'

Ethan swallowed. 'Why tie me at all?' he whispered hoarsely. 'I can't... can't get...' He gave up.

'Well, if this conversation goes well, perhaps I won't. Perhaps you'll get a meal and a bath and a bed and won't have to sit all night in your cooling piss. You've only to help me a bit.' He waited, but Ethan didn't try to speak. 'Just clear up a few matters.'

'Answer... questions?' Ethan almost snickered. He coughed, then swallowed again several times.

'Good point,' Brett conceded, and fetched a pitcher of water. He held Ethan's head up and helped him drink. 'Better?' Ethan nodded. 'There's more where that came from. Not just yet, though.' Brett returned to the chair. 'Tell me about the Doctor.'

Ethan looked bewildered. 'The Doctor?' he rasped.

'Yes, the chap who was in the field with you that night. The mysterious scientific adviser for UNIT. Who is he?'

'I don't know his name.'

'That's all right. Neither do UNIT. How did you meet him?'

'He came to see me.'

'Why?'

'He's...' Ethan's head rolled, as if he were about to pass out. Brett nudged him with his toe.

'Come along, now. He's what?'

'Interested in entropy.'

Brett had expected that. And there was really only one reason this elusive Doctor would show up at just this time investigating entropy.

'Did he make the circle?'

'Circle...?'

'In the field.'

'Yes.'

Again, not a surprise.

'Where can I find him?'

'I don't know. He always came to me.'

'To your flat?' Ethan nodded. 'How did he find you?'

'I don't know.'

That made sense to Brett. Probably found him through UNIT. They seemed to know everything. He lit a cigarette and smoked for a few minutes, thinking. 'He wanted you to continue with Unwin's equations.'

'Yes.'

'Did he say why?'

'No.'

Brett bent over him. 'Are you sure?'

'Yes.'

Brett pressed his cigarette against Ethan's cheek. He cried out and jerked spastically away. 'Absolutely sure?'

Ethan nodded. His eyes were closed, but Brett knew that when he opened them there would be tears there. 'A cigarette's nothing, you know. Even a hot kettle can do more damage. And one can escalate from there.'

'I'm sure,' Ethan whispered desperately. 'I am.'

'And you're also sure you don't know where to find him?'

'I don't.'

After some firm touches with the cigarette, Brett decided to believe him. He was clearly not dealing with a professional who'd been trained to resist this kind of treatment. It wasn't that civilians were less brave, but they weren't mentally prepared. 'How do you contact him?'

'He just comes by.'

'You don't know how to contact him?'

'No.'

Brett lit a fresh cigarette and after a few minutes' interrogation decided again to believe him.

'How often does he drop in?'

'I don't know. Once a week maybe.'

'Now,' said Brett, 'you are lying to me.' He jerked off Ethan's right shoe and sock and snuffed the cigarette on his sole. Ethan screamed. 'How often?'

'When he feels like it. Every day or so.'

'Was he supposed to come by today?'

'I don't know what today is,' Ethan groaned. 'Please...'

'It's Monday.'

'He comes when he wants.'

'Oh hell.' Irritably, Brett lit a third cigarette. 'Don't treat me like a fool. If he's got you working on those equations of Pat's, he's coming by all the time. And wants to be certain you're there.

Now, was he supposed to see you today?' And he pressed his thumb into the burn.

He had to do this several times before Ethan blurted out that yes, he was, that morning. Brett dropped his foot and considered. That meant today was probably wasted; by the time he could get up to London it would be past lunchtime. He sensed that the Doctor was not the sort to sit around waiting on events. He'd be trying to find his missing friend. There must be ways to exploit that...

He burned Ethan a few more times, to give him something to think about, and went upstairs.

He found Unwin in the long gallery, already half drunk. 'I could hear him,' Unwin slurred. 'I could hear him!'

'In future I'll gag him.'

'Future? For God's sake...'

'Oh shut up, Pat. He's a tougher little sod than he looks. He should have been sobbing and blabbering; spending the night in that chair was supposed to soften him up.'

'You won't do that to him again, will you? I don't think –'

'No. I'll just leave him down there.'

'But...'

'He's not tied,' said Brett impatiently. 'I left him water. How much longer will it take you to analyse what he's done with your numbers?'

'Several hours at least. His ideas are really quite soph–'

'Good. He'll be nicely impressionable by then. He's going to help you, of course.'

'Of course,' said Unwin miserably.

I KNOW WHO MADE THE CIRCLE
HAVE YOU STOPPED HIM
I DON'T HAVE HIM YET
WHO IS HE
HE'S CALLED THE DOCTOR

Brett waited for a few minutes.

ARE YOU CERTAIN

YES

More minutes passed.

THIS IS DISTURBING

WHY?

HE IS DANGEROUS

YOU ALREADY KNEW THAT

VERY DANGEROUS

YOU KNOW OF HIM?

HE IS KNOWN IN ALL PLACES

Good God, Brett thought curiously. This was getting interesting.

THEN HE IS AN ALIEN?

HE IS NOT HUMAN

WHO IS HE?

HE IS NOT HUMAN.

Back to the Ouija board. Irritably, Brett typed:

I NEED INFORMATION IF I AM TO STOP HIM.

WAIT

Time passed. Brett leaned back with his feet on the desk and lit another cigarette. Through the smoke, he gazed musingly at the ceiling. There was, he realised, at least one way to try to contact this Doctor. A long shot, admittedly, but by no means a ridiculous one. He looked over as words began to appear on the screen.

HE IS A TIME LORD.

Well, that was a big help. Brett swung his feet back to the floor and typed:

WHAT IS A TIME LORD?

A LONG-LIVED RACE WHO HAVE MASTERED TIME TRAVEL IN YOUR UNIVERSE.

Brett was tempted to type 'Oh really?' but instead wrote:

WHAT ABOUT YOUR UNIVERSE?

WE DO NOT KNOW WE HAVE NOT YET ENCOUNTERED HIM

IS HE PHYSICALLY INVULNERABLE?

NO
HOW VULNERABLE IS HE?
ESSENTIALLY HE IS HUMAN
NO SUPERPOWERS THEN
WHAT
NEVER MIND Brett thought for a couple of seconds. *IS HE EMOTIONALLY VULNERABLE?*
UNCLEAR
DOES HE HAVE FRIENDS?
TRAVELS WITH HUMANS
'Ah,' Brett murmured. 'Does he indeed?'
STOP HIM
I HAVE TO FIND HIM FIRST
CAN YOU FIND HIM
You know, Brett thought, I believe I can.
YES
AND STOP HIM
AND STOP HIM
Brett returned to the cellar. Ethan was curled beneath the blanket. Brett twitched it away. 'Just one or two more questions.'

The Doctor contacted the Brigadier then headed for the chart room. Ace followed him.

'How long will it take?'

'Several hours, I'm afraid.' The Doctor was at the control panel. 'It's a complicated process.'

'What if we don't have several hours!'

'UNIT may have luck.'

'And if they don't?'

'What do you expect me to do, Ace?' There was an edge in his voice. 'This is one of the most sophisticated locating devices in the galaxy. I can't use anything better.'

He glared at her. Ace glared back. 'We got him into this.'

'It was necessary.'

'It's always bloody necessary.'

'Yes!' he said. 'It is. This is the universe, Ace. You may have heard of it. Everything alive, not just one man.' She looked away and he softened. 'I understand. You... like him. It's hard.'

'I can't just do nothing.'

'Go back to his flat. It's quite possible we've panicked for nothing. If we have, he'll show up. He may have already shown up.'

'Right fools we'll look.'

'I hope so.'

'Yeah,' she said.

Ace didn't really expect the Doctor's optimism to be rewarded, and it wasn't. She looked at the messy flat and felt like crying. Sod that! She bloody well wasn't going to cry. She wasn't going to stay around here either, when she could be... what? Ace sat down miserably. The Doctor was right. It was a waiting game, which was one of the games she was rotten at. She knew she was doing something but it felt like doing nothing, and she couldn't, she couldn't –

Hang on. Ace shoved a hand into her jacket pocket. Yes! The number plate! The Brigadier would take her call. They'd be able to look up this sort of thing at UNIT, probably had their own files. The number might not be a lead at all, but she had to try. She jumped up and ran to the phone. That was when she noticed the message light blinking. Oh God, let it be him. Or at least good news. Or at least not bad news. She pressed the play button.

'This is a message for the Doctor,' said an upper-class voice. Ace sniffed. Posh plod. There was a click – he'd switched on a tape recorder. On the tape, the same upper-class voice said, 'What is your name?'

'What?'

Ace inhaled sharply. It was Ethan. He sounded like something was wrong with his throat.

'Your name.'

Ethan sounded puzzled. 'You know my name.'

'Tell me again.'

'Ethan Amberglass.'

'How's your foot?'

Sounds of a struggle. Not for long.

'Feeling better, are we?' said the upper-class voice.

'What's that?' It sounded to Ace as if Ethan had spotted the recorder. 'What the hell are –' Then he began to scream.

Ace just stopped herself from smashing the machine in fury. She stepped back, catching her breath. The little click came again, then the voice. 'I know you'd like to hear him speak to you himself, but he can't talk just now. He can't move very much either, or see.'

'You're dead, you bloody sod,' Ace breathed.

'I want to meet you. Tonight would be good, but, since you may not hear this message today, any of the next few nights will do. I think the field would be appropriate. You can have the guards called off, can't you? That's how I'll know you're there. And no trouble, please. If I'm not back here in three hours, Mr Amberglass will be killed.'

The message clicked off.

'Dead,' Ace repeated between her teeth. 'Dead and in pieces.'

She rushed from the flat and was almost down the stairs before she realised she wasn't sure what to do. If she fetched the Doctor, he'd have to stop programming the search function or whatever it was, and that was the only certain way to find Ethan. What could the Brigadier do except have his people trace the call, and she had no doubt that the caller had made sure that was impossible. Or UNIT could hide a few people on the road to the field and for every passing car note down the –

Number plate.

She felt quickly in her pocket, as if afraid the paper had vanished, but it crumpled in her fingers. She ran back up the stairs.

Brett had deliberately left a false impression in his message. In fact, Ethan was in better circumstances than he had been. After the tape-recorded session, Brett had brought him something to eat and drink and taken him upstairs to the toilet and then to the bath. He gave him an electric razor, ointment for the burns, and bandages to wrap around his abraded wrists. Ethan's clothes being beyond saving, he was provided with a shirt and old suit of Unwin's, which hung rather comically on his slight frame – he had to roll up the sleeves and trouser cuffs, and discarded the jacket as useless. As he couldn't really walk on his wounded foot and flinched at the thought of trying to force on a shoe, he simply donned Unwin's socks – grey wool with a subtle burgandy stripe.

Gripping his arm, Brett helped him down the hall to Unwin's computer room. Sunlight was falling in the narrow windows and Ethan almost cried with happiness at the sight. This sign of weakness frightened him.

Unwin was watching him nervously; Ethan looked back with disgust. Brett shoved him down onto a little rolling chair. 'Pat needs a bit of assistance. You'll help him, won't you?'

'Yes,' Ethan said flatly.

'Then I'll leave you to it.'

Ethan stared dully at Unwin, half afraid he was going to fall off the chair and half not caring.

'I need –' Unwin began.

'You're something a dog wiped his arse on,' Ethan said. 'Did you know that?'

Unwin paled. 'I'm not having any of that. I don't approve of what Brett's been doing, but you're going to help me.'

The chair had an ergonomically designed low back, but Ethan managed to slump against it. '"Don't approve"? Didn't do anything to stop it, did you? You're afraid of him.' Unwin said nothing. 'You're a weak bastard, and you're afraid of him. It's all right. I'm afraid of him too. Dab hand with a cigarette.'

Unwin called up a series of equations on the computer screen. 'Why did you decide to build on my work in this direction?'

Ethan peered at the screen. 'I can't see it.'

'Sorry?'

'I don't have my glasses.'

'Where are they?'

'You might,' said Ethan after a long minute, 'try the floor of the car.'

Unwin went into the hall and called to Brett to check the car floor, then returned, flushed and evasive-looking. 'In any case, you needn't see the specific numbers to answer my question. You took off in a direction I hadn't anticipated.'

'Music.'

'I beg your pardon?'

'Mu-sic,' Ethan repeated slowly. 'I thought I'd try to work in overtones. Thirds and fifths.'

'But that's nonsense.'

'Well, of course it is, literally. But if you look at what I was doing, you'll see what I mean. Not that it matters,' he yawned as Unwin turned back to the screen. 'Because the whole idea is nonsense. None of it can possibly go anywhere. Any equation now, we'll run things through a function and come up with gibberish.'

'If that's so,' said Brett smoothly from behind him, 'then why were you even bothering?' He dropped Ethan's glasses in his lap. Ethan ignored them. 'Just curious? Nothing left to do?' Brett walked around to face him. 'As a favour to the Doctor?'

When Ethan didn't say anything, Brett knocked him onto the floor. Unwin jumped up. 'Stop it, Sherry! I don't want any more of that!'

'Well, you certainly don't want to see any more of it.' Brett hauled Ethan up and dumped him back in the chair. 'Like to keep your hands clean and your conscience unsullied.'

'I am a genius!' Unwin roared, startling both Ethan and Brett. 'All I want is to do my work! It is not my fault that I can't without ugly things happening. I don't want them to happen. I only want to do my work, and it's not possible without...' He shot an anguished look at Ethan. 'Without things like this. I didn't want it this way. The agency wouldn't listen to me I'm going to solve the problem of existence itself, and all the support I can get is... is...'

'An unpleasant fellow like me,' Brett finished calmly. 'It's a difficult life, but someone has to live it.'

'I don't want to live what you call life,' Unwin spat. 'I never have. All I want is the equations. They go on forever, and this ball of mud is nothing but a mote in the eye of eternity.'

Brett smiled, not entirely mockingly. 'You're a mystic, Pat.'

Unwin, stopped, flustered. He ran a hand through his hair. '...Yes.'

'Still, you shit just like the rest of us.' Brett took Ethan's collar and gave him a little shake. 'So, was it the Doctor's idea?'

'The Doctor isn't important,' Ethan said. 'The numbers are what matter. I won't talk to you; I'll talk to Unwin.'

Brett raised an eyebrow at Unwin, who looked equally surprised. 'Very well, then. Enjoy yourselves.'

When he was gone, Unwin was perplexed. 'Why will you talk to me?'

'It's rather horrible, actually.' Ethan snickered and a little blood ran from his nose. He wiped it on the sleeve of Unwin's fine linen shirt. 'You remind me of myself.' He bent, very slowly, and retrieved his glasses from the carpet. 'Show me what you've been doing.'

Ethan went over Unwin's latest computations. After sitting and thinking for another half hour, he returned to the beginning and scrolled slowly through. Then he sat back with his arms folded, carefully so as not to press any burns, and mused some more.

'Brilliant work,' he said at last. 'It had to be the primes, of course. The immutably random element in the orderly realm of numbers.'

'If we work together...'

'We'll do some very pretty maths, and in the end it will come to nothing. Why can't you understand that? Equations describe the physical world, they don't create it.'

'All matter,' Unwin said seriously, 'can be reduced to mathematics.'

'No it can't!' Ethan yelled, surprising himself with his vehemence. 'A quark is not a mathematical entity. You can't create it or nudge it or bounce it up and down or turn it into rice pudding with numbers, no matter what hoops you make them jump through. You might as well try to push reality around with words –' He faltered, remembering his conversation with the Doctor about exactly the power that written words, nothing more than collections of symbols called letters, could in fact have on reality. And Unwin nodded.

'But we do,' he said quietly. 'All the time.'

'It's too many twists,' Ethan objected, almost desperately. 'Words have meanings from which we can derive abstractions. Or else they form a pattern of self-referential hermetic relationships that...' Again he trailed off. Again Unwin nodded.

'You can't do it.' Ethan was fixated on the equations; he couldn't seem to look away. 'You can't do it. You haven't the power. Unless...' His hot dark eyes shifted to Unwin, 'unless you have help. From outside. From very far outside.'

Unwin looked at his hands. 'I wouldn't tell Sherry you've worked that out.'

'Why not? He's going to kill me anyway.'

'Well,' Unwin's eyes remained down, 'there are ways to die, and then there are ways to die.'

Neither of them said anything for a while. Ethan again became distracted by the sunlight, until he rested his cheek on his hand and jerked back with a hiss of pain. 'What's wrong with him anyway?'

'Sherry?'

'No, you bloody fool. Ken Livingstone.'

Unwin's mouth twitched in embarrassment. 'Sherry hates the world.'

'Everyone?'

'Not just the human beings. Everything.'

'Everything alive?' Ethan gaped. 'But that's –'

'Everything,' Unwin said simply. 'The rocks and stones. The wind. The water. Sound and heat.'

'Is he completely mad?'

Unwin shrugged. 'I don't know. He says it's like a clock, reality – ticking away to nothing. He says he can almost hear it crumbling, atom by atom. Smell the rot as everything decays and passes.'

'He's mental.'

'Is he?' Unwin's voice was calm. 'Life is terrible. We're comfortable enough. But what about the wretched of the earth, who are, as you know, the majority? What about grief and illness and the suffering of children?'

'You've both read too much bloody Dostoyevsky. *The Grand Inquisitor*.'

'I never believed Aloysha's return argument to Ivan – kissed him on the cheek, as I recall. Love. God loves us. Do you believe that?' Ethan was silent. 'You see? And Sherry's in a position to do something about it.'

'Destroy reality?'

'No!' Unwin was shocked. 'I'd never help him! No, he wants everything to continue. Forever.'

'Including the suffering.'

'There won't be any suffering. The universe will be at peace.'

'"At peace".' Ethan echoed. 'It sounds like an inscription on a gravestone.'

'This is going to happen,' Unwin said flatly. 'There's nothing you can do about it.'

'Other than not help you. And you're not getting there on your own, are you? Not quite.'

'It's the primes!' Unwin pleaded. 'Your particular interest.'

'Oh, that's all right, then. I'd be delighted to screw up existence to indulge my hobby.'

Unwin flushed angrily. 'It's not a hobby! It's the way to the heart of reality itself.'

'And then you stop the heart.'

'I can't talk to you.' Unwin stood up. There was no place to go in the small room except the window, so he went there. Ethan closed his eyes wearily. 'I have another set of equations I'm working on. They have nothing to do with entropy.'

'What have they to do with?'

'Some sort of code-breaking, I think.'

'More mysteries. I don't think so.'

Unwin's lips tightened. He switched on the computer next to Ethan and brought up a screen. 'Don't be a fool. Look at this.' He scrolled slowly through several screens. Ethan frowned:

'That's interesting.'

'Isn't it?' Unwin highlighted a number of lines in bold. 'Very complex. Very impressive.'

'Stumped you, has it?'

Unwin reddened. 'Do you think you could do anything with it?'

'Oh yes. But no.'

'For God's sake. Do you want to go back to that cellar? Be tied and tortured? It can get much worse.'

'So he does this often? Just curious.'

'Listen to me.' Unwin shook him; Ethan cried out. 'Exactly. How much more of that do you think you can take? *Work* on this.'

Say yes, Ethan thought desperately, say yes. But when he spoke the word came out, 'No.'

'Well, I tried,' Unwin said, with the air of a man letting himself off the hook. 'You can't say I didn't.'

Ethan didn't reply. He was shamefully aware of tears in his eyes. He was afraid he was going to vomit up the only food he'd had in 36 hours.

'So how's our lad?'

Ethan started. He hadn't heard Brett come in.

'He's going to help,' Unwin said quickly.

'Is he?' Brett took a handful of Ethan's hair and yanked his head back, looking down into his burned face. 'What a good boy he is. Still, he seems a bit nervous to me. Are you sure he's come round?'

'Absolutely.'

Brett narrowed his eyes. 'I don't know. He looks shifty.'

'Don't put me down there again,' Ethan whispered.

'Oh I think one more night might do you good,' said Brett, and he heaved Ethan over a shoulder and carried him back to the cellar.

Hiding behind the library door, peeking through the narrow gap between the hinges, Molecross watched fearfully.

CHAPTER THIRTEEN

Much earlier that same morning, a dreadful thought had jolted Molecross awake. What if his interview had not gone quite as successfully as he'd first thought? After all, he'd given some things away. Mentioned the Doctor. Mentioned Amberglass. Of course, this Brett fellow wasn't interested in the least, but... Was it really a coincidence he'd been at the field the very night the pattern first appeared? Coincidences did happen, but a good journalist distrusted them. He had let down his profession.

Molecross got out of bed. More investigating must be done! He'd get in touch with one of his contacts who could match the Jaguar plate number with an address. Then he would return to Amberglass's flat, question him again. Get the Doctor's whereabouts from him, or at least a contact email address. Yes, that was the plan. He was on the case.

But when he got to Ethan's flat, he saw that the case was temporarily eluding him. The door was unlocked and no one was inside. He found a plate in the sink with crumbs on it, but there was no telling how long that had been there. Molecross surveyed the sitting room. There must be something. Of course – he remembered seeing an answering machine.

The last message hadn't been erased. Molecross pressed the play button and listened eagerly. After a few seconds, he sat down, staring at the machine. When the message ended he knew that he could not play it again. He simply could not. This was fear, he realised, real and sickening fear. He wished he could turn time back and never hear what he had heard, never know. Never, ever know.

And there was something else, something almost as frightening.

He recognised the voice on the phone.

Molecross gaped at the huge house with its mullioned windows and elaborate seventeenth-century chimneys. In spite of the Jaguar, he hadn't expected this kind of money. He was out of his depth here. A wealthy torturer. It was too much power to fight on his own. He ought to have notified the police. But the place was so big, and the owner so smooth. Amberglass could be anywhere among those rooms, and after a cursory look, they would leave. After all, it had only been an anonymous call...

He could go in and tell his story in person, but that wasn't likely to be more persuasive. Probably he'd be warned off, which was no good at all. And in the meantime, what would be happening to Amberglass? In a part of his mind he didn't want to examine, he knew that, whatever it was, it was his fault.

Molecross crept around behind the boxwood hedges. He was safely out of sight, but the hedges didn't go all the way up to the house. Someone could be looking out of any one of those dozens of windows. And how was he to get in? Surely there was an alarm system. But likely it wasn't turned on till night. Still, he was beginning to wish he had come at night. It would be bloody cold of course; even now he could see his breath. Molecross had exchanged his safari hat for a fleece-lined one with ear flaps, yet he was still shivering. Of course, that might be fear.

The house had so many windows, and they were so old – some of them were bound to be in disrepair. At least he hoped so, since he hadn't worked out any other course of action. And once in, how was he to find Amberglass? Brett's message had implied he was gagged. Of course, he'd be easy to hear if he were being tortured.

Molecross shivered violently. This was fear, all right. His stomach felt colder than the air around him. He thought he might pass out. What if Brett found *him*? He'd probably kill him immediately.

Molecross had been savvy enough to leave a note at his cottage telling exactly where he was going and why, but at the moment that was little comfort. He didn't want to die. God, he really didn't want to die. This was a fool's errand.

Well, he'd been a fool. And because of that, an innocent man had been put through agony.

He began to move carefully behind the boxwood screen towards the back of the house. He felt like he was pushing through the cold, as if it were a jelly sucking closed behind him. The windows were well above the ground. How could he even get to one? He spotted a garage and darted to it.

The garage was a large converted stable and contained several fine cars, including the Jaguar with the number plate. Molecross explored and, as he had hoped, discovered a storage room containing tools and other building apparatus. Stood to reason. Grand as it was, the mansion was only a house after all and needed repair like any other house. He found a ladder and carried it with difficulty to the garage door. He was learning, miserably, how much heedless use he had formerly made of his left hand. The big problems, such as learning to use a keyboard one-handed, he had anticipated. But he was thrown by the tiny, unanticipated ones: he couldn't open a jar; he couldn't hold his toothbrush in one hand and the tooth glass in the other. This petty hell was his new life.

Cautiously, he examined the house. Oh, why bother? If anyone happened to be looking out of one of the back windows (and how many people were in there, anyway? Were there servants?) he was for it. As quickly as he could, Molecross hauled the ladder across the lawn.

He was fortunate. The rear of the house was apparently unused, and there were a number of windows in doubtful condition. He propped the ladder below the one that looked easiest to get through and climbed up. Pressing his face to the cold glass, he saw a large, empty room; the only sign of former habitation was a faded wallpaper of delicate trees and exotic birds. The window frame was almost rotten, and, clumsily because of his hand, he climbed inside.

His entry stirred up dust that drifted languidly in the weak sunlight. The room had several doors, and he cautiously cracked open each one. Three led into other abandoned rooms, and one to a cold hallway. The remaining door also opened on a hall, but this one was a little warmer and Molecross guessed it connected to the occupied part of the house.

There was no noise at all. The silence made Molecross uneasy. Using the trace of heat as a guide, he crept nearer and nearer the front of the house, until a final door led him into a library. It was cold here too, but not the same deep chill as the empty rooms. In spite of himself, Molecross paused to gaze at the evidence of wealth: double levels of books, the top one with a gallery reached by a spiral stair. Well-worn leather armchairs. A fireplace. A soft, intricately patterned rug. Hesitantly, as if it were a person who might haughtily dismiss him, Molecross approached a shelf. Some of the bindings were lettered in Latin, their leather covers patinaed with use and age. Molecross touched one wonderingly. Could the man he'd heard on the phone use this room that indicated such respect for learning and human knowledge? Molecross reminded himself that both Al Capone and Hitler had loved opera.

He crossed to the room's other door, which was slightly ajar, and looked out. Another hallway, but this one with dust only along the baseboards – a passageway that was travelled. Molecross was about to venture out when he heard a noise on the stairs and ducked frantically back into the library. Afraid to risk being seen in the doorway, he squinted to see what he could through the hinge crack. Only wall and carpet, but the noise – someone walking heavily and awkwardly, someone groaning – was coming nearer. Molecross nearly jumped when a figure crossed his line of vision. It was gone by the time he put together what he'd glimpsed: a tall man carrying a smaller, struggling man over his shoulder. Molecross caught his breath.

That had to be Amberglass. What should he do? Follow them? He'd be seen in an instant. Wait, then search?

As he stood dithering, Molecross heard a door open. Trembling, he dared to stick his head out and look down the hall. The open door was only a couple of yards away. Molecross withdrew and considered. This simplified things. All he had to do was wait. Unless, he thought, heart sinking, he was about to hear a torture session. He knew he'd never be able to stand that, and his panic would give him away. Oh God, what was he doing here? He couldn't handle this. He'd make things worse. But before he could actually succumb to hysterics, the cellar door closed and Brett passed by again and went up the stairs.

Molecross was at the door as soon as Brett's footsteps faded. It wouldn't open. The lock appeared to be as old as the house itself, the sort that would need a very large key.

All right. That was it. He'd done what he could. He knew where Amberglass was, and now he could go to the police. Right now. He hurried down the cold halls and through the old doors, back to the room he'd first entered. By this time he was almost running, and he headed straight for the window. He'd already swung a leg over the sill when he looked down and saw a girl halfway up the ladder.

Molecross stopped dead. He knew her – the girl who'd been with the Doctor. She looked as surprised as he supposed he did. 'Oi,' she said. 'What the hell are you doing here?'

'Rescuing... I mean finding... Amberglass is in there.'

'Why haven't you got him out?'

'He's locked up. In the cellar.'

'Sounds manageable. Let's go.' The girl came up the ladder, pushing him aside to get in the window. 'I can't remember your name.'

'Adrian Molecross.'

'Oh yeah. I'm Ace. Where is he?'

'It's a job for the police,' said Molecross weakly.

'Right. Where's this cellar?'

'We have to be careful. There's a man here –'
'Does he have a gun?'
'I don't think so.'
'No worry, then.'
'How did you find –'
'Later, git. Take me to him.'

Ace eyed the lock and snorted. She took a set of picks from her pocket and knelt in front of the door. Molecross, sweating, kept glancing up and down the hall, though he knew he'd hear anyone before he saw them. Was Brett the only one in the huge house? It seemed unlikely, but he certainly hadn't heard any other footsteps. He watched Ace work at the lock. She was very angry, he realised. Frighteningly angry. He hoped she didn't get some mad revenge idea in her head.

Looking anxiously around again, he was startled when she grabbed his sleeve. He just managed to close the door as she led him down the steps, her torch darting around the cellar proper, leaving him to stumble in the dark. She suddenly jumped down the remaining steps and darted across the room. In the narrow beam of the torch, Molecross glimpsed someone under a blanket. Ace pulled this aside and began to swear. He'd never heard a woman use those words. He'd never heard anybody. Amberglass was squinting into the light, confused. His shirt was open and he had marks on his chest and a few on his face and throat – bruises, Molecross thought sickly. 'Is he all right?'

'No,' she said through her teeth.

'Ace?' said Ethan unbelievingly. 'Where... what...?'

'Later. Can you walk?'

'Not very well. How did you –'

'Help me with him, Molemoss. Which foot is it?' she said to Ethan, gently helping him up. 'He hurt one of your feet.'

'Right one,' Ethan panted. 'Don't...' He shifted her supporting arm. She swore again. 'Come on,' she hissed at Molecross.

What with the darkness and Molecross's limited carrying

abilities and trying not to make noise, it was a hard job getting Ethan up the stairs. He was in better shape than Molecross had expected, just lame in the one foot, but disorientated and off-balance. How the hell was he going to manage the ladder? Presuming they even got to the ladder. Presuming Brett didn't suddenly show up, with a gun. Unarmed, Molecross suspected he might not be a match for Ace, not in her present state.

'We have to go to the police,' he whispered urgently. 'Amberglass will tell his story and they'll arrest Brett.'

'Mm,' said Ace noncommittally.

'Or UNIT,' Molecross added eagerly. 'You know *they* can take care of this.'

'Balls to UNIT,' said Ace. 'The Brigadier wasn't there and no one wanted to hear my story; it was all I could do to get the address and car.'

'You can't do what you're thinking.'

'And what's that, mate?'

Tear Brett into shreds, Molecross thought, but couldn't quite manage to say it.

'No, you can't, Ace,' rasped Ethan.

'Shows what you know.'

'I mean you mustn't.' Ethan pulled back and actually managed to stop them. 'These people have to be taken by the authorities; they can't suspect anything. In fact, the safest thing to do would be to return me to the cellar so they don't realise –'

'Oh, stuff it!' Ace hissed. 'You've got about as much common sense as a bin-bag. We just got you *out* of the cellar, and you're staying out. Come on.'

'I mean it, Ace. You have to leave Brett alone. If you make this personal –'

'*Personal?* If I hadn't made it *personal,* you'd still *be* in that cellar – unless you think whatsisname here –'

'Molecross,' Molecross said unhappily. 'Will the two of you shut up? We must get *out* of here.'

To his surprise, this had some effect. No one said anything

more until they had manoeuvred Ethan down the ladder and hobbled through a patch of forest to a farm vehicle track where Ace had parked a UNIT jeep. She helped Ethan into the back seat, where he lay on his back, teeth chattering. Seeing his wounds clearly now, Molecross realised they were burns. He felt dizzy and held on to the door. 'Right.' Ethan settled, Ace got into the driver's seat. 'You have a car?'

'Down the road.'

'All right. Thanks.'

And before Molecross could say anything, she drove away. He gaped after her. The bitch! After all he'd done, the risks he'd taken. Amberglass hadn't thanked him, either – well, he wasn't in very good shape, and maybe he didn't owe Molecross thanks for getting him out of a situation Molecross had got him into. But that Ace girl was the limit. And where had the Doctor been? He was the real cause of all this trouble. Dropping in and getting people tortured. Hadn't even bothered to help with the rescue, only sent this obnoxious girl to do the heavy lifting. He'd been in real danger in there and –

It struck him that he was in real danger now, if Brett happened to check the cellar and come searching the grounds. He ran for his car.

CHAPTER FOURTEEN

Yet again, Molecross returned to the UNIT hospital ward. His maimed wrist needed attention. The effort involved in rescuing Amberglass had caused splitting and bleeding. It also turned out, when the nurse undid his bandages, that one of the stitched wounds wasn't healing properly and had become infected. Molecross was discovered to have a fever of over 40°C.

He exhibited signs of emerging feverish hysteria. 'You must help me,' he kept saying as they took him to his room and administered medicine and gave him hospital pyjamas. 'I've seen the Doctor.'

'Not yet,' said the nurse soothingly.

'The other Doctor! You must tell the Brigadier. There was a kidnapping. You must tell the Brigadier.' He repeated this over and over, in spite of the staff's assurances that the Brigadier wasn't in. It was nearly four hours before Sergeant Ramsey arrived to hear what Molecross had to say.

'It sounds as if there might be something to it, sir.'

The Brigadier closed his eyes and rested his forehead on his hand, his elbow propped on the yet-unfinished paperwork spread across his desk. 'That's not possible, Sergeant.'

'Well, sir, you're always saying nothing is impossible.'

Yes, damn me, I am, thought Lethbridge-Stewart. Never share opinions with your staff. 'All right. Tell me.'

'He claims this fellow Amberglass was kidnapped and held prisoner and that he, Molecross that is, and the Doctor's companion rescued him. She then drove off with Amberglass, presumably to join the Doctor. This can fairly easily be checked by a visit to the house Molecross described.'

'That doesn't sound very complicated.' Lethbridge-Stewart thought for a moment. 'Go ahead and send some men to check things out. I'd better contact the Doctor.'

Who, of course, wasn't answering his pager. Lethbridge-Stewart almost swore. What did the fellow have against telephones? He travelled through time and space in a police call box, yet acted as if phones were some kind of baffling gadget he couldn't figure out. With a resigned sigh, the Brigadier realised he was going to be making a trip to Allen Road.

Ace answered the door. Her face relaxed and brightened in relief, and the Brigadier was reminded of how young she was. 'How'd you know?' she said happily. 'Did the Doctor reach you?'

'No,' said Lethbridge-Stewart, perhaps a bit pointedly. 'That ass Molecross came babbling to UNIT again, and he actually seemed to make sense. Something about you and Mr Amberglass and a kidnapping.'

'It's all true,' she said grimly. 'Come in. It's bloody freezing. I'll fetch the Doctor – he's in the TARDIS.'

She dashed out the back door, relieved that a grown-up had arrived. All right, all right, she thought, pushing open the TARDIS door and running in, that wasn't entirely fair. But the Doctor's personality whipped back and forth between a sage and a young boy, with very few stops in the middle ground of dull, but sometimes extremely welcome, adulthood. He wasn't in the console room, and she darted down a corridor, calling for him.

Inside, Lethbridge-Stewart poured himself a Scotch and sat down in one of the club chairs, stretching his feet towards the fire. Typical of the Doctor's hospitality that he should keep liquor when he didn't drink. The fire was pleasantly warm. Lethbridge-Stewart had no doubt that a similar one was burning in all the fireplaces of the house. He looked around the room. Same as always. Simple and comfortable, which was odd since the Doctor was a complex, uncomfortable being. Maybe one of him Lethbridge-Stewart had never met, past or future, had actually furnished the place.

There were a few oil paintings – fine small nineteenth-century English landscapes. Lethbridge-Stewart was fairly certain one of them was a Constable. No portraits, which wasn't surprising, but no photographs either – neither of the Doctor alone nor with any of his companions. That made sense on a security level here, but the Brigadier doubted there were any in the TARDIS either. The Doctor never looked back if he could help it. Lethbridge-Stewart tried to remember that line about rising on the stepping stones of one's dead self, but he couldn't get hold of it.

'Brigadier!' the Doctor said happily, hurrying into the room. 'Just the man I wanted to see.'

'Then why didn't you respond to your pager?'

'Ah.' The Doctor patted his pockets. 'I must have put it down somewhere. Not to worry – I'm sure it will turn up.'

'Where's Mr Amberglass?'

'Upstairs. He may be awake enough to talk to you.'

But in the bedroom, Ethan was in a dead sleep, so still he hardly seemed to be breathing. Lethbridge-Stewart grimaced as he got a close look at him.

'Swine,' he said shortly.

'Very nasty,' the Doctor agreed. 'An unpleasant character, our Mr Brett. I suppose your people can get all the stats on him?'

'Of course. What did he want from this boy?'

'Mathematical assistance. It's a bit complex.'

'I don't need the particulars. This is something to do with those crop patterns, isn't it?'

'I'm afraid so.'

Ace entered with a blanket. 'Out, you two.'

Meekly, they withdrew to the landing. Lethbridge-Stewart watched Ace throw the blanket over Ethan. Dear me. He'd never seen this side of her.

'She's fond of him?' he asked as they descended the stairs.

'Yes,' said the Doctor uncomfortably. 'That may cause some problems.' He sighed. 'Still, one thing at a time. The long answer to your question is: these men who had Amberglass – one of them is Patrick Unwin, by the way, the AWOL mathematician – appear to be involved in constructing some kind of computational bridge over which our invaders can enter.'

'Forgive me, Doctor, but I...'

'Doesn't make much sense, does it?' They sat by the fire. The Doctor gestured to Lethbridge-Stewart's glass, but he shook his head. 'But if these beings are, for example, pure equations, then no doubt they could manage it. You know mathematical graphs quite often have more than three dimensions. Fractals can be graphed in one and one-half dimensions. It's more flexible in there than you'd think. Of course, it's also completely rigid.'

'Of course,' said the Brigadier unperturbedly. Over the years, he'd discovered that it was perfectly possible to work with the Doctor without understanding even half of what he said. 'But if they are equations or some such, how would they function in this world?'

'It's a problem, isn't it?' said the Doctor unhappily. 'It's very, very hard for any being with a body to conceive of their reality; I'm guessing more than I like.'

'Are they likely to break through?'

The Doctor went quiet for a few minutes, leaning back with his hands clasped, watching the flames. 'I wouldn't think any time soon. The computations from our end are extraordinarily difficult. People can take decades solving mathematical problems. Some were posed centuries ago and remain unsolved today. Even on Gallifrey, there are things that, so far, are beyond us. To use an Earth phrase, they exist only in the mind of God.'

This was getting too mystical for the Brigadier. 'So – what can I do?'

'Oh, nothing, I would think,' the Doctor shrugged, eyes still on the fire. 'There's no military solution at this point. And if they get through, there probably won't be a military solution either.'

'Nice to be needed,' said Lethbridge-Stewart, but he didn't smile. Neither did the Doctor.

'I thought there would be more snow.'

'It doesn't necessarily snow a great deal in the Swiss winter – sometimes it's too cold.'

'*I'm* bloody cold,' said Unwin. 'Couldn't you have found somewhere warmer?'

'It's supposed to have central heating, and I'm quite comfortable. It's only you, Pat. Go over by the stove.'

The stove was a rectangular one, almost as tall as Unwin and covered with Delft tiles. Unwin drew a chair close to it and sat down sullenly. Brett was gazing out the window at the night.

'I can't work out how he escaped,' Unwin said.

'He had help.'

'From whom?'

'Presumably the elusive Doctor. What a pity we missed him.'

Unwin touched one of his cold fingers to a tile and jerked it back quickly. 'I still don't see the point of our coming here.'

'I've told you,' Brett said patiently, still looking out. 'Kent was the first choice, this is the second. The membrane, so to speak, is not quite as thin here, but it's passable. If you can finish those equations...' He turned, eyes bright. 'And can you, without our little friend?'

'In time,' said Unwin miserably. He hated the blond-wood-panelled room. He hated Swiss austerity.

'The boundary is at its most penetrable now. It won't be for much longer.'

'It's not my fault!' Unwin shouted. 'The problem is fiendish. It's the sort of thing that takes people years.'

'I just told you, they don't have years.'

'So what? If I fail, I fail. There's nothing they can do about it.'

'If you fail,' said Brett softly, 'I will be very disappointed with you.'

Unwin avoided his eyes. 'Well, where are they going to enter? They need a more or less flat place, and we're in the middle of the bloody Alps.'

'I should think that would be obvious, young Pat.' Brett turned his hungry gaze back to the darkness and the hidden, ice-topped peaks. 'They'll come through on the top of a glacier.'

CHAPTER FIFTEEN

Ethan didn't remember much of his journey with Ace. Pain and exhaustion had caught up with him and he was hardly conscious. At some point, Ace pulled into a lay-by and brought him up front to be nearer the heater. She also pulled her jacket around him. He was aware of being led up a walk, then up a stair, then he wasn't aware of anything until he woke up in a soft bed under a pile of blankets. The window was dark, a little mica-shaded lamp glowed on the bed table, and the Doctor was looking down at him with concern:

'How are you feeling?'

'Better.' Ethan looked around the room. Old wardrobe. Pier glass mirror. Chest-of-drawers. Armchair. Fireplace with fire in it. A comfortable little bedroom. Somehow his glasses, or glasses indistinguishable from them, had made it to the bedside table. 'Where is this?'

'This is my house in Kent.'

'You have a house? I thought you lived in –'

'– a spaceship. Not all the time. Do you mind if I look at your face?' The Doctor lifted the lamp and bent closer. 'Not as bad as it was. How do they feel?'

Ethan touched one of the burns on his throat. 'It's hardly... What did you do?'

'Spaceman medicine.' The Doctor pointed to a capped tube on the bed table. 'Any time you think you need more, there it is. Are you all right otherwise? Was anything else done to you?' Ethan shook his head. 'Forgive me, but I must ask. Did you –'

'No.'

'One could hardly have blamed you.'

'Did you catch them?'

'No,' said the Doctor. Ethan didn't like the look in his eyes. 'They must have discovered your escape almost immediately. By the time anyone got to the house, the vulture had flown. Vultures, you say. Unwin was there too, I suppose.' Ethan nodded. 'Anyone else?'

'I don't think so. I can't be sure. Did they take the computers?'

'Oh yes. Ripped them right off their wires. Did you get to see any of the work?'

'Some of it.' Ethan moved his neck to get the stiffness out. 'He hadn't got much farther with the entropy rubbish, and he hadn't built on anything I'd done. He showed me a different problem he was working on, but it didn't look like much.'

'Difficult?'

'Well, certainly beyond Unwin's abilities,' Ethan said thoughtfully. 'I'm fairly certain I could have done it. Might have taken some time.'

'Any idea what the second problem was about?'

'Not the foggiest.'

'Hm.' Not really to Ethan's surprise, the Doctor had his umbrella with him. Now he tapped his chin with it, humming thoughtfully.

'Unwin's quite brilliant,' Ethan admitted. 'But not brilliant enough to deal with entropy.'

'None of you is.'

'None of us?'

'Humans.'

'Ah yes, I forgot. But your lot are.'

'My lot, and others.'

'Oth– Hang on, you mean them? The ones who want to come through?' The Doctor waited for him to work it out. 'Unwin can't get there on his own. But coming from the other side...'

'And from the other end of the computations.'

'... *they'll* join up with *him*.' Ethan's eyes darted unseeingly around the room as he put things together. 'But that means that they're... that they've solved entropy.'

'Or at least controlled it to such a degree it hardly functions.'

'But the laws of physics –'

'In this universe.'

There was a pause.

'Oh, of course,' Ethan said a bit giddily. 'I should have thought. Naturally there are other universes.'

'Yes.'

'Loads and loads, I'll bet.'

'A great many. Do you want any food?'

'Hang food! What are we going to do?'

Ethan started to sit up, but the Doctor gently pushed him back. 'I'm working on that.'

'You have been from the beginning, haven't you? You sussed it out right away.'

'Not quite right away. And not entirely. Even now, I'm not sure of our invaders' motives. I don't know what they want.'

'They tried to pull you through,' said Ethan.

The Doctor, who had begun to pace, stopped. 'Sorry?'

'They tried to pull you through,' Ethan repeated. 'Perhaps it's you they want.'

'Dear me.' The Doctor tapped his chin some more. 'I think you have a point. That's not a good thing at all.'

'As opposed to invading Earth?'

'As opposed to invading Earth if I'm not here.'

'What?' Ethan said blankly.

But as if he hadn't heard him, still tapping his chin, humming, the Doctor left the room. Like the white rabbit down his hole, Ethan thought dazedly. Down his hole to another, magical, frightening world. Then he, like the dormouse, curled up and went to sleep.

'I should have broken the sod's bones,' Ace said.

'Darjeeling?' said the Doctor. 'Or Earl Grey?' Since he'd come into the kitchen, he'd been preoccupied, to Ace's annoyance, with making tea.

'Bones,' she said. 'Bones, bones, bones. Now he's got away.'

'Oh, I don't know.' The Doctor turned grim eyes on her. 'I don't think that's necessarily true at all. I think I may be able to find him.'

'How?'

'It's complicated.'

'You always say that!'

'That's because it always is!' He caught himself. 'And this time, even more so than usual. I understand your anger, Ace. But you would have put all three of you at risk. We don't know how many people were actually in that house. You did the right thing, and you got Amberglass out, which is what matters most. It was very brave and very bright. You threw a spanner in their works. Brett will get what's coming to him.'

'But not from me.'

'We can't have everything we want,' said the Doctor, in such a mild, faux-pedantic way that she found herself laughing. She jumped and perched on the counter.

'You really think you can track them down?'

'I'm almost positive.' He frowned at the tin. 'This isn't Darjeeling. I was certain I had Darjeeling.'

'Probably another one of you popped in and drank it all.'

'I wish I'd stop doing that. I'm going to have to start leaving notes. All right, Earl Grey it is.' He lifted the second tin. 'Bother.'

'I guess all of you like the tea you like.'

'They could at least replace the things they use. I always do.'

'Yeah, well, you're the responsible one, aren't you? The others all sound as if they were a bit loopy.'

'My fifth incarnation wasn't,' he said stiffly. 'A gentleman, in his way.'

'More than I can say for you.'

'Kind hearts are more than coronets,' he sniffed. 'English Breakfast it is, then.'

She watched him warm the pot. 'Suppose Ethan wants some?'

'Certain of it,' said the Doctor.

When Ethan waked this time, he felt Ace's warm nakedness against his back. He put his hand back and found her thigh.

'I've got tea,' she said.

'It's not tea I want.'

She kissed the nape of his neck, but said hesitantly, 'Your chest. It'll hurt if you're lying on... well, you know what I mean. Pressure, and all.'

He snorted. 'Don't tell me that you, of all people, have never heard of Girls On Top.'

'You're feeling all right,' said Ace.

'I'm feeling wonderful.'

'No, I mean, all right. No headaches. No hallucinations.'

'No,' he said, pleased but bewildered.

'You'd think...' She stopped. 'I mean, with everything...'

'The physical reality doesn't influence the illness,' he said, settling her closer against him. 'If it did, the last hour would have cured me.'

Aced laughed happily. 'Seriously, if you need some medicine from your flat – only that's not such a good idea. The Doctor may have something in the TARDIS.'

'It's a chemist's as well as a spaceship?'

'It's lots of things. I can't wait to show you.' She sat up. 'Come on.'

'I'm ill,' he objected. 'I've had a dreadful time. I must stay in bed, and I can't be left alone.'

She lay down immediately, 'All right, slacker.'

A log fell, but no embers sparked onto the hearth.

'It's all right,' said Ace. 'Nothing landed on the rug.' She turned over and put her arms gently around him. 'D'you suppose...?'

The log fell, scattering embers on the hearth.

Ethan and Ace sat bolt upright, still holding on to each other.

'Erm...' he said.

'Oh hell,' she muttered.

'Wasn't that... Didn't that happen before? Just now? Only the embers...'

'Yeah.'

The log fell. Embers flew out onto the rug.

'Bollocks,' said Ace. She started to get out of bed, but the embers faded to black.

'What's happening?'

The fireplace was cold and empty.

Ace said, 'Balls!'

'What's going on?'

'The thing. Only it shouldn't be happening to you. It only happens to me. And the Doctor. Because we've travelled so much in time. But everyone else, it changes for them. It should change for you.'

'Right,' he said bewilderedly.

'It's Time! Time's just spinning in place. Well, not exactly, it's repeating itself with tiny changes, only you shouldn't be seeing that, you should just be changing –'

'That was a time shift? I just saw a time shift!?'

'– only I can't work out why you're not. Oh!' She squeezed his hand. 'We were touching.'

'We were touching, yes. And that means...?'

'That's why it happened to you too. Wicked!' She jumped out of bed. 'I've got to tell the Doctor.'

'Put some clothes on!'

'Oh, this wouldn't bother the Doctor. He's not interested in sex with aliens.' Nonetheless, Ace pulled on her jeans and jumper. 'I'm not sure he's interested at all. I think his lot reproduce by being woven from DNA or something naff like that. Not much fun, is it?' She headed for the door. 'Probably accounts for him being so gloomy. I'm starving. Come down to the kitchen; we'll find something to eat.'

'You'll have to help me, I'm afraid.'

'Oh, right.' She winced, embarrassed. 'I forgot for a minute. It's because you're so capable otherwise,' she added, smiling.

'Praise from Caesar is praise indeed. You know I haven't any clothes. I'm not putting on that suit again.'

'Bugger.' She opened the wardrobe and pulled out a harlequin-patched coat.

'No,' he said immediately.

'As if you have any style sense. I rather like it.'

'No.'

She sighed and pulled out a brown velvet frock coat that was much too large for him. There were some trousers his size, but for a stouter man. 'There's nothing in here. I don't know why he keeps these; he'll never wear them again.'

'It looks like he can't wear them now.'

'Yeah,' she said. 'Well... We'll just have to borrow something from him. You're about the same size.'

'Does he even have other clothes? I've only ever seen him in that suit.'

'Oh yeah, he's got others. They're not so nice as the suit. He's well elegant now, but you should have seen him when I first met him. Something out of an old clothes bin he was. He must have *some* proper clothes in the house.' She darted down the stairs.

When she returned with a pair of checked trousers, red braces, and a sleeveless jumper out of some sartorial nightmare, Ethan thought he might just stay in bed. But the trousers fitted and the shirt was acceptable. She helped him downstairs to the kitchen. The Doctor was not to be found. 'Probably in the TARDIS.' Ace started rummaging in the cupboards.

'It's nearby then?'

'Yeah. Tinned soup. Surely he has more than that. He usually keeps cheese.' She opened the refrigerator. 'Right. And some eggs. Cheese omelette all right?'

'Anything.'

In the event, she made him three omelettes and he finished each of them in about ninety seconds then drank half a litre of orange juice in a gulp. Ace hadn't found any bread, but there was blackberry jam so they ate this from the jar with spoons.

The Doctor sat at a computer examining for the third time Unwin and Ethan's combined calculations. He took Ethan's word for it that he hadn't contributed any additions while he was a prisoner. Which meant that all Unwin had was the work Ethan had done under the Doctor's guidance, which, according to Ethan, Unwin hadn't managed to do much with. Nor would he, the Doctor was concluding. Even running the computations through the TARDIS computers, which were perfectly able to handle them, took several hours. At the rate Unwin was going, he'd be stuck for years before he worked out the next step. That would keep the threat at bay until the Doctor could find a permanent way to thwart it.

So the crisis was far from imminent. Still, though it hardly seemed necessary, he might as well check the status of that fragile place in the barrier. He pressed a button and the sensor panel lit up.

The worn spot was gone.

In the morning, it snowed. Ethan got out of bed, softly so as not to wake Ace. Balancing on the toes of his wounded foot, he hobbled to the window and looked out into the silence. The snow was already an inch or so deep. He wondered why the Doctor kept an old police call box in his back garden.

When he came down to the kitchen, he found the Doctor making pancakes. A bottle of syrup sat on the table, along with orange juice and hot coffee. The Doctor glanced at him, said without irony 'Stylish trousers' and flipped a pancake onto a plate. Ethan sat down and picked up the bottle. Maple syrup from America. A small covered dish contained a mound of fresh butter.

'The others on your planet, are they like you?'

'No.' The Doctor set a plate of pancakes in front of him.

'How are they different?'

'Oh, homebodies. No sense of curiosity or adventure.'

'So you just travel around doing what? Fixing problems with Time?'

'For the most part. You'd be surprised how many there are. Rents, unravelling, undone hems, grease spots.'

'Something odd happened last night. Ace said it was a time shift.'

'Yes, those are peculiar, aren't they? They're what first alerted me to this particular problem. Fortunately, we won't be having any more of them.'

'Why not?'

'Because it was the disruption of the aliens' partial emergence that was putting the stress on the time line. And they won't be doing that again.'

'No?'

'No. The potential entry has vanished.'

'How?'

'It could only have had a limited duration anyway. Its time was up.'

'So everything's all right?'

'Well, I still need to make sure nothing similar can happen again. And sort out Brett and Unwin, but essentially,' the Doctor grinned, 'the answer is yes.'

Ethan exhaled with relief. The Doctor sat down with his own pancakes and soaked them in syrup. 'These things are remarkably absorbent,' he said when he caught Ethan looking at him oddly. 'I've often wondered if they could be put to some sort of technical use. I must look into that some day.'

For a while, they just concentrated on the pancakes. Ethan poured himself a cup of coffee and discovered a jug of fresh cream behind the pot.

'I am curious about that other set of equations,' said the Doctor.

'Unwin thought they were meant to break some mathematical code, but he didn't know what.'

'No, I can't think why they'd need that. You say this program was also constructed of primes?'

'All of it that I've seen.'

'Mm.' The Doctor ate in silence for a while. Then he said in a different tone, 'I'm sorry about what happened to you.'

'You don't need me any more, do you? I'm serious: I am not cut out for this.'

'You've done very well.'

'I've been surprised at my stamina,' Ethan said dryly. 'But I don't expect it to last.'

'No mental episodes, though?'

'No.'

'And yet you've missed several doses of your medication.' Though the pancakes seemed to have absorbed little if any syrup, the Doctor drowned them again. 'I thought from the beginning it wasn't really good for you. How about your headaches?' His eyes flicked up inquiringly. Ethan thought he also looked worried.

'Nothing so far. But they don't follow a pattern.'

'Mm.' The Doctor chewed for a moment. 'I know you want to get back to your own place, but it would be safer if you stayed here for a while.'

'Where the hell are they?'

'I'll find them,' said the Doctor, a cool edge to his voice.

'Then what?'

'Then I'll stop them.'

'By yourself?'

'More or less. Not to worry, you won't be needed.'

'What about Ace?'

'Ace would murder me if I left her out. I suggest you don't become protective of her – it would insult her, and it wouldn't change anything. This is the life she's chosen. And I always shield her from the worst of it.'

'And she'd murder you if she knew that.'

'Please don't mention it. More pancakes?'

Ethan said yes. The Doctor's now pancake-free plate held a pool of leftover syrup. Ethan was half afraid he'd eat it with a spoon.

'Morning,' Ace yawned. 'Yes to pancakes.' She sat down and smiled at Ethan – a little shyly. For no reason either could quite explain, they were both unwilling to parade their relationship in front of the Doctor. *In loco parentis*, Ethan thought, a bit embarrassed by his embarrassment.

'There was one of those time shift thingys last night,' Ace said to the Doctor.

'Yes, Ethan told me. However –'

'But it was well weird, Professor. You know how before we watched things change but we didn't change with them. Only last night, that happened to him too.'

The Doctor turned from the stove, eyes bright. 'That's interesting.'

'I think it's because we were touching.'

The Doctor raised an eyebrow and resumed flipping a pancake. Ace reddened a little. Was he her father, Ethan wondered, or her uncle, or her older brother – or, in some undefined way, Ethan's rival?

'Well, there won't be any more of those shifts. The potential entry portal is gone.'

Ace didn't seem nearly as amazed and excited as Ethan thought the situation warranted. She only nodded in satisfaction, smiling. 'Knew you'd do it. Told you he always does,' she said to Ethan.

'It wasn't me this time, Ace, it just happened naturally.'

'Gross.' She'd spotted the syrupy plate. 'Why don't you just shoot it up?'

'Death by maple syrup injection. That would be a new one, even in my experience.'

'What are you going to do about Molecross?' Ethan asked.

'Nothing.'

'You keep saying that, and then he turns up again.'

'He *was* trying to help,' Ace admitted. 'It took a lot of bottle for someone like him to go there alone.'

'It wasn't very intelligent, either,' the Doctor said pointedly. 'If official channels had been used, both Brett and Unwin would be in custody now.'

'Look,' said Ace irritably, 'I couldn't find the Brigadier, I knew the police wouldn't believe me, I didn't want to interrupt you searching in case I was wrong, so I did what I could.'

'To my eternal gratitude,' Ethan added.

'Yes, yes,' sighed the Doctor. 'You're right of course. Under the circumstances, you made the only choice you could.' He gave Ace her pancakes. 'I'd best get back to work now.'

He left in his now-you-see-him-now-you-don't fashion. Ethan looked out of the window at the falling snow. It almost made the old police call box look beautiful. He was about to ask Ace about the Doctor's peculiar taste in garden staturary; when the Doctor himself came trudging through the snow, opened the box's door, and vanished inside.

'What the hell is he doing?'

'Hm?' Ace looked out the window. 'Where?'

'He just went into that call box!'

'Yeah,' she said. 'That's the TARDIS.'

Ethan went to the window. Every time he thought things were as strange as they could possibly be, they got stranger. '*That*'s his time machine?'

'It's bigger on the inside than the outside,' she said helpfully.

'How big?'

'I don't know,' she said simply. 'I don't think he knows.'

Ethan stared hard at the box, expecting to spot a shimmer in the air or the gleam of technology or *something* giving a clue that things weren't what they seemed. The call box modestly continued to be a call box.

'It looks at least forty years old.'

'Yeah, it got stuck that way.'

'... Stuck?'

'It's sort of complicated. I'll let him explain it to you.' She took his arm. 'But I can show you around this place.'

From what he knew of such things, Ethan guessed that the house dated from the 1880s with mid-twentieth-century updates of the kitchen, baths and toilets. It was comfortably, even warmly furnished, with an oddly welcoming feel for a place that was so often empty. There were window seats for curling up and reading in, odd nooks, mysterious cabinets. It was, Ethan thought, the house in which Peter Pan flew in the nursery window and a little-used room held a wardrobe that led to another world. And in the snowy garden, the sorcerer's magic box.

Even as he thought this, the Doctor came out of the TARDIS and stood admiring the snow. He was so ordinary-looking, Ethan thought, except for the wonderful, in all senses of the word, eyes. The Doctor removed his sad-looking hat, slapped it against his thigh to shake the snow off, replaced it, and returned to the house. In a moment, they heard him on the stairs.

'Right then,' said Ace as he joined them. 'What now?'

'Interestingly, this is one of those cases where having utterly superior technology isn't much use. I can't track two random human beings. UNIT, however, can follow the paper trails of tickets and credit-card receipts and hotel registrations, and the Brigadier has agreed to take care of that.'

'How long will that take?' Ethan asked.

'A while,' said the Doctor apologetically. 'I know you'd like to go home, but it's just not on yet. I'm afraid you'll have to stay here.'

'Hard cheese,' said Ace, and then snorted with laughter. She couldn't stop giggling. The Doctor was regarding her curiously, and Ethan had such a carefully composed straight face that the sight of him set her laughing again.

'So,' said the Doctor, when she had finally subsided. 'You'll be provided with your own computer, of course, and anything else you want.'

Ace began to guffaw and had to leave the room. The Doctor raised an eyebrow at Ethan but didn't say anything. Ethan didn't say anything either. Ace came back into the room, red-faced and precariously composed.

'How long will that take?' Ethan asked. Ace and the Doctor both stared at him in alarm. 'What?' he said irritably.

'Er.' The Doctor faltered slightly. 'I realise it's a bore, but until we have Brett and Unwin, I think it's advisable –'

'Yes, yes, I understand. Why are you looking at me like that?' he said to Ace.

'Oh, erm, nothing. I'd rather like having you here, actually.'

Ethan warmed at the words, but the expression still disconcerted him. 'Are you all right?' He turned to the Doctor for explanation, but the Doctor was gone. 'What the hell is going on?'

Ace hesitated, chewing on her lip. 'There was one of those time blips,' she said quietly.

'What? Just now?'

'Yeah. Only we weren't touching, so you were in it instead of just watching. You asked how long till you could go home, twice.'

'I don't remember that.' Ethan felt panic starting and tamped it down furiously. 'I've lost that.'

'It didn't really happen to you.' She was trying to sound reassuring. 'You're you, you know. That first bit was just a detour.'

'A detour! Oh good God!' Ethan ran his hands through his hair and started to pace. 'How much more of this is there? Aliens. Time machines. Threats to the universe. Sadists. Perception going all wobbly. Two of me that are really only one of me.'

'It's all right.' She put her arms around him. He didn't push her away, but he was rigid in her embrace.

'It's not all right,' he said tonelessly. 'It's rather horrible.'

She released him and stepped back, but he caught her hand.

'Let's not quarrel,' he said. 'You're the only thing about this I don't hate.'

'*There's* a compliment,' she snorted. 'You're back to your old self, right enough.'

He shook his head, dismissing their conversation. 'Why'd the Doctor vanish like that? What's wrong?'

She glanced uneasily out at the TARDIS. 'Well, you see, these time blip things were the result of the invaders trying to come through and stressing the continuum and all that. So when the place where they were trying to get in went missing –'

'– the time shifts should have stopped.'

'That's it, yeah.'

'That means there's another way in.'

Ace bit her lip and nodded.

Ethan did his hands-in-hair thing again. She watched helplessly. She wanted to reassure him, but things really were going pear-shaped.

'Ace! Ethan!'

The Doctor was standing in the snowy garden, waving them down.

'Come along! We're going to Switzerland.'

A bolt of pain burned through Ethan's skull.

CHAPTER SIXTEEN

At last they came to the ice. Unwin was panting and shivering. There had been no wind in the valley, but here at the edge of the glacier it was fierce. Brett didn't seem to feel the cold. He clambered up onto the till and surveyed the bright, blinding plain, almost too radiant to look at. Unwin sat down and took a canteen from under his parka.

'Do you want some water?'

Brett didn't answer. Unwin took a swallow. Bloody good thing it hadn't frozen.

'If you're without water,' said Brett, 'and you eat snow, you'll freeze to death.'

'Thank you. I hope never to be near ice or snow again.'

Brett smiled at him strangely then resumed squinting at the glacier.

'I don't see why they'd try to come through,' Unwin continued irritably. 'They know they haven't enough power.' Brett didn't say anything.

'They're not trying to come through, only to leave us a sign that they can, given the right circumstances.'

Unwin's teeth began to chatter. What if he couldn't finish it? The work Amberglass had done on his own, before they got hold of him, opened up new doors, but how long did the numbers go on beyond those doors? He might have to spend his life on the problem. Unwin wouldn't have minded that; it was Brett's threatening haste that made the task so hard. Perhaps impossible. He glanced up at Brett's straight, implacable figure. Perhaps he ought to run away. Find some far-off place to live with his beautiful equations. A tear leaked from his eye and froze.

'I can't take much more of this cold.'

'It's the alcohol in your veins. They expand and release more heat from your body.'

'Is that true? I don't believe that's true.'

'There are no marks; they haven't tried yet.' Brett came carefully down across the rubble. 'I'll have to check later.'

'I'm not coming up here again. I don't know why you insisted on my being here in the first place.'

'I thought it would interest you,' said Brett, stepping past him and starting the descent to the road and the car.

Or possibly, Unwin thought with trepidation, you were afraid I might run if you left me alone. Had Brett sensed he was wavering? Would he tie *him* up in a cellar? He'd thought he knew the man in front of him, but he hadn't. Not at all. He was in a terrible position.

He watched Brett moving cautiously in front of him. What if there were an accident...? Brett looked back. Unwin started and smiled nervously, and knew he could never do it. Never, never do it. And Brett knew it too. Unwin hated him again. As if he had read the thought, Brett smiled.

'Come along, young Pat. Back to the warmth.'

Lie, thought Unwin as he followed him. Lie. He would never come out of the cold again.

Ace wondered guiltily if Ethan's headache, which had literally knocked him over, had been brought on by the succession of so many weird things so quickly. The Doctor had done something that relieved the pain and left him to rest in the quiet dark. Ace sat by the bed for a while, not saying anything, until his breathing told her he was asleep.

She missed him. She wanted to show him the Alps. Show him that there were good things about travelling with the Doctor, that it wasn't all torture and dreadful threats and chaos. Except, she admitted to herself, it mostly was. 'This isn't life,' she whispered as she left. 'You mustn't hole up in your flat again. Life can be wonderful.'

In his sleep he heard her, and he dreamed of her and wonderful things.

When she returned to the console room, the Doctor had made one of his mysterious departures.

'Bugger,' said Ace. She went outside. The car the Doctor had rented was gone. Git. He'd gone on without her. Sulkily, she kicked a stone. He knew how much that irritated – all right, all right, hurt – her. And he should know that most times he turned out to need her after all.

She surveyed the scene morosely. The TARDIS stood in a cluster of dark green firs on the slope of a shallow valley. About a quarter of a mile distant lay a little Swiss village, at the end of which glinted a frozen pond complete with ice-skaters. Ace had sniffed to the Doctor that it looked like some naff Disney film, and he had replied, in that know-it-all way of his, that it ought to since the major designer for Disney's early animated features was Gustav Tenggren who came from... She couldn't remember. Some place with Alps.

There wasn't even much snow.

She moped back into the TARDIS. Ethan was asleep. The Doctor was gone. What was she supposed to do? Bake biscuits or something? Well, what the hell. She went into the little kitchen annex off the food-machine room. A can of green pea soup with the lid missing sat unappetisingly on the counter.

Maybe she'd take a swim.

In bathing costume and terry-cloth robe she started down the corridor that led from her bedroom to the pool. It was about a five-minute walk with, it had always seemed to her, a needless number of turns. Why couldn't the Doctor just reconfigure things so that the trip was shorter? She'd asked him, and she knew he'd meant to, but something else always took his attention. Giant metal insects or something. It's not as if it would take that much time, she though irritably as she turned a corner and walked into Molecross.

* * *

The Doctor examined the glacier. Though the wind was fierce, he still wore only his suit, his one concession to the temperature being a disconcerting paisley scarf. He had driven the car up to a lay-by from which a footpath snaked steeply through the till. The climb turned out to be neither long nor difficult; he presumed that in the summer this was a destination for walkers.

The glacial ice was greyish, which didn't surprise the Doctor. He knew that silt from erosion made all glaciers, except the pristine ones of the sea, look dirty. Of course, if clouds hadn't come up, the glare would still be bad enough to call for sunglasses.

He worked out a rough sense of the area in his head. Three acres, more or less, for the flattest expanse. The rest was either too uneven or too steep. He stepped onto the ice and, with a graceful, half-skating gait, headed out across the glacier. About fifty metres in, he stopped and turned in place, using something that looked like a penlight to laser a shallow circle in the ice. He moved on and made a second circle. Then a third. This was going to take some time, but he couldn't be sure exactly where the landing attempt would be made. And if anyone showed up who objected to the circles, several dozen of them would be harder to erase than one.

'I've got it set up,' said Unwin. 'We can communicate through the computer again. Don't need to go to that bloody glacier.'

He was drunk again. Brett watched, tight-lipped, as Unwin wove to the sofa and collapsed. Useless, completely useless. He wished he could get rid of the lush now. But he couldn't until he had another, hopefully more competent, mathematician to replace him. And how that was going to happen, now that Amberglass had slipped through their fingers, he couldn't imagine. Perhaps Amberglass would have been stymied in the end too, but that wouldn't matter: if he had Amberglass, sooner or later he'd have the Doctor. Only he didn't have Amberglass.

Brett dismissed the matter as useless speculation and went to the computer.

WE WILL TRY TONIGHT BUT WE STILL MAY NOT HAVE THE POWER THE BRIDGE IS UNFINISHED

BUT SOME ADDITIONAL WORK HAS BEEN DONE YOU MUST TRY

FIND THE DOCTOR

Like a broken record, Brett thought.

I'M TRYING

FIND HIM

WHY Brett typed in exasperation *WHAT CAN HE DO*

STOP YOU

HE DOESN'T EVEN KNOW WHERE WE ARE

HE WILL YOU MUST FIND HIM FIRST

Brett reread the message uneasily.

HOW WILL HE FIND US

HE WILL

Brett regarded these last words soberly, then shrugged. When he would he would. In a few hours, it might not even matter.

Ace and Molecross both leaped back. 'What are you doing here?' she yelled.

'Oh thank God.' He was almost in tears. 'I thought I was lost in here forever.'

'How in hell did you get in?'

'I was so frightened.'

'Where've you been hiding?'

'I don't know. I've been trying to find my way out. You know,' he added conspiratorially, 'there are all these little constructions in the halls. Devices. Very mysterious.'

'Tell me how you got in,' she snapped.

'I really need something to eat,' he said pathetically. 'And a toilet.'

'Tell me.'

'You rushed in and left the door ajar. I slipped in after you. I'd followed the Brigadier to the house.' Molecross cringed as if he expected her to hit him. Not far wrong either, Ace thought angrily.

'You can't stay here.'

'I don't want to,' he assured her.

She directed him to a toilet and the food machines and waited in the console room. This was a right cock-up. What was she going to do with the prat? At a movement, she looked up sharply. But it was Ethan, his hair smoothed down inadequately, polishing his glasses on the edge of his shirt. He put them on and peered at her.

'What's wrong?'

Molecross came in, stuffing a cream pastry into his mouth.

'Oh dear God!' Ethan didn't actually leap towards the ceiling, but it was a near thing. 'What are you doing here?' He turned to Ace wildly. 'He's not really here, is he? Tell me he's not.'

'Afraid so,' she said glumly.

Ethan went over to a wall and banged his head against it.

'Stop that!'

'It feels good,' he assured her. 'Really, it does.'

'Well, stop it anyway. It gets on my wick.'

Ethan stopped but didn't turn around. 'Why is he here?' he said mournfully. 'What horrible configuration of the planets caused this?'

'He stowed away.'

'On the TARDIS? He stowed away on the *TARDIS*?'

'Why are you talking as if I wasn't here?' Molecross asked.

Ethan eyed him sourly. 'Just wishful thinking.'

'I saved your life, you know!'

'Yeah,' said Ace. 'And good luck for you I was there to help.'

Molecross sulked, but didn't correct her.

'Balls to this,' said Ace, and went off to change back into clothes.

For a minute or so, neither Ethan nor Molecross said anything. Molecross broke the silence.

'You look better. I mean, than when I last saw you.'

'I'd hope so,' Ethan snapped.

Again, a few minutes in which no one spoke.

'What did they want? Those men who took you.'

'I'm not going to talk about that.' There was just no safe place, Ethan thought disconsolately. People charged into his apartment, they charged into the TARDIS. Was he never to have any privacy?

'Where are we?'

'Switzerland.'

'Really?' Molecross was excited. 'I've always wanted to see the Alps. Is there a window?'

'No.'

Piqued, Molecross went to the console and began to examine the layout. Good luck, thought Ethan. As if anyone but the Doctor could make sense of it. 'I think you might want t- *don't touch that!*'

Molecross jumped. 'I was just seeing what it was made of.'

'Alien stuff, all right? Just write that down: "A source said it was made of alien stuff".'

Molecross looked curiously at a lever. 'That's odd. Bit old-fashioned, isn't it? Everything else is buttons and switches. Now don't get upset. I'm just going to feel if it's made of different -'

Ethan rushed him, but too late. At Molecross's touch, the lever automatically moved, and the TARDIS doors slid open. Molecross stepped out, gaping at the landscape. Ethan was about to shut the doors and be rid of him, when a nasty thought hit him: Molecross might go wandering down to the town and bump into Brett. Brett had never seen him, of course, but Molecross would recognise Brett. And almost certainly panic and give himself away. And the rest of them. Plus get himself killed.

'Come back in,' he called. 'I'm freezing with the door open.'

'There should be more snow.' Molecross sounded deeply disappointed.

'Well, there isn't. Will you please come in?'

'There's a town down there. Do you know the name?'

The Doctor had mentioned it in passing, but Ethan couldn't remember. 'It's just a bloody Swiss town, Molecross. Old churches. Pastry shops. Cute buildings.'

'Local colour,' said Molecross. 'Not to mention something to eat.' He started off.

'Hell,' Ethan said, and lunged out the door. He tackled Molecross and brought him down flat. 'Hey!' Molecross gasped. Ethan clung to him as he rolled back and forth; it was like riding a small whale. 'Shut up,' Ethan panted. 'Stay still. Brett's down there.'

Molecross froze. 'Oh my God,' he said in a small voice. Ethan slipped off him and sat catching his breath. Molecross lumbered up. He found his safari hat and crammed it back on his head.

'Sorry,' Ethan said. 'I hope I didn't hurt your arm.'

'He's down there?'

'More or less. He's in the vicinity. Probably. Or soon will be. Anyway, I'd stay here.' Ethan got to his feet. 'Let's go back inside.'

Back in the console room. Molecross sagged in the armchair. 'I could use a real drink.'

'I don't believe there is anything.'

'Brett's really here somewhere?'

'Looks likely.'

'This is frightening.'

Ethan sighed deeply. 'Molecross, what are you doing here? What do you think is going on? Haven't you worked out that it's dangerous and ugly?'

'I don't know what's going on,' Molecross said sadly. 'But I want to. Don't you understand? Sitting in this room, we're on the edge of the transcendent. The Doctor is immortal and lives among the stars. Haven't you worked out how that's wonderful and miraculous?'

'Okay,' said Ethan after a moment. 'But don't touch anything.'

They didn't speak for a while. Molecross ate all the biscuits.

Ethan fetched some more and also found a small wedge of cheese, which Molecross took care of in three bites.

'You're all healed,' he observed.

'Yeah.'

'That was horrible when I found you,' Molecross said in a small voice. 'I mean, of course it was more horrible for you. Obviously it was. But it was awful. I'd never seen... And I heard you, on the answering machine.'

'Let's drop it,' said Ethan tersely.

'Life is terrible,' Molecross went on. 'Isn't it? Suffering and death. Even the best life has those. I always knew there was something else. Something beyond all that.'

'A place where when people stand up from the toilet they leave behind candy bars?'

Molecross flushed. 'There's no need to –'

'Yes there is. You're off in the moonglow. You want to live with the fairies. You're scared of life and you want to get out, only without dying.'

'I want the marvellous,' said Molecross. 'Why shouldn't I?'

'We don't live in Eden.'

'But Eden is where we belong.' Molecross's voice was simple and innocent. 'Not here, among all this pain.'

CHAPTER SEVENTEEN

Rain was coming, thought Brett. And what kind of rain would it be? Not water. Not fire. Certainly not pennies from heaven. He grinned and turned from the window. As usual, Unwin was passed out on the couch. Probably he hadn't accomplished anything, even with Amberglass's numbers to build on. Brett's spirits fell. He had to face facts. This attempt would probably be a failure, like the ones in Kent. They still weren't far enough along.

Nonetheless, he needed to be there in case anyone, any... thing, did arrive.

The Doctor felt the snow on his cheeks and lips. He put up his umbrella.

He hadn't enjoyed sitting around for hours waiting for an alien invasion that might not even happen. But they would want to come through, or at least attempt to, as quickly as possible. Not immediately – they'd need to connect up to whatever else Unwin had been able to work out – but soon. So he had to be here, in case something went wrong. If it did, he had one more spanner to throw into the works.

He searched along the glacier's edge until he found a pair of boulders that, particularly if he wedged his open umbrella between them, would make an excellent shelter and hiding place.

He didn't construct this immediately. The snow was very beautiful. The Doctor watched it soften the hard ice, turn the grey white. He wasn't worried about his circles vanishing. Their effectiveness didn't depend on their visibility.

The Doctor thought about ice. Vapour to liquid to solid – reverse entropy. Achieved, of course, by an expense of energy somewhere else. A freezer was a little anti-entropic chamber, but outside the chamber electricity was what enabled the laws of physics to be suspended.

He stiffened, mouth slightly open, eyes fixed. A race of equations. Entropy. Energy. Transcending entropy was such a radical physical achievement that only an enormous amount of power could keep any such system intact. But to create and preserve a situation of no wasted energy, you'd have to use more energy than you were saving. So obviously the energy couldn't come from the system itself.

They didn't want to come here. They wanted to take something away.

'Ah,' he breathed angrily. He should have known. He'd let the idea that he was fighting an invasion prevent him from seeing any other options. What a fool he'd been. An eddy of snow enclosed him. He wanted to bat it away, like a cloud of gnats. The snow was falling more heavily now – large, feathery flakes. But he could still see through it. And he saw Brett.

The Doctor took an automatic step back, but Brett wasn't looking in his direction. He was standing several hundred feet away, smoking, eyes on the ice. He couldn't see the circles, the Doctor thought with relief, not that he'd have been able to destroy them all anyway – that would take much longer than making them had.

Wind pushed the snow aside, and he got a good look at Brett. Tall. Aristocratic features. Dark hair brushed back from his forehead. Who are you, the Doctor wondered. Why would you bring such destruction down on your own planet?

Brett was shivering but he didn't notice. His lips were parted, his heart racing. Blood rushing through his veins, hot blood. Well, there'd be no more of that. Perhaps soon. How peaceful the silence was. It lulled him. He half shut his eyes. Perhaps very soon.

* * *

'Balls to this,' said Ace. 'I'm going down to that bloody village.'

'Good.' Molecross was enthusiastic. 'I want a proper meal.'

'Am I the only one here with any brains?' Ethan asked, though he was pretty certain he knew the answer. 'What can you do in the village, except possibly run into Brett?'

'We don't even know he's here.'

'Right. He's left England, the entry point is here – what's he done, gone to Cancun?'

'We must have got here ahead,' she insisted, running from the room. Her voice echoed back, 'He doesn't have a time machine!'

'No,' Ethan muttered. 'Only jet travel.'

Molecross was beginning to look doubtful. 'He's never seen me.'

'You're not bloody going, Molecross. That's all she'd need.'

Ace ran back in, carrying an armful of coats. She tossed one to each of the men. Neither looked as if it would fit. Ethan was also provided with a soft, wide-brimmed hat that looked to have gone a few rounds in its day.

'Ace, do you happen to have a plan?'

'He's taken the car. We might see it on the street and find him that way. It's not a big place.'

'What in hell would he even be doing there?'

'Sniffing out information. Who knows? I'm not hanging about doing nothing.'

'Maybe he doesn't want you interfering, did you think of that?'

She glared at him. 'You're just afraid! Right, don't come. Don't either of you come. The last thing I want is to have to take care of a pair of nerds.' She slammed down the door lever. Snow blew in. 'Bugger.'

For just a second she was nonplussed, then she charged out the door.

'Oh hell.' Ethan struggled into the smaller of the two coats. 'I have to go after her.'

'No you don't,' Molecross objected. 'She can take care of herself. She's damn tough.'

Ethan jammed on the hat. It was too big. 'And you bloody

stay here, Molecross. Do you hear me? Stay. Here. If you touch anything, I'll murder you.' And he ran after Ace.

The snow was heavier, but it wasn't yet sticking to the ground. Ahead of him he could see Ace's leather jacket and bouncing ponytail. He yelled her name, but she didn't stop. Stuff this, he thought, and sped up. If he couldn't catch a girl running downhill, he might as well go home and jump out the window. When she heard him approaching, she glanced over her shoulder.

'Go away!'

'Not bloody likely. You child!' he shouted as she turned away. 'You stupid, stubborn child! You're still in the playground! You think this is a game and you're going to win.'

She spun on him. 'What do you know about it? You don't know anything. You don't know the things I've seen, the things I've got clear of, things I haven't got clear of in time. All you know is bleeding numbers and pills.'

'I know you're a fool.' He caught up to her, panting and angry. 'You don't have any idea what you're doing. You've just panicked and run off. Find him by his car! What's he going to be doing, then – having a drink in some quaint Swiss inn?' He bent over, hands on knees, trying to catch his breath. 'All you want is to smash things, Ace.'

'All you want is to hide.' But she was sullen rather than shouting.

'Not having much luck, am I?'

She shoved her hands into her jacket pockets. 'Some things need smashing. A lot of things.'

'There's a philosophy. Do they need blowing up too? Have you still got that Nineteen Nine?'

'Nitro Nine,' she said scornfully. 'You really are a nerd.'

He straightened, wiping the snow from his face. 'I can't begin to estimate the number of non-nerds on this planet who have never heard of Nitro Nine. I imagine a great many of them have never blown anything up, either.'

'It's not like I blow up buildings,' she sulked. She kicked a tree, but not very hard. 'You're talking like I'm Guy Fawkes or something. I only blow up small things, like Daleks.'

Ethan didn't want to know what Daleks were. 'Sometimes you act like you're 13, Ace. You're not 13.'

'I hated my life,' she said in a small voice, 'before I met him. I lived in this lifeless bloody suburb and I was going to grow up and marry some local prat and have kids and yell at them. I hadn't the brains to go to uni, not the right sort of brains anyway. Then I got caught up in this time storm and carried away to this ice planet and what happens? I'm a waitress! And I get involved with a prat anyway, only he's about forty years older than I am. Out of the frying pan, e'nt it? And then the Doctor came. And it turns out there's this dragon on the planet nobody'd known about – not a real one, a biomechanical or something. But still... a dragon. Like out of a fairy tale. It was like he brought it with him. Not the bad part, just the magic. He needs me.' She looked Ethan straight in the eyes. 'Because there's only so much magic can do. And I'm not magic.'

'You're wrong.'

'You know what I mean.'

He nodded and brushed snow from her hair. 'What shall we do, then?'

'Not wait in the TARDIS. Not nothing.'

'All right.' He put his arm around her shoulders. 'We'll go down to the village, and if we can't find him we can at least have a drink.'

They started walking.

'And if we run into this Brett,' she said, 'he's for it.'

But Brett was still standing at the edge of the glacier. He'd donned gloves and a dark fedora, but otherwise hadn't moved. The Doctor could just see him from inside his improvised shelter, into which he'd retreated after knocking snow off his hat for the fifth time. Why the man hadn't frozen, he had no idea. Ice in his veins. The Doctor bore cold easily, and even he was uncomfortable.

And bored. The vigil looked to go on into the night, and he hadn't even brought a pack of cards. He played with his yo-yo for a while.

When it grew dark, how would Brett know what was happening? How would *he*, for that matter? The phenomenon was lightless. Soundless. Like the depths of the ocean.

The Doctor was a bit worried about his experience in the field in Kent. Without anyone to hold him down, he'd be plucked up like a weed. But that had been when he was in the middle of the scars of ice, right under the entry. This time he was at the edge, not even on the glacier itself but crouched on the gravelly till.

To be frank, he wasn't entirely sure why he was there. One circle had blocked the invaders in Kent; a few dozen ought to really banjax them. Still, this was the sort of thing one ought to keep an eye on. Life was full of surprises, and so many of them were nasty.

The Doctor cocked his head: what was suddenly different? Yes. The wind had stopped. He stood up and peered through the greying light at the sheet of ice. Nothing appeared to have changed. Brett, he noticed, was rigid, keenly alert. Without the wind, the silence was profound, almost unearthly. Well, the Doctor thought, it is unearthly, isn't it? I don't think I've ever not heard anything like it. He narrowed his eyes. Was there movement above the ice, like the rippling swell of a curtain? In the dimness, he couldn't be sure. Yes. No.

Yes.

The Doctor took a step forward. The air had definitely gone wrong. It was clear, yet he couldn't see through it. A little, soundless thrill ran round the glacier's edge; it passed through the Doctor like an electric shock. What was happening? He sensed an awful heaviness, as if the atmosphere had remembered its massive weight and was falling, falling...

Then he saw something terrible.

Under the invisible pressure, the ice was melting. The Doctor flinched back onto the till. The surface of the glacier was becoming slick as glass. As he watched, his circles filled with their own melting water and sloshed to nothing.

The Doctor shot out onto the wet ice, almost falling in his haste. They probably wouldn't make it through anyway, a small part of his brain reminded him. He thought the small part of his brain had gone round the twist. Probably the Chernobyl nuclear plant wouldn't melt down. Probably the pile of mine debris wouldn't slide down and destroy the village. The edge of the disruption billowed towards him and he fell back and grabbed at his pocket and sent the round lid of a soup tin flying across the ice.

Then Brett landed on him.

He'd forgotten Brett, and wasn't happy to remember by having his breath knocked out. 'What did you do?' Brett was screaming. 'You little bastard, what did you do!' He was beating the Doctor's head against the ice. Very direct chap, the Doctor thought dizzily, not that he hadn't already gathered that.

'Too late, Brett,' he gasped. 'It's over.'

'Who are you!' Brett grabbed his throat. The Doctor choked. Brett hit him savagely in the face. 'Do you know what you've done?' His voice was rising hysterically. 'Do you have any idea –' He broke off abruptly. 'Why, of course,' he continued calmly, as if they'd just been introduced at a party, 'you must be the Doctor.'

A few yards away, what light there was vanished. There was no sound, but the Doctor thought he felt a ripple of shock. 'Don't go over there,' he advised Brett. Then he realised the shock wave was something else. 'More to come.'

'What?'

'Hold on,' said the Doctor, and surged towards the disruption.

He wasn't moving, but Brett felt him go. Astonished, he fell across the Doctor again and gripped his shoulders. He had never had to hold onto anything so tightly in his life. Beneath him, the Doctor was stiff and mute. Brett wrestled with him, with his stillness, with his *leaving*. They want him, he thought suddenly, why am I holding him, I should let him go. But even as he fell back, he heard the wind, and everything was peaceful.

'Goodness,' said the Doctor, 'that was intense, wasn't it?'

'You are the Doctor, I presume. If you're not, you're a very weird creature indeed.'

'I am a very weird creature indeed,' the Doctor sat up and looked around for his hat, 'and I am also the Doctor.' He located the hat, put it on, then raised it politely. Brett hit him and knocked him over.

'Aren't you cold?' The Doctor used his scarf to wipe blood from his lip. 'We're both rather wet: I should think you were freezing. Why don't we get off this glacier? Only a suggestion, of course. Don't mean to rush you.'

'What did you do?' said Brett levelly.

The Doctor sat up again. His hat had stayed on. 'Soup tin lid.'

'What?'

'Soup tin lid,' the Doctor said patiently. 'I threw one onto the ice. Homely solution, I know, but pi is pi. Did you ever hear the joke about the American boy who returns from college to his illiterate family, and when they ask what he's learned he answers, 'PiR^2,' and his mother says, 'You idiot. Cornbread are square, pie are ro–'

Brett hit him again. He hit him for a long time.

CHAPTER EIGHTEEN

'Good God.' Unwin rose unsteadily. 'Is that Amberglass? Oh,' he said as Brett dropped his burden on the floor, 'no. Who is he?'

'That,' said Brett dryly, 'is the Doctor.'

'Him?' Unwin gaped at the small figure, Brett had certainly been at him. Unwin could hardly see his face for blood. 'That little chap? It can't be.'

'Oh it can, believe me.' Brett went to the stove, rubbing his cold hands. 'He ruined their entry with a soup tin lid.'

'A what?'

'A soup tin lid!' Brett yelled.

'But I thought...' Unwin sat heavily on the sofa. 'I mean... I'd have thought he'd use some extraordinary alien machine.'

'No.'

'Are you absolutely –'

'Feel his pulse,' Brett said impatiently. 'Apparently he has two hearts.'

Unwin declined. He continued to stare at the Doctor, who lay unmoving except for the rise and fall of his chest. 'What are we going to do with him?'

'They want him dead, but first I'd like to get his advice on a few matters.'

Unwin blanched. 'Sherry, please...'

'You can go for a walk,' Brett said shortly. 'You can drink yourself into a stupor. I can hit you with the poker and knock you unconscious.' Unwin flinched. 'Actually, I don't believe you have to worry. He seemed quite chatty.'

* * *

I HAVE THE DOCTOR
  WE HAD HIM NEARLY
  NOW I HAVE HIM HE WILL DIE
  SOON
  YES WHY COULDN'T YOU ENTER
  CIRCLE
  WAS THAT ALL
  NOT CERTAIN OF POWER LEVEL NECESSARY
  SO YOU MIGHT NOT HAVE BEEN ABLE TO COME THROUGH
ANYWAY
  YES
  BUT WE CANT BE SURE
  FINISH THE COMPUTATIONS
  PERHAPS THE DOCTOR WILL HELP
  DESTROY HIM HE IS DANGEROUS
  Yes indeed, Brett agreed silently. Not in the way he'd expected,
but definitely dangerous.
  HE MAY BE OF USE
  NO RISK KILL HIM
  FIRST LET ME QUESTION HIM
  DANGEROUS
  YOU SAID
  DESTROYER OF WORLDS
  'What?' Brett said aloud. Quickly he typed:
  ELABORATE
  DESTROYER OF WORLDS SKARO
  WHAT IS SKARO?
  HE DESTROYED IT

Brett hadn't actually managed to beat the Doctor unconscious,
but he had put him in a somewhat confused state in relation to
events around him. Consequently, when he became more clear-
headed and found that he was only cuffed to a bed by one wrist
and could stretch out easily and even sit up with both feet on
the floor, he was greatly relieved. His jacket was missing, but his

hat, he saw happily, hung on the bed post. On the bedside table sat a bowl of water and a hand towel; the Doctor wet the towel and wiped his face. The cloth came away red.

He looked around for his jacket. It was flung over the seat of a chair. Scattered on it were objects from his pockets – his yo-yo, a Wodehouse paperback, a pair of spoons, something the Doctor couldn't identify. Brett must have done a quick search for a weapon, which of course he wouldn't find. Or wouldn't know he'd found – he'd hardly think twice about a penlight.

The Doctor eyed the chair with frustration. It was about six feet away, which might as well have been a mile. As he was reviewing the logistics of the situation, the door opened and Brett came in. 'With us again. How are you feeling?'

'Surprisingly comfortable.'

'I see Mr Amberglass has been talking to you about my hospitality.' Brett took a chair and turned it around, then sat, arms folded along the back. 'You're an entirely different case. I don't think trying to soften you up would be very effective. I wouldn't mind seeing young Amberglass again. I don't suppose he's with you.'

The Doctor sniffed. 'Drag a human along with me? I have too much to do.'

'Ah yes, you're not human. What are you?'

'I'm from Gallifrey. Ever heard of it?'

'No.'

'Well, there you are. It's a lot like here. Mountains, valleys, oceans, trees, carbon-based life forms – which our would-be visitors aren't, I gather.'

'Nice segue,' said Brett. 'No, they're not. They want you dead, you know.'

The Doctor nodded. 'It is the usual thing.'

'They say you're dangerous.'

'Goodness.' The Doctor adjusted his expression to its most inoffensive mode. 'Do they really?'

Brett ran a sceptical eye over him. The Doctor straightened his tie, aware that, what with the blood, he wasn't looking his best.

'I admit you don't look it.'

The Doctor smiled modestly.

'They also call you Destroyer of Worlds, which fits even less well with your appearance.'

'Well,' said the Doctor, 'that one happens to be true.'

Brett paused with his cigarette halfway to his lips. The Doctor was willing to bet it was the only time in his life he'd ever looked shaken. 'What do you mean?'

'I blew up a planet. Well, technically speaking, I blew up a star, which burned the planet out of existence. And to be perfectly accurate, I didn't do the blowing-up – I manipulated someone else into it. Still, I have to take responsibility.'

Brett still hadn't quite pulled himself together. 'Why?'

'Very nasty civilisation. Wanted to take over the universe. Killed several billions trying. It was time for them to go.' The Doctor looked at the floor. 'Yes,' he said, as if to himself, 'it was time.'

'How in hell did you manipulate someone into exploding a star?'

'Oh, you know. The old don't-throw-me-in-that-brierpatch routine. Don't push that button, don't push that button, oh please please *please* don't push that button.' The Doctor shrugged. 'So naturally he pushed it.'

'And this was deliberate on your part?'

The Doctor raised his eyes to meet Brett's. 'Oh yes,' he said quietly. 'Quite deliberate.'

Brett drew on his cigarette and exhaled the smoke slowly. 'Perhaps I should kill you.'

'Why haven't you?'

'Curiosity. Wondering if you might be of some help.'

'No,' said the Doctor.

Brett smiled. The Doctor had seen a lot of bad smiles in his life, and this one ranked in the top ten. 'What's wrong with you, Brett?'

'I don't know,' Brett said casually, looking around for some place to tap his ash.

'Perhaps you're a sociopath.'

'It's certainly a possibility.' Brett fetched a pin tray off the chest of drawers and sat down again.

'Though even for a sociopath, ending all life on this planet is rather extreme.'

'You should know.'

'It wasn't my home planet I was destroying.'

Brett smiled again. 'Well, it's early days yet. They say the second crime is always easier.'

'Whereas this is your planet,' the Doctor continued, as if Brett hadn't said anything. 'Everything else aside, when it goes you'll go.' Brett shrugged. 'What is this – suicide by annihilation?'

'You know what the philosopher said: "Life should not be, and the only good is the passage from being to nothingness".'

'Yes, I've read Schopenhauer, thank you. He didn't kill himself, or anyone else.'

'No, he held on, didn't he? People do cling to life; it's all they have.'

'And they have a right to it.'

Brett raised an eyebrow. 'What a silly thing to say. They want it, I agree, but there's no right to life. It's not written down in some cosmic book.'

'So you think you have the right to obliterate it all.'

'No I don't. I'm just going to do it. Eventually it will happen anyway: heat death of the universe and so on.' He smiled again. 'Like the centre of Hell, the centre of life, is ice. I'm only speeding things up.'

'Because you hate life?'

'Because life is unforgivable.' Brett crushed his cigarette in the pin dish. 'The complexities and, indeed, wonders of human existence are possible only because they are supported by gobbling selfishness. Mozart should not have written music; he should have been working to alleviate suffering. Da Vinci should never have painted, Shakespeare should never have written, Einstein should never have worked out his incomprehensible theories of reality. Everything we call culture is based on a dereliction of moral duty. No journalist should write, no architect should build, no teacher should instruct, no vintners should make wine. No miner should take home his pay and enjoy his family, no garbage collector should buy himself a beer, no nurse should take a hot bath at the end of her shift, no child have a pet, no reader lose himself in a book. They all stand in blood. And there's no "salvation" from some postulated good society. Every civilisation, from the villages of Africa to the hideously complicated structures of western Europe, rests on cruelty, and is corrupt.'

'No, you're not a sociopath,' said the Doctor. 'You're a saint.'

Brett laughed. '"Kill them all; God will sort out His own."'

'Except that there is no God.'

Unwillingly, despite his revulsion, the Doctor was impressed. This was nihilism so complete it achieved a perverse visionary grandeur. Pure darkness is, after all, pure. 'So the fabled Shining City on the Hill will shine because it's made of ice. I think I'll stick with being over nothingness.'

'Unless it's expedient to do otherwise.'

'The death of billions that allows many billions more to live isn't quite the same as the death of billions with all lives, everywhere, lost.'

Brett shrugged. 'It hardly matters now, does it?'

'I stopped you before.'

'Yes, and that was very, very clever. But you weren't handcuffed to a bed then.'

Good point, the Doctor thought glumly. 'I don't believe they have the power to come through. Even without my interference.'

'You may be right. That's where I need your help.'

'Now who's being silly?'

Brett smiled. 'Touché.' But he still unlocked the handcuff, twisted the Doctor's arm up behind him, and shoved him out the door.

Unwin's computer station was set up on the lower level of a

bunk bed. He had to hunch uncomfortably over the keyboard, which he was doing when the Doctor and Brett came in. The Doctor raised his hat.

'Mr Unwin, I presume.'

Unwin started. 'He's all right,' he said to Brett in some disbelief.

'Yes, he's a sturdy chap.'

'Hello,' said the Doctor. 'I'm here. I can be talked to.' Brett pushed him over to the computer.

'Take a look at this.'

The Doctor did. Relief almost made him tremble. The computations were nowhere near far enough along. As if he'd read the Doctor's mind, Unwin looked shamedly at his hands.

'Well?' said Brett.

Trying to look unhappy, the Doctor didn't answer.

'Yes, that's all very well,' Brett said dryly. 'But how can I be certain you're not faking?'

'How can you be certain either way? You could beat me to a pulp and never know whether the answers I gave you were true or not – you haven't enough information to judge.'

'He's right, Sherry.'

'Oh, I don't know,' Brett said imperturbably. He yanked the Doctor's arm up. 'Are you sure you don't have any friends with you?'

'I'd know, wouldn't I?'

'That's not really an answer.'

Unwin turned from the keyboard: 'He's all right.'

'Yes, I just told you.'

No, thought the Doctor desperately. Not now. And not Brett. With a cry, he tried to wrench loose, grabbing with his free hand at the keyboard. Startled, Unwin pushed him away, and Brett caught him up tighter: 'What the hell –'

'Oh my God,' whispered Unwin. He was staring at the equations. He scrolled down, then back, unbelievingly. 'It's here. This is it, Sherry! This is what it should be. I couldn't get here, but somehow –'

'Save it!' Brett roared.

'But what –'

Brett threw down the Doctor, put a foot on his back, and leaned past Unwin to hit Save. The Doctor's writhing almost tipped him over. Unwin flinched back: 'What's happening?'

'I don't know,' Brett hissed, 'but I like it.' He stomped hard on the Doctor. 'Stay still, you little bastard. It's too late.'

The Doctor grabbed a leg of Unwin's chair and pulled himself toward it, trying to throw Brett off balance. Brett stepped on his neck. The Doctor tugged helplessly at the chair leg. He heard the click of the eject button, the hiss of the disk sliding out, then Brett was down close to him. 'You're the stable point, aren't you?' he grinned, and jammed the disk into the Doctor's rear pocket. The Doctor squirmed frantically. 'No, don't get up.' Brett put a knee in the small of his back. 'Let's wait this out.'

'What the hell are you talking about?' Unwin was pressed back in the chair, gaping at them. 'What's... How did...'

'Oh, do shut up, Pat. We just had a little time miracle, that's all.'

'He's all right,' said Unwin in surprise.

The Doctor groaned and smashed his fist against the floor.

'What's my line now?' Brett mused. 'Oh yes – "He's a sturdy chap".'

'What are you talking about? Why is he on the floor?'

'Look at the numbers,' Brett ordered, rising and dragging the Doctor up by the back of his collar.

Unwin looked. 'They're just as always.'

Brett extracted the disk from the Doctor's pocket. 'Try this.' The Doctor made another lunge, but Brett pulled him away from the computer and looped an arm around his neck. Unwin shoved in the disk and opened the file. 'Oh my God,' he breathed.

'All as it should be?'

'So beautiful,' Unwin whispered. 'So perfect. Stop!' He leaped to his feet. 'What are you doing?' Brett had jerked off the Doctor's tie and twisted it against his throat. 'Don't kill him!'

'He's no further use.'

'You don't know that!' Unwin shouted. The Doctor tried to give him an encouraging nod. 'We're still in unknown territory – we might need him.'

Brett loosened the tie. 'Are there going to be any more time slips?' he said in the Doctor's ear.

'Oh, really, as if I'd tell you.' The Doctor gulped for breath. 'But I don't know.'

'Don't you?'

'No. This is a new one to me. I always like it when that happens. It's so rare. Grk.'

Brett had choked him again, though only enough to keep him quiet.

'For God's sake, leave him alone! You know I'm right, Sherry.'

'For once,' Brett admitted grudgingly. 'Go over those numbers.'

He took back his disk, hauled the Doctor back to the little bedroom and cuffed him to the head rail again. The Doctor lay back, eyes shut in either pain or despair.

'Check and mate,' said Brett. 'What happened back there?'

'The pressure of the attempted entries puts a strain on the continuum. It causes small time glitches. Usually they're self-correcting.'

'But this time I made that impossible.'

The Doctor nodded. He looked a hundred years old, Brett thought. How long had he lived?

'Accident intruded,' said Brett.

'Accident is generally on my side.' The Doctor's voice was hoarse.

'This one time rather cancels out all the others.'

'They still may not have enough power.'

'Then we'll solve that problem,' Brett said calmly. 'Just as we solved this one.'

For a long time after Brett left, the Doctor simply lay still and waited. Near dusk, he heard the front door open and shut. Brett going to check the site? In any case, Brett going. He sat up and eyed the chair. The situation was far from ideal. The bed was iron and disposed to stay put. With a resigned little sigh, he pulled off the top sheet and, humming quietly, proceeded to tear it into strips.

Once he had tied the strips together and formed a loop, the Doctor studied the logistics again. He was certain he could get the loop over the chair back, but after that difficulties presented themselves. The chair was facing him, the most awkward possible position in which to be dragged. There'd be maximum resistance, and if he weren't careful, he was liable to tip the thing over. That the bed sat on a rug was also discouraging: it would be hard to get the chair legs over the edge.

Well, one step at a time. He crouched clumsily on his knees and, after a few tries, got the makeshift lasso spinning. Easily, as if simply setting it in place, he dropped the loop over the chair back. So far, so far. A discomfiting thought occurred to him. What if Brett had taken the remaining contents of his pockets away to poke through later? He was scuppered then. Well, no sense worrying about it. Slowly, he started to edge the chair towards him.

'You've got to get out of here.'

The Doctor froze, then, very carefully, looked over his shoulder. Unwin was closing the door with finicky precision. He nodded at the Doctor. 'I am going to get you out of here.' His voice was a thick whisper. He was so drunk the Doctor was amazed he was upright. 'Get you out of here.'

'That's good,' the Doctor said supportively.

'What are you doing?'

'Oh... just a thing.' The Doctor sat down. 'If you'll only hand me my jacket, I'll be on my way.'

Unwin sank onto the end of the bed. 'He's going to kill you.'

'I rather assumed that. Good of you to come rescue me. If you'll only –'

'I don't know what happened,' Unwin continued, tears running down his cheeks. 'We were at school together. I only ever wanted to do my work. I didn't know all this would happen. This cruelty.'

'Unwin,' said the Doctor slowly, 'what did you think was going to happen? When you finished the computations?'

Unwin waved a careless hand. 'Some Utopian something-or-other. Brett's idea. Save the world.'

'Freeze-dry it,' murmured the Doctor.

'I didn't care about any of that. Results aren't the point. The work is the point.'

'Thank you, Dr Oppenheimer.'

'What?'

'Never mind. You know, if you'd only get my jacket for –'

'The world is hideous,' said Unwin, 'but the work is beautiful. Mathematics doesn't rot. It doesn't fade. Numbers are eternal.'

'Well, more or less. Once the universe is drained to nothing, there won't be anything to count.'

'Numbers exist independent of their referents.'

'And there won't be anyone around to know that. Unwin, Brett might return to us any minute. Please get my jacket.'

'Where is it?'

'On the chair.' The Doctor took Unwin's head and turned it. 'There. See?'

'Why don't you get it?'

'Because I am cuffed to a bed.'

'Oh.' Unwin squinted at the Doctor's wrist. 'Right. How'd you get like that?'

'Remember this Brett who's going to kill me?'

'Not if I can help it!'

'And you can. Please – the jacket.'

Unwin wobbled around the bed and picked up the jacket. He stared at it. The Doctor beckoned encouragingly. Unwin turned his watery eyes on him. The Doctor winced at his expression – a blank, stunned pain, like an animal surprised by a bullet. 'What have I done?' he whispered.

'Nothing good. But I can fix it.'

Unwin handed him the jacket. The Doctor searched frantically through the pockets. Unwin sat on the bed, then lay down. He began to snore. The Doctor found the laser and severed the handcuff's chain. Quickly refilling his pockets, he gave Unwin a nudge. No response. Completely unconscious.

The Doctor stood and pulled on his jacket, biting his lip. 'Unwin,' he hissed. He followed the hiss with a couple of slaps and a good shake. 'Unwin, it's you he'll kill now. You have to come with me. Wake up.' Reluctantly, he found and pressed a cluster of nerves in Unwin's neck. The only reaction was a small jerk. The Doctor shook him again. 'Wake up!' Useless. The Doctor tried to lift him, but the dead weight was too awkward for a good grip. There was no way he'd ever get him out the window and away. But to leave Unwin here was to kill him.

Of course, there were advantages to that.

The Doctor abruptly stepped back, as if Unwin were infected. The computations were finished, he told himself, Unwin's work done – there was no need for him to die. He couldn't do any further damage. Except... The Doctor had begun to sweat again... except, possibly, with that mysterious second set of equations. A back-up if the first set failed? Ethan had said he didn't think Unwin could solve those, but that was no guarantee. The equations might not even be dangerous. But there was no guarantee of that either. Without realising it, the Doctor had been backing away from Unwin. Now he hit the wall.

Beside him was the window. In front of him lay a man he almost certainly couldn't carry through the snow but who would certainly die if he left him. 'He meant no harm,' the Doctor muttered. But harm had been done. And would be done. And whatever could stop it must be done. The Doctor raised the window, swung a leg over the sill, and dropped into the night.

'It's bloody cold,' said Ace. 'Why are we out in the cold like this?'

'Because we're drunk,' Ethan explained.

They were walking, with a somewhat casual approach to direction, along the snowy street, having searched every inn in the village for the Doctor. At the final one, they'd sat down to rest and consumed some warming drinks, the exact number of which temporarily escaped Ethan.

'I'm not drunk!' she said indignantly.

'As you like.'

'In Perivale, I used to put back twice that of an evening.'

'As you may have noticed, we're not in Perivale. There's an altitude difference. And cheap ale isn't exactly as strong as what you've been having.'

'Bollocks,' she sniffed. 'I'm well sober.'

If there were any justice, Ethan thought, she would now slip and fall. But she continued agilely on. They passed lozange-paned windows glowing warmly gold; the cold modern glare of the corner streetlights was dulled behind curtains of snow. A thick-maned pony passed by, pulling a wagon-sled of milk canisters, its bundled-up owner hurrying beside it.

'You ought to tell me about this maths stuff sometime.'

'Next time you need to get to sleep.'

'No, I'm serious. I hated maths in school, but you're talking about a whole other thing, aren't you?'

'All right,' he said resignedly. 'But you won't like it.'

She took his hand.

Using a torch from his pocket, the Doctor picked his way among low-hanging branches. Should he have attempted to retrieve the disk? No. Brett probably had it with him. A branch dropped its snow down his neck. He must get that umbrella back. Of course, he didn't want to run into Brett again, who might go up to the glacier and start scrabbling desperately beneath the snow, trying to find the obstructing tin lid. More luck to him. The adage about the needle and the haystack came to mind. And as long as any circle was on their landing field, they were blocked.

Of course, that only meant that the whole operation would move again, as soon as this weak spot closed up. Brett needed to be hobbled. But Brett was nothing compared to these others. They were what he really had to stop.

Abruptly, he found himself on level ground, the lights of the village a few hundred yards ahead. The Doctor smiled. He could easily orientate himself to the TARDIS now: there was less than a mile to walk. He proceeded slowly through the soft, yielding snow. All the way down through the forest, he had kept an ear out for sounds of pursuit. It was much more likely that he might be apprehended here, out from under the trees and so near to the main road. But – he looked back – his tracks were already blurring; the ones farther up must be completely erased. He had no idea how far Brett's chalet was by road, but driving tonight would be a challenge. And why come after him, really? They had what they needed and, in spite of his ingenious employment of the tin lid, might presume he wasn't much of a threat. He smiled again, but thinly.

Brett must be thinking – or desperately hoping – that at full power the invaders might just blast through the barrier created by the lid. Only it wasn't a barrier so much as a hole – a fighter plane might as well fire down at a canyon it was falling into. No, for the moment, that was taken care of.

Would they run when they found him gone? He snorted. To where? And how? The roads were becoming unpassable, and a simple alert to the police on his part would prevent their sliding down to the village and departing by train. And of course, they'd hardly want to leave the vicinity of the possible entryway, not when, at long last, they had the proper equations.

If they were still a "they", not a "him". The Doctor shivered and put Unwin from his mind. Ahead he saw the TARDIS, its roof-light shining through the flurries like a welcoming lantern. Exhausted, he opened the door and stepped inside.

'It's you!' cried Molecross.

CHAPTER NINETEEN

The Doctor took a minute to recover, then raised his hat. 'How do you do? Mr Molecross, isn't it?'

'You really are him,' said Molecross. 'I knew it all along.'

'Well,' said the Doctor weakly, 'there you are. Ace anywhere about?'

'They went down to the village.'

'Well, you seem quite comfortable in that armchair. Biscuits I see. Lime squash. I'll just be off.'

'Don't you want to know how I got here?'

'Not particularly, no. I'll just –'

'What happened to you?' said Molecross.

The Doctor felt his face, looked at his clothes. 'Oh… you know.'

Molecross nodded sagely: 'The sorts of things that happen when you're saving the Earth.'

'Exactly those sorts of things. Well –'

'You're saving us from aliens, aren't you? Not that you're not an alien yourself, of course. I mean unfriendly aliens.'

'They do seem to be unfriendly,' the Doctor agreed, edging towards a door.

'Do they want to take us over?'

'Not exactly.'

'Look,' said Molecross, with sudden firmness. 'You owe me *something*. I've gone to a lot of trouble to get this story,' – the Doctor glanced at his maimed arm – 'and I'm here, so why not talk to me?'

'I'm not giving you an interview, Molecross.'

'Right.' Molecross held up his remaining hand understandingly. 'So we'll just do it on deep background, OK?'

The Doctor frowned. 'You mean "off the record"?'

'That's a common misperception. "Off the record" actually allows some attribution, whereas "deep background" –'

'Yes, yes,' the Doctor sighed. 'All right, I'll answer a few questions. You deserve that much.'

'I can't take notes any more,' Molecross said in a small voice.

Pity stung the Doctor like a slap. 'Well, we'll work something out. That arm looks as if it could use some attention.'

'It does hurt,' Molecross admitted.

'Well, come along then. We'll take care of it, and you can ask me questions in the meantime.'

'You mean,' Molecross seemed afraid to believe his luck, 'I'm going to see the real TARDIS? Not just the corridors?'

'Parts of it, yes. Come along, don't sit there staring in awe, it's not as interesting as you might think.'

Brett leaned against the wall, arms crossed, watching Unwin sleep. Or – his lips twitched sardonically – whatever it's called when you're passed out drunk. It was just possible that Unwin had come in after the Doctor had gone, and collapsed across the bed. But the odds were against it. Very much against it.

Had he made a mistake with Unwin? He'd known he was weak. On the other hand, without him nothing could have been done. There would have been no contact. None of the bridge could have been constructed. It was Unwin who had brought Amberglass into the equation. True, he hadn't had time to get from Amberglass what he needed, but the boy was connected to the Doctor in some way and was no doubt the reason the Doctor had shown up. And served a very useful purpose.

And made Unwin obsolete.

With some difficulty because of the dead weight, Brett hefted Unwin into a fireman's lift. He took him out the back door of the chalet and up under the dark, snow-laden trees, where he dumped him and looked around. He kicked at the snow, walked another few feet and kicked again. At last he spotted an area where the trees thinned, and went to examine it. A little dip, almost a ditch, filled with pillowy snow.

Brett dragged Unwin over and rolled him into the hollow. Unwin landed in a tangled position only a drunk could maintain. Brett began to kick snow over him. He didn't hurry. After a bit, he had to crouch and shove the snow with his hands. It took longer than he expected. The last thing to vanish was one of Unwin's feet, slipping quietly beneath the icy powder. Brett piled the snow till it was slightly higher than the ground around it. He tamped the resulting mound down a bit, but didn't bother hiding the marks he'd made all around. No one was coming up here.

Molecross sat on an examination table with what was left of his wrist stuck in a box filled with blue light. The Doctor had removed the bandages and examined the healing wound. Now he was looking at computerised diagrams of Molecross's arm. 'I think I can accelerate the healing process.'

'Thank you,' said Molecross humbly.

The Doctor glanced up at him sympathetically. 'I'm sorry I can't regrow the hand for you, but we're not at that stage yet with humans.'

'"We"?'

'My people. There are some medical problems even we haven't solved – though, I admit, not many.'

'Will it hurt?'

'No. You won't even know anything is happening.' The Doctor began to work with some buttons.

'Can I ask some questions now?'

The Doctor sighed. 'Go ahead.'

'How often have you saved Earth?'

'I've lost count.'

'Lost count?'

'Everyone wants to take over the Earth,' said the Doctor. 'You'd be amazed.'

'Why?'

'Well, it's strategically located. Also unusually rich in resources. Blessed, you might say. Of course, that attracts the would-be conquerors. No silver without a cloudy lining.'

'Have you saved other planets?'

'Yes. Don't ask me how many. It's all in files somewhere.'

'How?'

'Sometimes one way, sometimes another. I depend a great deal on improvisation. It's never a good idea to go into a situation with fixed ideas.'

'There's an invasion happening now, isn't there?'

'Trying to happen. I wouldn't call it an invasion – more of a gleaning.'

'What do they want?'

'Power. You'll find most problems are caused by desire for power – to wield it, to consume it, to overcome it. The condition is universal.'

'Can you stop them?'

'Oh yes.'

Molecross went quiet for a moment, digesting this. 'Do you ever fail?'

'Not often.'

'All this,' Molecross said after another moment, 'it must take... How do you have... How old are you?'

'Hm' The Doctor frowned. 'I'm not entirely sure. Nine hundred and something, I think.'

'Nine hundred and something!'

'Don't hold me to it.'

'Then... is that why you've had so many bodies?'

'I beg your pardon?'

'The available information suggests you don't always look the same.'

'Silly idea.'

'There are photographs.'

'Not of me.'

'Oh.' Molecross mused on this. 'Are you sure?'

The Doctor looked at his eager, innocent face. Oh well, why not? 'All right, yes. I change bodies. Regenerate. This is my seventh.'

Molecross simply stared at him, his mouth slightly open. The Doctor looked away, embarrassed.

'It's all true,' Molecross whispered.

'Probably not. Goodness knows what sort of nonsense about me is out there.'

'You don't understand. This is... For me this is...'

'Go on with your questions, please.'

Molecross was momentarily at a loss about what to ask next. 'I've seen a bad photograph of one of you who's very tall.'

'Long scarf?'

'Yes.'

'That's the fourth me.'

'Do you have any choice about how you look?'

'Unfortunately no. I usually come out a bit odd, though my third and fifth incarnations weren't bad. I admit that at some point I'd like to be really handsome. Petty vanity, but there you are.'

'Why do you have a Scots accent?'

'I have no idea. Came with the package.'

'Do you live forever?'

'No,' said the Doctor softly. 'I don't think so.'

'Tell me about your planet.'

'Nothing to tell. Basically like Earth with a different colour scheme. Stultifying place. I never go there if I can help it.'

'You never go home?'

'No.' The Doctor's eyes were fixed on the box of blue light. 'I never go home.'

Molecross brooded on this. 'My parents are dead,' he said unexpectedly.

'I'm sorry.'

'Do you have parents?'

'It's complicated and I'd rather not go into it.'

'Do you grow on plants or something, like fruit?'

'Molecross, if you insist on bringing up these ludicrous science-fiction ideas, this conversation is over.'

Chastened, Molecross went quiet again. The Doctor continued to push buttons. The box hummed softly.

Molecross cleared his throat. 'You don't understand. You're a miracle.'

'Oh for heaven's sake.'

'No, listen to me.' His seriousness made the Doctor look up. 'You *don't* understand. Time and space are yours. The mysterious is as ordinary for you as eggs for breakfast. But my life is small. I never... I'm not good with people. At school...' He swallowed hard. 'But I always knew, you know, that this wasn't it. I mean, why would we be made to feel wonder if there wasn't any to feel? It had to be somewhere.'

'Somewhere else,' said the Doctor gently.

'Not here, that's for bloody certain. But on the edges of everything there's... strangeness. Second sight. Hauntings. UFOs. Astrology. I mean, *Newton* studied alchemy.'

'Newton is paranoid schizophrenic.'

'You've met him, then?'

'He's a difficult man.'

'But *he* knew. There were truths out there, truths no one had ever seen, and he saw them. If he *hadn't* had the sort of mind that could accept something as weird as alchemy, would he have recognised anything as weird as the laws of motion? Where does the crank end and the genius begin? Where does the ridiculous end and the transcendent begin?' Molecross rubbed the side of his face, suddenly embarrassed. 'I always knew there was something more,' he finished. 'And it's you. Everything you are, everything you represent.'

The Doctor's sad eyes didn't meet his. 'You don't want this world Molecross. But there's no way out. Suffering and corruption expand with the universe.'

'But you try to stop it. People get up in the morning and ride the bus to jobs they hate and come home to a family that hasn't any use for them and pay taxes and get sick, and there's nothing they can do, is there? But you *can* do something. And you do. I don't...' Molecross took a deep breath. 'I just wanted to know you existed. That things I couldn't imagine existed. That there was something else.'

'That was the story you were after.'

Molecross nodded. 'And now I've got it. And I'll put it on my site and no one will believe me.'

The Doctor smiled consolingly. Part of him wanted to argue with Molecross, explain to him that there really was no escape. He told that part to shut up. So many ways to deal with the pain of existence. Run away from it, fight it, shut it out, deny it. He thought of Brett. Murder it. So many solutions to the insoluble problem. 'Let's have a look at your arm.'

The skin was smooth and scarless. Molecross stared at it and began to weep – huge, gulping sobs, like grief. The Doctor turned away uncomfortably. He wondered whether he should leave Molecross alone for a bit, go and check to see whether Ace and Ethan had come back. Though no doubt she and Ethan were doing quite nicely, thank you.

'I need to go,' Molecross said between sobs. He was sniffing loudly.

'I'm sorry?'

'Go...'

'I can't take you home yet, Molecross. The situation is too –'

'No. I mean, go to the village. Get a room. Look at the sky and breathe the air and see people. I can't...' He was beginning to shiver. 'This is too much.'

'Ah.' The Doctor understood. 'Overload. Not to worry – it shouldn't last more than a day or so. In the meantime, we'll find you an inn.'

* * *

'You know,' Ace said, 'you're better.'

'Than anyone else you've known?'

She began to laugh, then hiccup. 'Conceited sod.'

'Understandably, the question consumes me.'

'What I mean is,' she said solemnly, 'you've not been seeing things.'

'There've been periods before when I haven't.'

'But you're not taking your meds.'

'No,' he agreed. One for the Doctor.

'Only I'm wondering,' she said, 'whether the meds might have caused them. The hallucinations.'

Ethan thought about it. He'd been put on anti-psychotics several years before, after a breakdown that a psychiatrist had diagnosed as schizophrenic. He'd had all sorts of nervous episodes and instabilities before that, a few of them, such as hysterical deafness, fairly exotic. But had he experienced visual delusions? He hadn't even had an imaginary friend when he was a boy.

'What were they like?'

'Nothing very dramatic. People would appear in my flat and talk to me.'

'Like tell you to kill yourself or murder people or that you were Margaret Thatcher?'

'No, they just talked. It made sense at the time, but afterward I could never remember what they'd said. Most of them didn't talk, actually. They just sat and watched me work.'

'What did they look like?'

'Oh, all sorts. An elderly woman, a young Jamaican boy, bloke who looked like a rugby forward. Once a pair of twins.'

'No little green men.'

'No. Nor spiders. Some people in the institution saw spiders. Very nasty.'

'But you've not seen anything lately.'

'No. The Doctor kept telling me I shouldn't be taking those pills. Perhaps he was right.'

By this time, they were walking up the rise to the TARDIS. Ethan stopped to look back at the pretty little village with its snowy streets and warm windows.

'He's always right,' Ace said. 'It may not look like it, but at the end of the day he is.'

'Ace...'

She turned, and stopped dead when she saw his face. 'What is it?'

'Get the Doctor.' She hesitated and he gave her a desperate push. 'Get the Doctor, for God's sake! They're coming through!'

As she ran toward the TARDIS, Ethan stared at the air above the pond. It looks like lightning, he thought. How can it look like lightning when it's cold? It doesn't look like lightning. It looks like a step graph. It looks like a grid of lozenges. It looks like all of them and none of them. He half fell to the cold ground. How quiet everything was. The branches above him were still. No wisp of wind shivered the snow. The village was silent. Surely, nothing was actually happening.

'Not to worry, Ace.' It was the Doctor's voice, coming closer. 'The site was on top of the glacier. I scuppered it.'

'It's not there, it's here!'

'It can't be here, there's no flat place –' The Doctor came hurrying up and followed Ethan's gaze. He gasped.

'It's happening,' Ethan said quietly. 'It really is.'

'The equations are complete!' The Doctor began to run. Ace shot after him. 'Stay there, Ace!'

'Oh right – bloody likely,' she said, and dashed past him.

The Doctor swore and grabbed Ethan's arm: 'Come with me.'

'Forgive me for asking,' Ethan panted as they ran and slid down the rise, 'but what exactly can you do?'

'I don't know,' the Doctor groaned. 'I should have realised they could use the pond. What's happening now?'

Ethan looked up. The grid hung in the darkness, an angled net of non-light spread over the Earth. 'They don't seem any closer.'

'Perhaps they can't do it,' the Doctor breathed, half to himself.

'Perhaps they haven't enough power after all, even with the bridge.'

'How did that happen? The computations being completed?'

'In a way, it was my fault. Just as this is my fault for being so smug and certain.' His fingers dug into Ethan's arm. 'They're trying to open a door to annihilation. I was supposed to stop them. *Stop* them!'

His voice cracked in anguish. Ethan tried to think of something useful to say but couldn't. He concentrated on keeping his feet as he slipped and stumbled on; the Doctor was as agile as a snowshoe rabbit.

'Do you see Ace?' he said agitatedly. 'I hope she hasn't gone onto the ice.'

'She's not stupid.'

'Hardly. But she's extremely impulsive. If she runs into Brett, the least he'll get is a broken jaw.'

'Brett?' said Ethan sickly.

'Obviously he arranged the new site. He'll be there to greet them.'

'But won't he get fried, or withered, or whatever happens?'

'I don't think he cares.'

They had come to the edge of the pond. 'Perhaps it's not big enough,' Ethan said without much conviction.

''Tis enough, 'twill serve. Ace!'

'No need to shout.' She peeked out from behind the spreading branches of a spruce. 'You two are well exposed out there.'

A bit shamefacedly, they joined her. A load of snow slid from a branch and landed on the Doctor. He bore it with dignity.

'They're no lower,' Ethan said, eyes on the sky.

The Doctor closed his eyes and let out a long breath. Ethan looked around. 'Where's Ace?'

'Oh no,' the Doctor whispered. 'She must have spotted Brett.'

'Where!'

'I don't see him. Do you?'

'No,' said Ethan frantically. He pointed. 'What's that? That hut.'

'It's where the skaters change their shoes.'

They started running.

Brett was, in fact, standing on the other side of the hut, his eyes alert and bright. He had been staring at the ice so long he was beginning to feel as if he weren't really seeing it, so he glanced away – just as something hurled itself into him and knocked him over.

'You're done, you bastard!' cried a young female voice. 'You're past tense!' and a fist slammed into his face. Brett seized her wrist, bewildered – who was this *girl*, and why was she attacking him? She jerked back and to her feet, then kicked him in the head. He rolled away and she landed on his back, got a handful of hair and started pounding his face into the snow. He rolled again and grabbed for her as she fell. She was screaming obscenities, and when he caught her wrist she lunged forward, grabbed his ear in her teeth and ripped. Brett yelled. It was like fighting an animal. He knocked her away and held her down.

'Who are you, you little bitch!'

'I'm the frigging angel of frigging death,' she snarled. 'Say your prayers, scumbag!'

Brett hit her, but this turned out to be a mistake since he had to let go of one of her wrists and she went right for his throat. He couldn't believe how strong she was. He grabbed her wrist again and she switched her grip to his collar and pulled him down to her teeth.

'Ace!'

For just a second, she was distracted, and that second was all Brett needed. He hit her awkwardly, managed to stand and stumbled away. Choking and spitting, Ace started to get up, but the Doctor and Ethan each caught an arm.

'Ace, Ace,' the Doctor's burr was soft and calming, 'no more, Ace.'

'Go after him!' she screamed, trying to rise, slipping in the snow.

'How badly are you hurt?' said Ethan.

'You've let him go, you've let him go!' She began to sob in rage. The Doctor stroked her hair.

'He's much bigger than you, Ace. It was only a matter of time till he won.'

'I'd have killed him! He ought to be dead!'

'Yes, yes.' The Doctor pulled her head to his chest and she sobbed against him. Ethan fell back, watching them. 'It's all right. They couldn't get through. He can't do any more harm.'

'He ought to be dead,' she repeated, and wailed like a child.

Something flashed at the edge of Ethan's vision. He looked at the sky.

'It's over.'

CHAPTER TWENTY

Ethan must have paced around the console room to a distance of two miles before the Doctor appeared.

'How is she?'

'Fine,' said the Doctor soothingly. 'Bruises and cuts like that can be healed in fifteen minutes.'

'She got the bloody better of him.'

'Indeed she did. I try not to encourage that kind of behaviour.' The Doctor sounded a bit guilty. 'But there's no denying it comes in useful.'

Ethan thought 'useful' wasn't really adequate but didn't say so. 'What now? Brett's still out there.'

'I rather think Brett and Unwin have been cut off at the knees. If our visitors couldn't come through when the computational bridge was complete, then they can't come through. They simply haven't the power. Which is not surprising in an anti-entropic civilisation. I'd like to know how they managed to accomplish what little they have.'

'Some alternate power source.'

'I think so. That was why they wanted the Earth – and, of course, the rest of the universe. They must have drained their own stars dead.'

'They ought to be under arrest.'

The Doctor looked at him oddly. 'Well, I suppose so. But I really can't see how – oh. You mean Unwin and Brett, don't you?'

'Yes,' said Ethan patiently.

'I think we're all right there. I stopped by the police station on my way back from my meeting with Brett: they won't be able to leave by train. And now that Brett's wandering around oozing blood, he'll be –'

'Let's go back a bit.' Ethan said carefully. 'You met with Brett?'

'I have to catch you up, don't I? Time for a cup of tea.'

Humming to himself, the Doctor prepared a tea tray, which he then carried, Ethan following, to a small, fire-lit parlour. As he was pouring out, his hand shook slightly, sloshing some tea in the saucer. 'Sorry.' He tipped the contents of the saucer back into the cup, and put both on his side of the table. 'That was a bit of a near miss out there. I never like it when the universe comes within a hair of blinking out. Gives me a bit of that "So glad I cancelled my trip on the Titanic" shiver.' He massaged his forehead with the tips of his fingers. 'All I can do is be grateful that, at the end of the day, it didn't work. Little thanks to me.'

'You stopped them in Kent and on the glacier.'

'Very good of me – what a shame not stopping them at the pond would have made those first two accomplishments meaningless. This wasn't a situation where doing one's best was doing enough. Anything that could be done had to be done.'

'Anything?' Ethan said curiously.

'Of course!'

'Yet you didn't kill Brett or Unwin.'

The Doctor removed his hat to run a hand through his hair. 'In the first place, Brett and Unwin aren't the primary problem. As long as the threat of the aliens existed, someone, somewhere would find a way to build that bridge. Brett is unlikely to be the sole nihilistic maniac on the planet, nor Unwin the sole idiot savant working on a mathematical answer to entropy. Fortunately, now that we've seen that even with a complete bridge our friends can't come through, the issue is resolved. Other Bretts and Unwins can work on computations till the end of time – without the necessary power, the computations aren't enough.'

'What if they find the power?'

'How? It seems pretty clear they can't get it from their own world, and without being able to enter here, they can't get it from ours.'

'What about other universes than theirs or ours?'

'Yes, indeed. I'll probably have to do something about that. At any rate, you can see why our earthly villains aren't the real problem. In the second place...' The Doctor stopped, rotating his hat in his hands and watching it as if it were some absorbing film. 'In the second place, I believe I did kill Unwin. I left him there, passed out drunk, for Brett to discover.'

'Could you have taken him with you?'

'Probably not.'

'Then why –'

'"Probably" not, not "Certainly not". I knew there was a chance I was abandoning him to his death. But I chose to leave him. One less threat to the existence of the universe. One life against possible billions. But then... it turned out that the bridge didn't work, so I needn't have let him die after all.'

'He may not be dead.'

'No thanks to me.'

The Doctor firmly replaced his hat, as if corking up any further thoughts on the matter. A little shiver passed through Ethan. He remembered the conversation in the bar in London. He was a chilly thing, the Doctor, under the good manners and cosy charm.

Ace bounced in. 'Oi, tea!' As far as Ethan could see, her face was unmarked. She gave him an embarrassed smile. 'I was a right girl back there. Crying like that.'

This remark left Ethan speechless. She sat on the arm of his chair, leaning on his shoulder. 'Enough tea for me as well, Professor?'

'Of course,' said the Doctor, producing a third teacup, apparently from a pocket. 'And there is butter and honey for the toast – as soon as there is toast.' He started fitting a slice of bread on a toast fork.

Ethan cleared his throat. 'You were saying...'

'Hm? Oh yes.' The Doctor found a spot for the bread not too near the flames. 'Where to begin? Well, I was up on the glacier making certain nothing could come through up there, and I encountered Brett, or vice versa, and he took me back to this rather dreary little chalet he's rented – just bunks for skiers, really.'

Ethan sat up. 'Then you know where he is?'

'I couldn't find it again. I wandered all over the place after I escaped.'

'What did he do to you?' said Ace in a disturbingly quiet voice.

'Not to worry.' He smiled at her disarmingly. 'The major difficulty is that there was a time slip while Brett had the unfinished bridge up on his computer, and suddenly the computations were complete. Brett was smart enough to suss this out, and he copied it and shoved the disk in my pocket before the moment snapped away. Then he gave the disk to Unwin. Who later helped me escape.' The Doctor's face sobered. 'I worry about Unwin.'

'Likely he's offed him,' Ace said indifferently.

'Ace, I've told you that this borrowing of American slang must stop. Your speech is undecipherable enough as it is.' The Doctor turned the toasting bread over. 'But you're right,' he sighed. 'I'd be very surprised if Unwin weren't dead.'

Ace glanced at Ethan's face. 'Don't tell me you're sorry.'

'He was just weak.' Ethan couldn't understand why the idea of Unwin's death caught at him. 'He had no life but numbers. He didn't know anything about the world.'

'He didn't want to know,' the Doctor snapped.

'Well,' Ethan said, 'why should he, really? Everyone shuts out the world to some degree or other. Otherwise, it's unbearable.'

The Doctor eyed him keenly, and Ace pulled his ear. 'Thanks a lot.'

'There are always exceptions,' he murmured. She ruffled his hair.

'Toast,' the Doctor reminded them sternly. 'With honey. And

possibly jam will make an appearance. Didn't someone say that the only true pleasures of life are the small ones?'

'I've got something to show you,' Ace said. The tea was drunk and the toast eaten (jam *had* made an appearance) and she'd led Ethan to a door that she opened into a music room dominated by a shining grand piano. A Bosendorfer, Ethan thought, impressed.

'You have a piano in your flat. So you must play.'

'Sometimes. Does the Doctor play?'

'Some of him.'

Ethan let that pass. He tapped middle C. The tone was full and clear.

'So play something.'

'You wouldn't like it.'

She grimaced. 'Old stuff?'

'Eighteenth century, mostly.'

'I don't so much mind that. It's all those naff songs about the white cliffs of Dover.' She watched Ethan stroke one of the smooth ivory keys, as if he were petting a cat.

'It would be the finest piano I've ever played,' he admitted.

'Go on, then.'

He sat on the bench and ran a few scales up and down. The sound was voluptuous; he thought he could almost breathe it, like wine-sweet air. Ace leaned on the piano, chin in hand.

'The Professor says music and maths are almost the same thing.'

'He's not wrong.'

'D'you compose then?'

He tried out a few phrases from Mozart. 'Not exactly.'

'What's that mean?'

'I mess around. Try to turn maths into music.'

She frowned. 'And what's *that* mean?'

'You really don't want to hear about it.'

'Stop telling me what I won't like!'

213

'Seriously. It'll bore the hell out of you, Ace. It bores most people.'

She plunked stubbornly down on the bench beside him. 'Try me.'

'OK, then.' Ethan made a mental bet with himself as to how long it would be before her eyes glazed over. Less than three minutes or more than three minutes? There was always something dispiriting about watching the interest drain from a listener's face. 'By plucking a string, Pythagoras worked out that a note's relation to its overtones was always a fraction: $1/2$, $1/4$, $1/3$, $1/5$. For reasons having to do with the human ear and brain, we find the correspondence between any given note and its third and fifth harmonics the most pleasing. I'm losing you, aren't I?'

'No,' Ace said bravely.

'Here. I'll show you on the piano.' He picked out the keys. 'Our main note, its third, and its fifth. Now I'll do the same thing in D. Already, you see, we have a whole and its fractions turned into music.'

'Wicked!'

He glanced sideways to see whether she were having him on, but she was grinning, happy at learning something new. Well, that was why the Doctor travelled with her. One reason, anyway.

'Well, you remember that a prime number –'

'– is divisible only by itself and one.'

'Right. The only even prime number is two, for obvious reasons.' She nodded encouragingly, but he could tell she wasn't quite following. He really wasn't much of a teacher; it was difficult to work out how to get past his own knowledge and explain something to a novice. 'Well, never mind about two. Not important. What matters is that as far along the number line as we go – and it goes on forever since the number of integers... Forget about that. The number line is infinite. Now, most numbers or combinations of numbers form a pattern along the line. The simplest example is the odd or even numbers, which follow one another, odd, even, odd, even, and so on, forever. The primes are a consistently definable entity, in the same way, for example, even numbers are always multiples of two. But where even numbers occur regularly, the primes appear to be randomly scattered. The question is, why something that is such a building block of maths – all numbers can be reduced to multiples of two primes – has a disorderly sequence of appearances in the number line.'

'So what does this have to do with music?'

'Stay with me a minute. The Riemann hypothesis – that we talked about that time on the street...?' She nodded. 'The Riemann hypothesis, if proved, would mean that there is in fact an organisation of the primes on the number line. But no one's ever been able to work out a mathematical proof for it.'

'That's why everyone's so excited about working it out.'

'Exactly. It was listed at the beginning of the twentieth century as one of the greatest unsolved problems in mathematics. Well, it's the twenty-first century, and we're no nearer than we were a hundred years ago.'

She grinned. 'Well mysterious.'

'Yes,' he said. 'A beautiful, tantalising mystery. The mathematician's Grail. Only it's more like the Questing Beast, running away from you up the number line. This all has to do with music,' he went on, cutting off her question, 'because...' He paused, very tempted to say, 'Because it does'. This was harder than he'd thought. 'Erm, the thing is if you restate the occurrence of the primes in the number line as a graph, the results indicate they might have an order. And each prime point on the graph has a specific vibration. Fundamentally, at the subatomic level, everything is vibrations – let's drop that. The point is, you can restate those vibrations as musical notes.'

Ace appeared to be trying to suppress any indications that she thought he was mental. 'You know that makes no bloody sense at all.'

'Well, no,' he conceded. 'But it is true.'

She smiled. 'Let's hear this mathematical melody, then.'

'It's not very melodic,' he cautioned. 'It's definitely, erm, post-modern.'

'You mean it just sounds like noise?'

'Careful. That's what your grandparents said about rock and roll.'

'Play!' she ordered.

Ethan played. He concentrated on the keys so as not to see her reaction, which he presumed would be of the 'uck' variety. But when he finally snuck a glance at her, she looked startled. He slowed down, almost stopped. 'What's the matter?'

'It's... Keep playing.' There was a knock on the door, and the Doctor peeked in. 'Professor, listen!' The Doctor came in, smiling expectantly. 'It sounds like your tune! That naff tune you've been humming for weeks.'

Ethan wasn't following this. He turned and saw that the Doctor had stopped, his face almost as white as his suit.

'What is that?' he whispered.

'It's just an experiment of mine,' Ethan said, puzzled, 'turning the vibration-value of certain primes into music.' The Doctor came a few faltering steps into the room, then stopped; he appeared stunned with confusion. Ace stood up.

'Professor, what is it? Are you all right?'

'Someone...' The Doctor's voice was so hoarse he stopped and swallowed. He licked his dry lips. 'Someone is trying to hack the TARDIS.'

The Doctor bent over a screen and swore in a language Ethan had never heard. He tapped some keys, swore again. He'd plucked Ethan out of the music room and hurried him to yet another collection of computers, then abandoned him, bounding frenziedly from computer to computer, cursing at each of them. At least, Ethan assumed he was cursing. It certainly sounded that way.

'Well,' the Doctor took control of himself, 'it could be worse.

They've only breached the first firewall.' He exhaled deeply. 'If they tap into the power of the TARDIS, nothing can stop them. They won't need a bridge of equations. They won't need a weak spot in the cosmic fence. They'll push right through and take everything they want. Which is everything.'

'I'm not following this. You've been humming that piece I played for Ace?'

'Not that piece specifically, but near enough. A piece composed of the music of primes. The primes that make up Unwin's second set of equations – the hacking code for the TARDIS.'

'You *heard* the equations?'

'The TARDIS and I have a telepathic link of sorts. I don't have time to go into it now.'

'How in God's name could they get into the TARDIS at all?'

'The simplest answer for you is, an extraordinarily sophisticated form of wireless connection – the way the TARDIS stays in contact with the data base on Gallifrey. Certain waves can travel between universes where matter can't.'

'Is there anything I can do to help?'

'You almost helped them,' the Doctor said sharply. 'Unwin had worked out the first part of the hacking program that got the worm through the initial barriers. You were to bring the worm all the way in.'

'That was the code he wanted me to work on.'

'Yes. He really is brilliant, I have to hand him that. That he got as far as he did is remarkable. But he was finally stumped. That's where you came in. You say you saw the program?'

'Yes. I have to say, it looked like something that could be deciphered, given time. But Unwin couldn't work it out.'

'No. Only you could.' The Doctor's eyes were on one of the computers. 'Probably you're the only person on Earth who can.'

'I doubt that. I'm sure the Chinese have someone, probably others as well. Only Brett and Unwin wouldn't be able to find them, so –' Ethan stopped, staring at the Doctor, who nodded.

'You're the only one.'

The silence went on for a long time. The computers hummed. The Doctor stood perfectly still, as if he were something that had never moved, something inorganic.

'You little monster,' said Ethan. 'You're going to kill me, aren't you?'

The Doctor cocked his head, his eyes bright and blank, like a bird's. His face suddenly didn't make any sense to Ethan – it was just a collection of human features pulled together to cover something that wasn't human at all.

'I was right,' he said slowly. 'Oh, I was right. She doesn't know. She couldn't guess. And how she loves you – stupid little girl. What a fool you've made of her.'

The Doctor still didn't move, but his eyes may have darkened.

'She'll never know. You'll dispose of my body very efficiently. Feed it to an acid-mouthed alien predator or something. Atomise it. She'll just think I've run off from her. She'll get over that. But if she knew about you, it would hurt for the rest of her life. But then perhaps you'd cut that short – out of mercy, of course.'

'We are talking about the universe.' The Doctor's face didn't change, but there was an edge of pleading in his voice. 'You know what the end of entropy means, don't you? Watch water turn to ice.'

'What are you trying to do – persuade me to kill myself and save you the trouble?'

'It's one life against the whole of existence.'

'It's my life, and I'm not going to do it.'

'The *universe*!' cried the Doctor, anguished.

'You're trying to take it off you – murder without murdering. You think I'm going to make it *easy*?'

The door opened, and they froze. Ace poked her head in. 'I can bloody hear the two of you in the hall. What's all the noise about? I bet it was you.' She went and kissed Ethan lightly on the cheek. 'You'd get on anyone's wick. Doctor, what's wrong?'

He'd turned rapidly away; head down. She ran to embrace him. 'Are you OK? What is it?' He tried ineffectually to escape her arms. 'Doctor, look at me!' The Doctor wouldn't. He sank to his knees and she went down with him. 'Where's your hat?' she looked around helplessly. 'You've lost your hat.'

Ethan had crossed to them. Now he picked up the hat and handed it to her. She pushed it onto the Doctor's head. 'He never loses his hat,' she said. Her voice faltered. 'I used to think it was part of his head, some weird alien thing.' The Doctor shuddered. 'Oh don't,' she whispered, holding onto him. 'Doctor, don't. It's all right. Whatever it is, it's all right.'

Almost in one gesture, he pushed her away and stood up. Ethan half expected his face to glisten with tears, but it was dry, and expressionless. He helped Ace to her feet and .put a hand to her cheek. 'I'm all right,' he said softly. He looked at Ethan with his strange, sad eyes. 'I'm sorry. There has to be another way.'

He left the room without looking back.

'Well weird,' said Ace, staring after him. 'What was that all about? He never apologises.'

'We'd been arguing about the best way to deal with the equations. I don't know why he was affected so strongly.'

'He's exhausted,' she said sympathetically. 'This has all got to him.'

'He's dealt with this sort of thing before, hasn't he – alien invasions, and such?'

'All the time. He always works it out.'

Ethan put his arm around her shoulders. 'One way or another.'

CHAPTER TWENTY-ONE

In Kent, the temperature had edged above freezing. The Doctor's back garden was a stale, slushy mess, and the call box showed its battered age. Well, not really, Ethan thought, looking out the kitchen window. Its age if it were really a sixties call box, not its true number of God-knew-how-many years. The Doctor had shut himself up in it, leaving the three of them – for Molecross, unaccountably, was still along – in the house.

In a way, Ethan was glad he was around. Molecross's presence put a certain damper on the intimacy with Ace, and Ethan had developed some ambiguity there. Not about Ace herself – about being with her when he knew what he did about the Doctor. It separated them. He was always lying to her now, even when he wasn't saying anything. Ace sensed something, of course, but she blamed it on Molecross. Who, admittedly, was one of those people on whom it was easy to blame things. Ace was convinced he'd broken the sugar bowl and hidden the pieces.

She'd been mopey about being banned from the TARDIS, as she put it, though this wasn't really the case – the TARDIS door was unlocked and she could go in. But the Doctor himself was nowhere to be found. Checking the corridors, she had come across new small and mysterious constructions.

'He's definitely at work,' she'd told Ethan. 'Don't know when we'll see him.'

Never would be soon enough, Ethan thought now, turning from the window. The kitchen was cold. He made some tea and took it into the fire-warmed parlour. Bored and restless, Ace had headed out to the nearest Waitrose, Molecross with her. This

220

hadn't been Ace's idea, but when he followed her out to the car like a hopeful dog she relented.

What the hell were they going to do about Molecross? Ethan wondered, stretching his feet out to the fire. That question kept coming up, but nothing ever *was* done about Molecross. He had become the lingering guest no one could quite tell to go home. Not that he had much of a home, according to Ace. Well, let him stay here, where it was warm and he had some company.

And of course Brett was still alive. Somewhere. Defeated, to be sure – but nobody thought he was down. The Doctor was particularly nervous about his encountering Ethan again and prying knowledge from his head. Ethan wasn't mad about the idea himself. He wanted to go back to his flat, and even in his most paranoid moments he couldn't actually imagine Brett's lying in wait for him there. Nonetheless, it wasn't a good idea.

'Hello,' said the Doctor.

Ethan jumped. So help him, if he ever got out of this situation, he'd sit with his back to walls for the rest of his life.

'May I join you?' The Doctor was hatless and in his shirt-sleeves, his demeanour hesitant. Ethan made a what-the-hell gesture, and the Doctor sat in the armchair opposite. As usual, he wasn't quite in scale with the furniture – the discrepancy made him look almost childlike. Right, Ethan thought cynically. 'I haven't been able to trace Brett.'

'What will you do when you find him? Kill him too?'

'Keeping time on course,' snapped the Doctor. 'What do you think it takes? A tap dance and a smile?'

'Something with no conscience.'

A spasm of pain crossed the Doctor's face. 'I told you, I'm going to find another way.'

'What else can you do?'

'I'll have to carry the fight to them.'

'How?'

'I don't know yet.'

'It was you they wanted in the first place. They tried to pull you to them. I felt it.'

The Doctor blew out air slowly, not quite a sigh. 'Well, you see, that's the problem. If they want me, they probably shouldn't have me.'

'Is that a new hint I should off myself?'

'No,' the Doctor said sharply. He leaned toward the fire, and Ethan saw that his face was drawn. 'Perhaps it was only the TARDIS they wanted,' he muttered to himself. 'I was only a way to the TARDIS.'

Why do I feel sympathy for this bastard? Ethan wondered furiously. Why do I want to help him? Is he hypnotising me somehow? 'Look,' he said, 'take me somewhere, and leave me. Some other place or time. I don't want to be around you.'

'I can't. You know too much.'

'As if anyone would believe me.'

'Not about me and the TARDIS. About maths. If I take you to the past, you'll introduce knowledge that mustn't be revealed until the next century. If I leave you in the present, Brett or the invaders may find you. I can't leave you in the future because then there will be two of you; and I can't take you to the future after you're dead because you'll be alive when you shouldn't be.'

Ethan's stomach went cold. He sat up. 'I'm going to die, aren't I?' he whispered. 'Soon, so it wouldn't have mattered if you killed me. But you needed to hurry up the process – because I wasn't meant to die until after I might have helped these aliens.'

The Doctor raised his eyes. They were so blue, blue as the sky. Fly away in them, Ethan thought dizzily. Fly free, fly forever. 'No,' the Doctor said. 'You weren't meant to die soon, and you aren't going to. You only die if they get through. Along with everyone else.'

'Even you?'

'No,' said the Doctor, a trace of self-disgust in his voice. 'Not me. I'll just pop into the past and start trying to fix the disaster from there. If that can be done. Ace will be all right too,' he added.

'Ace,' Ethan snarled. 'Your travelling companion. Lucky, lucky Ace.'

The Doctor was silent.

'You want to go by your house?' Ace asked, as she and Molecross drove out of the Waitrose car park. 'Since we've got the car?'

'No. I can't check my email, and there's nothing else there.'

'Clothes,' she suggested. Like Ethan, Molecross had been wearing leftovers from the TARDIS, and they did little to improve his appearance.

'No.'

'You have to go home sometime.'

'I don't want to.'

'Well, you can't stay at the house.'

'Perhaps the Doctor could use a caretaker. For when he's not here.'

Ace rolled her eyes. 'You don't live in the real world, Molecross.'

'Not if I can help it,' he agreed.

The Brigadier didn't really think it was necessary to revisit the crop patterns; but the Doctor was insistent. So they found themselves wandering through the muddy field checking out the lines in which ice was still frozen. The Doctor poked at this with his umbrella for no reason Lethbridge-Stewart could see. But then the Doctor's motives were so often a mystery. Why, for example, had he come with a small entourage that included Molecross? 'He's been very useful,' the Doctor had said, and explained no farther.

Aside from Molecross – who, the Brigadier had to admit, was noticeably subdued – the Doctor had brought with him Ace and Amberglass. Ace, of course, was to be expected, but Amberglass didn't look as if he ought to be up and around. He'd been put through it. People who associated with the Doctor so often were.

To preserve the Doctor's circle, Lethbridge-Stewart had had it filled with cement. The Doctor poked at this too, as if testing its firmness.

'I assure you, it's not coming out of there.'

'No, doesn't look like it.'

'We've been monitoring this location, and there haven't been any new markings.'

'Yes, this entry seems to have closed up. In any case, they won't be trying any more. The bridge wasn't enough, and that was all they had.'

'So we are here because...?'

The Doctor tapped his chin with his umbrella. 'Because it never hurts to check.'

More to give them something to do than anything else, Lethbridge-Stewart had dispatched Amberglass, Ace and Molecross to the far edges of the field to check for suspicious marks. Molecross, understandably, was unwilling to return to the spot near the trees where he'd been maimed, so Ethan took that area. Ace sloshed around about a quarter mile away, and Molecross went down into a small dip and out of sight.

Work for work's sake, Ace thought irritably. In the mud. All right, she'd been getting restless and was glad to leave the house. Still, this wasn't what she'd signed up for. Especially when she could be home in a warm bed with Ethan – Molecross and the Doctor both gone, plenty of room and privacy. Ethan had been a bit off lately – distracted, back inside himself. Something was going on between him and the Doctor, she knew it. But she couldn't work out what. If it were something they weren't telling her, she'd be right pissed off. But it might just be some weird, difficult code problem. The Doctor, certainly, had been more or less distraught since discovering the hacking attempt. She looked over at him and the Brigadier, standing on either side of the cemented circle and apparently finding it interesting. Well, she thought resignedly, at least she had found

her wellies and wasn't stamping about in ordinary shoes like
Ethan and Molecross.

Molecross's feet were damp, but he hardly noticed. He was
happy. He was helping the Doctor, which meant helping save
the universe. Were such tiny actions usually part of so huge a
task? Perhaps so. Perhaps it wasn't so often like movie special
effects but more like this, treading around in the mire, getting
your feet wet. They also serve who only stand in mud.

It was decent of Amberglass to take that... that other part
of the field. He'd volunteered, sympathetic in a taciturn sort of
way. Fine chap, really. Molecross tried not to pay attention to the
knot of guilt in his stomach; it was bad enough just thinking
about what he'd let Amberglass in for. As is said of the dying,
Molecross's whole life had been passing before him these past
few days. He didn't like the look of it. Silly and self-pitying.
And timid. He'd told himself he was an explorer, when all the
time he'd only been avoiding everything difficult about life.
Working for a living, knowing people, taking responsibility for
someone other than himself. He was ashamed. He felt grateful
that he was allowed to perform this one small, soggy chore.

On higher ground than Ace and Molecross, Ethan wasn't
worried about his feet. He was trying to work out a solution to
the hacking problem. Apparently, the TARDIS made regular
update connections to the data banks on the Doctor's home
planet. That was the vulnerable point.

'I don't understand,' he'd said to the Doctor. 'Why hasn't
anyone tried this before?'

'Because the codes are virtually unbreakable.'

'But I can break them, you say, and I'm only human.'

'The work's actually been done by two humans, both of them
among the best mathematicians on Earth. Your planet's headed
into a dry spell there: Erdos is gone, and he was the last of the
great abstract thinkers. As for other civilisations, obviously there

are some advanced enough to be a threat, but they're locked out of the network entirely.'

'Why don't you simply reconfigure the TARDIS's defence system?'

The Doctor looked at him as if he'd grown a second head. 'Do you have any idea how complex the TARDIS is? Breaking down the defences alone would take one of your years.'

So here we are, Ethan thought unhappily, taking a long step over a muddy patch. The only solution – other than killing him – seemed to be for the Doctor to confront the potential invaders himself. Only he hadn't worked out the logistics – a fairly substantial difficulty. Did he honestly think they'd find something useful in this field, or was he just marking time till he could come up with a solution?

The path Ethan was taking brought him close to the trees, almost under them. He'd been walking slowly, examining the ground, and when he stopped and looked up he saw an irregular, almost torn-looking spot ahead of him. It wasn't large, and it took Ethan a minute to realise that this must be where Molecross had fallen. He grimaced and went closer, but there wasn't much to see – only the churned up, burned patch. Unexpectedly the sight saddened him. Poor bloody Molecross. Poor sod.

As he turned away, something caught the corner of his eye. A flash, a glint. Ethan peered tensely into the trees. In the overcast sky, the sun was only a blur, and the wood was already dark. He went to its edge and stood for several minutes, waiting for whatever he'd glimpsed to appear again. Nothing did. Hell, he might have only been seeing things; that had certainly been known to happen. Still, he lingered. Something told him that this wasn't his imagination, that it was real. Whatever that meant. A few days with the Doctor – God, had it only been a few days? – and your notion of the real began to stretch out of shape.

Then he saw it again.

It was light, only it wasn't light. As he watched, it flickered among the trees and was lost. 'Oh dear God,' Ethan breathed. He turned to call to the Doctor – and an icy shock went right up the bones of his neck into his skull.

Ace clumped wearily up to the Doctor and Lethbridge-Stewart, Molecross trailing after her, abashed. 'Look, Professor, this is well useless. We haven't found anything, and I bet Ethan hasn't either.'

The Brigadier was of her mind: 'I'm afraid she's probably right, Doctor.'

'Yes, yes,' the Doctor admitted gloomily. 'I suppose I'm overanxious about these marks. It's only that this is where the trouble began.'

Ace had been looking around. 'Oi,' she said. 'Where's Ethan?'

CHAPTER TWENTY-TWO

There was something cold on the back of Ethan's neck. It was a hand. He jerked away, but the hand caught his hair and twisted his head around.

'I must say,' Brett observed, 'you look much better than I would have expected.'

'You look like hell,' Ethan snarled. It was true. The wounds Ace had left on Brett's ear and face were redly swollen. He was uncharacteristically dishevelled, and needed a shave.

'I don't feel particularly well,' Brett admitted. 'I think my bites may be infected. You know, the saliva of the human mouth is much more dangerous than a dog's.'

Ethan had no idea what to say to that. He was trying to work out where he was – a sparsely furnished sitting room in a house that, from the look of the ceiling beam and the irregular walls, dated from Elizabethan times. There were numerous modernisations – the large fireplace, for example, had at some point been furnished with an iron stove, behind whose grate a fire glowed. Ethan didn't like the look of it.

'Whose house is this?'

'The fellow who owns the field. You know, *the* field. He's spending the winter in Australia, I understand.'

'But...' Ethan frowned, trying to pull his wits together. He was propped in a worn chintz armchair. His wrists were tied in front of him, with a few inches of rope between them. So I can use a keyboard, he thought. 'Why are you here?'

'I assure you, it's under compulsion. I now have to visit the site daily.' Brett was pacing, drawing near the stove as if he were cold, then abruptly striding away as if he were too hot. 'The barrier here is thinning again. We have to stay in touch.'

'You and Unwin?'

'No.'

'Where is he?'

'Pat's gone. Let's not talk about him any more.'

'Then who's "we"?' Ethan had a feeling he was talking in circles, but he was too groggy to tell. The back of his neck hurt horribly. 'What did you do to my neck?'

'One question at a time,' said Brett, but he didn't answer either of them. 'I'd like your help.'

Though he knew exactly what Brett meant, Ethan said, 'What for? They can't come through.'

Brett smiled bitterly, as if he were about to say something, but changed his mind. 'They need more power. Do you remember that second set of equations?'

'What second set?'

Brett turned his disagreeable eyes on him. 'Now, now,' he said softly, 'I really don't suggest being evasive again.'

No, Ethan thought. 'What about them?'

'I'd like them finished.'

'You're talking as if they're a crossword puzzle. It could take months.'

'It could, but it won't.'

'Whatever you do,' said Ethan, with a steadiness that surprised him, 'you can't make my mind work any faster.'

Brett shrugged. 'We'll find out, won't we?'

'What do you need them for, anyway?' Ethan kept his eyes away from the stove. 'How are they supposed to help?'

'Ah, yes. I skipped a step. They're a way to access the power our friends need.'

He should have killed me after all, Ethan thought sickly. The Doctor should have killed me. Because sooner or later, I'll give Brett what he wants. He'll burn it out of me.

'Why couldn't they have done any of this themselves? The

computations must be well within their capabilities.'

'There's a limited amount of energy available to them for any task.'

'Then it's true,' said Ethan before he thought.

'What's true?' Brett's tone was casual, but his eyes glinted. 'What's true, young Amberglass?'

'They've solved entropy. Or almost.'

'Now, you never thought of that. That was the Doctor's idea, wasn't it? What an interesting little thing he is. I'd like so much to get to know him better.'

'He's hard to know,' said Ethan. 'He's like those sets of mirrors that reflect each other forever. Like a whole hall of them.'

'Infinite riches in a little room,' said Brett softly. 'Have you been in that time machine of his?'

Ethan hesitated, and Brett shook his head disapprovingly. 'Yes,' Ethan said.

'Astonishing, I imagine.'

'Actually, it's fairly plain.'

'Actually, it isn't, I assure you. It's unimaginably complex – at least to us.'

'But not to them.'

'Oh no. They'll know exactly what to do with it.'

Ethan swallowed. 'It's the power source, then.'

'Potentially.'

'They don't only want the Earth. They want all of time and space.'

'And who can blame them?'

'But it's nonsense. If they expend any energy at all – and they have to expend some to harvest existence – then sooner or later they'll run down. And if they suck up all the energy there is, then at the end of the day the universe will die sooner, and they'll perish earlier than they would have if they'd let things alone. What's the point?'

'Oh, they'll harvest existence very slowly. Thread by thread, you might say. Their conversion process is extremely efficient.'

'What in God's name is in this for you?'

'I've already had that conversation with the Doctor.'

Without warning, Brett yanked Ethan up, tore his shirt back over his shoulders, and swung him against the stove. Ethan yelled, and Brett threw him down. 'Only a singe,' he said softly. 'Just a taste of things to come.' He bent and ran a thumbnail across Ethan's blistered spine, forcing a cry from him. 'Let's stop this nonsense. Eventually you'll do what I want, so why don't we simply jump to the end?' He took hold of an arm and helped Ethan up. 'I suppose I should do something about your back. I never remember what to put on burns. Is it butter?' Ethan only groaned. Brett sat him on the edge of the chair. 'I don't recommend leaning back.'

Ethan sat forward, exhausted, his face in his hands. 'What about ice?' he said between his fingers.

'Oh yes,' Brett repeated slowly. 'What about ice?' He walked around behind Ethan and laid a palm against the burn. Ethan's head jerked up – 'What...' He began to shiver, teeth nearly chattering. 'What have you...'

Brett came back in front of him. 'Feel better?'

'But your hands...' Ethan was still shaking. 'They weren't... Before, they...'

'Yes,' said Brett heavily. 'It comes and goes.'

'*What* comes and goes?'

'Never actually leaves, though.' Brett was standing by the stove now, his eyes tired. Then, almost as if pushed, he moved away. 'To be frank,' he said 'it's a bit of a bore.'

'Show yourself,' Ethan said quietly. 'I can see; show yourself.'

Brett looked bewildered. As Ethan watched, something like an aura began to appear around him, only in pieces, sliding in and out of his body. Triangles, squares, rhombuses, octahedrons – finally shifting so fast Ethan couldn't distinguish them. It was as if lightning flashed around Brett – but of course it wasn't lightning at all. It wasn't even light. A long narrow triangle plunged out of Brett's stomach, then zipped back inside.

'What are you looking at?' said Brett angrily.

'I can see it.'

'You can what?'

'See it. There's something funny about my eyes. Something came through, didn't it? Only a bit. Made a home in you.'

'My,' said Brett softly. 'You're full of surprises, aren't you?'

'It's feeding off you.'

'Well,' Brett moved to the stove again, 'I suppose you could put it that way. A cold fire consuming heat. It seems only able to make use of something organic. I wanted to find an animal for it, but I've discovered I can't go very far from the field, and there's no livestock nearby.'

'Is it... Does it...'

'Have intelligence? Not really. I think it's only a piece of some entity that does. All it seeks is survival.'

'It's killing you.'

Brett shrugged. 'Probably. It certainly needs my heat to maintain its stasis.' He strolled over and placed his hands on Ethan's bare shoulders, as if about to impart some important piece of advice. 'You know, I think I'd like to share the experience with you,' – and he sliced his long thumbnail into Ethan's collarbone.

Freezing energy slammed up Ethan's veins – he toppled into Brett, who held him up. Then a shriek like grinding ice shot through his head, and the thing was gone. Brett staggered as it dived back into him. 'Dear me. It doesn't seem to like you.'

He dropped Ethan and started pacing again – to the stove, away from the stove, to the stove... Ethan crawled to the chair, but was too weak to climb into it; he held on to the seat cushion like a life belt. Brett eyed him curiously. 'I wonder why it rejected you.'

Who cares? thought Ethan. He lowered his head to the cushion, afraid he was going to cry. His nose was running from the cold. Then pain sliced from one side of his skull to the other, as if someone were trying to take off the top of his head. He gave a small cry.

'What the hell is it now?' said Brett irritably.

Ethan couldn't answer. Blood slipped from his nose.

'Oh for God's sake,' said Brett. 'What is it? Migraine?' Ethan made a noise that sounded like 'urgh'. 'I'll take that as a yes.' He hauled Ethan to his feet again. 'I wonder if one pain will drive out another.'

'Well,' Ethan gasped, 'let's find out,' and he threw himself against Brett and drove him into the stove.

Brett screamed, and Ethan backed up. He couldn't make himself hold Brett against the metal, and doubted he'd have the strength in any case. He tottered back and collapsed on his side. The pain in his head nearly made him vomit. Brett had fallen on his face, and the non-thing, panicked, was slicing in and out of him. It shot toward Ethan, then snapped back, flashing around Brett in angles and planes, making no noise, though Ethan was certain it was screaming. Brett didn't move. He's dead, thought Ethan. And it's dying. The heat killed them both.

With what was left of his sleeve, he wiped the blood and snot off his face. Telephone. Somewhere in the house there had to be a telephone. Of course, the farmer might have had the service cancelled while he was away. Think positively, Ethan told himself, and that struck him as so funny that he laughed until a spasm of pain shut him up. After that, he curled in a tight little ball, fighting nausea, and didn't move for a while. He was still like that when he heard the front door open and, looking up, saw Molecross hurry into the room.

'This is a joke, right?' he said hoarsely. 'Why are you everywhere I turn, Molecross? Are we psychically linked? Is it karma? What? Just tell me, what?'

'I don't think you're quite yourself,' offered Molecross, crossing to the hearth. He gulped. 'What's wrong with him?'

'He's dead, you moron, that's what's wrong with him.' Ethan's head was beginning to clear, and a practical question occurred to him. 'How the hell did you get here anyway?'

Molecross was backing away from Brett's corpse. 'I drove. Oh – I see what you mean. Well, after you disappeared, the Doctor and Ace were searching all over, went back down to Brett's house, they may still be there. But I thought, perhaps he's gone somewhere nearby. I mean, we knew it had to be Brett. Not likely you'd have a lot of enemies. So I thought I'd check here.'

'Good reasoning,' Ethan admitted.

'How are... Are you...'

'I'm all right,' said Ethan. 'Particularly considering I've had an alien being shunted in and out of me. My back is... it's...'

'Yes,' said Molecross, looking. 'Hang on a mo'.'

He went away. Ethan shut his eyes. The whole situation seemed unbelievable to him, like a dream; not only a bad one but any sort of dream – unreal, unretrievable, of another quality of being altogether. He had the peculiar feeling that if he opened his eyes he would be back in his flat, and none of the last week or so would ever have happened. Nor would he mind – except for Ace. Thank God Ace wasn't here. It was getting embarrassing always to be discovered in a bloody heap. He sincerely hoped this was the last time it would happen.

'The power's off,' said Molecross, re-entering with a towel, 'but the water's on. Try this.' He'd soaked the towel in cold water; now he laid it gently across Ethan's back. 'Does that help?'

It didn't actually help much, but Ethan murmured, 'Thanks.' He heard Molecross walk away a few paces.

'There really is something wrong with him. Aside from being dead.'

What else could that possibly be? Ethan wondered distractedly. He didn't feel able to concentrate on the question. 'Never mind.'

'I suppose the Doctor will know.'

'Oh yes,' Ethan muttered, 'the Doctor knows everything.'

'Sometimes I honestly believe he does. I left him a note.'

'What?'

'A note. At my house. I'm sure he'll work it out.'

I'm sure he will, Ethan thought. Just as he worked out that the best thing to do would be to kill me. And he was right. I saved myself as much by luck as ability; if Brett had had long enough with me...

Molecross had gone away again. Now he returned with a dish cloth for Ethan to wipe his face. 'What happened, anyway?'

'Isn't it obvious?'

'Not really. I mean, it's clear what happened to you, but I don't understand why Brett is dead. He hit the stove and it killed him?'

'He hit the stove and it killed him.'

'Oh... The body is, erm, strange. Perhaps you should look at it.'

'I'm not interested in the body.'

CHAPTER TWENTY-THREE

But of course, the Doctor was. He arrived and sent Molecross packing on some errand. Ace wasn't with him, to Ethan's relief: he didn't want to be sympathised with and fussed over. And he wasn't. The Doctor examined his back, pronounced it not bad, and went straight to the stove. 'Hm,' he said. 'Tell me what happened.'

'I don't quite know. Something, or a bit of something, did make it through and attached itself to Brett. The heat of the stove was too much for them both.'

'Mm,' said the Doctor again, and tapped his chin with his umbrella handle. 'That would explain things.'

'What things?'

'Are you certain it's dead? Didn't it try to flee to you?'

'Brett tried to get it to earlier. But it wouldn't.'

'Wouldn't?' The Doctor blinked at him.

'I... It's hard to explain. It's as if something in me repelled it.'

'Ah.' The Doctor turned quickly away. 'The corpse has crystallised.'

'It's not ice, is it? Melting.'

'No, not like the Wicked Witch. Crystallised and dry. Freeze-dried,' the Doctor said quietly. 'The fate he had in mind for the Earth. Not to mention everything else.'

Ethan propped up on his elbows. 'Why did he do it? It's completely –'

'Mad?'

'– irrational. Who was he, anyway? Did anyone ever find out?'

The Doctor shrugged. 'Only child. Wealthy family; good

education; no history of hardship; no history of psychological disorder. He was married once.'

'You're taking the piss.'

'No, he really was. She drowned. Rumour had it he was involved. But rumour is always nasty.'

'What did he study, up at – Oxford or Cambridge?'

'Oxford. He only just managed a third in Philosophy.'

'Oh good. More irony.'

'It does seem to be one of the universal constants. Though generally in better proportion to events.'

'I suppose he was mad, in some sense.'

'Yes, I daresay it's possible to be morally insane. Goodness knows I've met enough examples to convince me.'

'You've had a very interesting life,' said Ethan. He meant for it to come out as sarcasm, but somehow it didn't.

'Yes I have. Long and interesting. Interesting and long.' The Doctor remained preoccupied with what was left of Brett.

'And does everyone who's involved with you get knocked about?'

'I get knocked about myself. Rather badly, sometimes. That's when I change.'

'Get a new body?'

'More like dying and returning in a different body.'

Ethan went quiet for a few minutes. 'You were right about killing me, you know. It was a near thing with Brett.'

'No,' said the Doctor sharply. 'I was not right At the end of the day, did you help him? No. Nothing is predictable. Chance rolls us like dice. I, of all people, should know that.'

'I have to give you credit, Molecross,' Ace said. 'You get more things right than not, and when you do, they're really right.'

Ethan nodded, agreeing. They were in the fire-lit sitting room of the Doctor's house. Ethan was drinking Scotch and Ace beer. Molecross had a glass of orange juice. He looked shyly pleased at the compliment.

Ace hadn't fussed, though she was clearly upset, and Ethan was grateful to her. She had, however, insisted on hearing the details of Brett's demise. They weren't gory enough for her.

'He deserved worse.'

'It was bad,' Molecross assured her. 'He was all in flakes.'

'Hm. Well, that's all right then, I suppose.'

'Glad you approve,' Ethan noted dryly. 'Do you run into this sort of thing often?'

'Bastards like him? He's a top boy. Mostly it's monsters and such.'

Ethan regarded her admiringly. What stamina she had. He felt as if he'd been through ten lifetimes, all of them unfortunate.

'Sometimes it's fun,' she said, as if reading his mind. 'Honestly. I wish I could show you some of the stuff that's fun.'

He smiled. 'That rather depends on the Doctor's success.'

'Not to worry,' she said comfortably. He was both moved and disturbed by her faith. 'And he says you're to help him. So with the two of you, I don't see how things can cock up.'

She's a child, thought Ethan. He felt suddenly tender towards her, and suddenly far away. What would happen when this was over? – presuming it ended well. On the one hand he wanted things to go on and on, wonderfully, as they had. On the other, he knew that eventually they'd drive each other mad. How she'd exasperate him, and how he'd bore her. He'd block out her sun, stunt her. The Doctor, whatever his faults, would never do that.

'Penny for them,' she said.

'No. I'm only being morbid.'

'Then cheer up,' said the Doctor, appearing in that sudden way of his. Ethan was almost positive he never actually entered, just popped into being like an elusive particle. 'We've work to do. Not you.' He nodded at Ace and Molecross. 'I need Ethan.'

Ace sulked but didn't object. Molecross was disappointed, but also kept quiet. The Doctor took Ethan's arm. 'Come along now.'

'How did that salve work?' he asked as they walked through

the TARDIS corridors. These all looked identical to Ethan: white walls patterned with concave hexagons. He couldn't imagine how the Doctor and Ace found their way around.

'Seems to have taken care of things.'

The Doctor nodded, satisfied. They were passing one of his odd little contraptions and, without pausing, he scooped it up to carry under an arm. He opened the next door, which led into yet another room containing several computer stations. A huge monitor covered a wall. 'Now,' the Doctor escorted Ethan to a numerical keyboard, 'here's the code that broke through the first level of the TARDIS's security system. You said you think it's based on primes?'

'It certainly looks like it.'

'Then break it down for me.'

'I don't understand,' said Ethan. 'You're from a far superior mathematical culture, why do you need me to do this?'

'Because I have other things to do.' The Doctor set his device on a table and began to poke around in it with what looked to Ethan like a pencil. The Doctor caught him watching and made a shooing motion. 'Don't you have something to do?'

Well, thought Ethan, yes. And he set to work.

'Bourneville Fruit and Nut!' said Moleross.

'Yeah.' Ace glanced at the chocolate bar in his hand. 'So?'

'You can't *get* these any more. They stopped making them in the eighties. But the food machine has dozens of them.'

'Have fun.'

Molecross chewed happily. He had brought several bars into the kitchen of the Allen Road house, and he sat with them in front of him on the table. Ace watched him sourly. All right, like she'd said, you had to give Molecross credit. But you didn't have to find him interesting. In fact, you couldn't.

'Are all your adventures this fraught?' he said.

'What? Don't talk with your mouth full.'

Molecross swallowed. 'Sorry. Fraught. All your adventures.

I mean, do you do anything, well, less intense than saving the universe?'

'Yeah, of course.'

'Such as what?'

'Lots of things. The first time I met the Professor, it was only a dragon causing trouble.'

'A dragon?' Molecross stopped chewing and gazed at her happily. 'A real dragon?'

'Well, sort of. It was on this ice planet –'

'An ice planet!'

He looked like a five-year-old ready for a story. Ace sighed and drew a chair up to the table. 'Yeah, you see, I was working as a waitress...'

'That was quick,' the Doctor said approvingly.

'All I did was create a program to do the heavy lifting. It ought to finish in about an hour. So what's that you're working on?'

'A thing.'

'And what is it when it's at home?'

'Still a thing. Thank you for your help. You can go now.' The Doctor waved a dismissive hand, his eyes on his little machine. There was something about his expression – grim, sad, afraid? – that made Ethan hesitate. He had the same peculiar feeling he had before – that somehow it was the Doctor who needed his help, not the other way around.

'I won't be able to find my way out,' he stalled.

'Do you love Ace?'

The non sequitur was so jarring Ethan thought he hadn't heard right. 'I'm sorry?'

'Do you love Ace?'

'I...' Ethan was aware that something enormous rested on his reply, but he didn't know what. 'I don't know,' he said awkwardly. 'I mean, yes, I love her. I'm not in love with her, nor she with me.'

'But it could happen.'

Ethan thought about this. 'Yes. I think so.'

'She loves me,' the Doctor said simply. 'And she trusts me. And you're right – perhaps she shouldn't.'

'I never said that.'

'Near enough.'

'Do you love her?'

The Doctor's shoulders shifted uncomfortably. 'These human emotions... They're very hard for me to comprehend.' He still hadn't looked away from his machine. 'Ace is hard for me to comprehend.'

'What are you going to do? When she's an old woman and you've hardly changed?'

'She'll get tired of me before then. She'll start wanting a real life.'

'Travelling with you isn't a real life?'

'A human life. I look like one of you, but I'm not one of you. Not in the least. At the end of the day, she'll have to leave me.'

Ethan waited, but the Doctor appeared to have finished. He poked at and adjusted his device. Finally he said, 'Please go now. I have work to do.'

Without quite knowing how, Ethan found his way to the console room. He left the TARDIS and crossed the slushy garden to the house. In the kitchen, he found Ace and Molecross at the table. At least ten rumpled chocolate wrappers lay at Molecross's elbow.

'Bourneville Fruit and Nut,' Molecross explained, embarrassed. 'Go on,' he said to Ace.

'Well, that's it, really. UNIT put them away in one of their super-security prisons, and I suppose they're still there.'

'Sheherezade,' said Ethan. She smiled at him.

'It's all more extraordinary than I even imagined,' said Molecross dreamily.

Ace glanced at Ethan, then leaned across the table toward

Molecross. 'Look,' she said in a low voice. 'I'm not supposed to do this, but… How'd you like to spend some time in the TARDIS library?'

Molecross gasped. She smiled and guided him out the door.

'Right,' she said to Ethan when she returned. 'Alone at last.'

CHAPTER TWENTY-FOUR

Molecross sat engrossed in a holograph book of the canyons of Cevitor. Faced with the immensity of the library, he had at first only wandered dazedly. For a half hour or so, he was entranced by the merely familiar: Newton's notes for his *Principia*; several Shakespeare manuscripts; scrolls labelled with Greek names, noted as survivors of the fire that destroyed the library of Alexandria; a number of Napoleon's battle plans in the general's hand; a notebook of pencil sketches by Goya; handwritten scores by Mozart... In addition to these recognisable marvels, there were papers and volumes by authors he'd never heard of on subjects that baffled him. And all this before he reached the rooms devoted to other planets.

'Oi, Molecross!'

He looked up. Ace was grinning down at him. 'You've been in here for bloody hours.'

'Has it been that long?'

'Time flies when you're having fun, does it?' Ace glanced around at the shelves. She wasn't particularly keen on the library. 'Seen the Professor?'

'No.'

'Come help look for him then. You can come back later,' she said when Molecross's face fell. 'Only I need to find him. He gets engrossed in these projects and forgets to eat. He says it doesn't affect him, but then he's all cranky.'

Ethan was waiting in the corridor. He glanced past them at the expanse of books.

'I wouldn't half mind...'

Ace shut the door firmly. 'Later.'

'You know he's all right,' Ethan said impatiently.

'No I don't, and if you'd been with him as long as I have, you wouldn't either.'

'He was working on *graphs*, for God's sake. How can anyone get into trouble with graphs?'

'You don't know him very well, do you?' She set off down the corridor and, with a sigh, Ethan followed. As usual, Molecross brought up the rear.

'I've seen the most amazing –'

'Not now,' Ethan snapped. He was jealous of Molecross's time in the library, and when he realised this, he was embarrassed. It wasn't as if his last few hours hadn't been extremely well spent.

'This it?' Ace had stopped at a door that looked to Ethan like every other door he'd seen.

'Might be.'

'Yeah,' she said, as if she'd spotted a sign invisible to the rest of them, 'this is the one.' She pushed the door open. The Doctor wasn't inside.

For a moment, Ethan didn't even notice – he was caught by the image on the monitor screen. He crossed to it slowly, his eyes following the lines of the graph as they swept into peaks and dropped into valleys.

'Where's he got to, then?' said Ace irritably. 'Oi, what's that?'

'It's a landscape. He's graphed himself a three-dimensional landscape from the elements of the code.'

'Right. Now try that in English.'

'You can take equations and state them another way as a graph. Translate them, in a sense. That's what he's done with the primes that formed the basis of the worm's code.' Ethan bit his lip, thinking.

'Why would he do that?' said Molecross. 'What's it for?'

'My God,' Ethan muttered, 'I think –'

'He's gone in there,' said Ace. 'The git! He's gone bloody *in* there, hasn't he?' She ran to the screen and slammed her hands against it. All she hit was a flat surface.

'Why would he do that?' said Molecross bewilderedly. 'Why on Earth would he want to go in there?'

Ethan ran his hands through his hair and crossed to the computer he'd used earlier. Its screen showed nothing but equations. He stared at these while Ace continued to beat helplessly at the wall screen. At last he said slowly, 'We've seen that the aliens can't properly exist in our reality. Nor could we in theirs, probably. So if you wanted to communicate with them, you'd have to construct a middle ground where the two of you could co-exist.'

Ace stopped pounding, her face white. 'You mean he's gone to *meet* them?'

'I think so.'

'Oh bloody hell!' She was almost crying in frustration.

'He's brilliant.' Ethan looked back and forth between the two screens. 'Absolutely brilliant.'

'And bonkers!' she cried angrily. 'He's gone in there without anyone to help him, and what if he fails? Pop goes the cosmos, right?' She kicked the screen. 'He thinks he can do *anything*!'

Looking at the graph, Ethan wondered if perhaps he could.

'Right then,' said Ace. 'We're going after him.'

'Very good,' said Ethan. 'Why don't you tell me how?'

'You work it out. You're the genius.'

'I could be Einstein, for all the good it would do us. This is beyond anything human.'

'There's a wall,' said Molecross. 'Like glass. How did he get through?'

'Ah, excellent point.' Ethan scrolled through the equations. 'I'm betting he arranged the wall to form after he'd gone through. It's a door. And he's locked it.'

'To keep himself in?' said Ace, confused.

'To keep us out, I imagine. And other things in.' Ethan went over to the screen and examined it closely. 'I wonder if there's any physical form of lock to correspond with the logorithmic one, since the graph corresponds with the computer's equations.' He lay flat and ran his fingers along the lower edge of the screen. 'Hm. Come here, Ace.' She knelt beside him. 'Can you feel anything?'

She placed her hand where his had been. 'Yeah, like a little box.'

'That's it then.' Ethan got to his feet. 'Not that it helps us. I've no more idea how to unlock this than I do the other.'

'Unlock it, balls!' Ace grabbed him and Molecross and shoved them into the corridor. She wheeled in the doorway, her hand going to her pocket.

'Oh no,' Ethan gasped. 'Ace –'

'Be prepared,' she spat, 'that's my bloody motto,' – and launched something like a tiny grenade at the bottom of the screen. The explosion knocked them all over, but Ace was up in an instant and, before Ethan or Molecross could stop her, shot across the room and leaped into the graph.

'Ace, no!' Ethan rushed after her, and slammed flat into the screen. Behind him, Molecross stopped in time:

'It's closed up again.'

'Thank you,' said Ethan, rubbing his nose. 'I'd worked that out.'

'But how –'

'I imagine the lock's self-healing, so to speak.'

'Let's blow it open again!'

'Fine. Have you any explosives?'

'Ah,' said Molecross.

'Yes.' Ethan strode back to the computer. 'The key's in here somewhere,' he said hopelessly.

'Why did it reseal, anyway?'

'Because the Doctor wanted to keep something...' The hairs on the back of Ethan's neck prickled, and, slowly, he turned around.

'Hello,' said Brett.

The Doctor climbed hills and slid into valleys. He hiked up mountains. Around him, the seeming landscape was white as snow. The Doctor found the going surprisingly easy, perhaps because he wasn't traversing actual heights. Where he had started, just inside the screen, the hills were low, but they had gradually and regularly, in precise ratio, become higher. In the distance a peak rose and rose, like a column, until it vanished beyond sight. The Doctor knew that it led to infinity.

In spite of the tension of his purpose, his journey was slightly boring. The perfect proportions surrounding him were as dull as computer animation – nothing to surprise the eye, only lines to lead it. The ground beneath his feet was featureless. There was no sound but his own breathing and the crack of his umbrella ferrule on the non-ice.

He was walking straight ahead, towards the higher ground. To his right the peaks gradually flattened out to an endless plain. He knew that on his left, over what looked like the spine of the mountains, there was nothing. Nothing at all. He had graphed only real numbers, and beyond the ridge was the territory of the impossible.

A soft rustle fell to him, like a light slide of snow. There was no snow. The Doctor stopped and looked around. In the depths of the false ice gleamed a blue shadow. It is coming to me, he thought, and waited, leaning on his umbrella. A hairline crack ran crookedly down the slope of the hill, then shuddered and widened, making an entry. No, the Doctor corrected himself, I am going to it.

He ventured forward and poked his head inside. In front of him a short passage opened into a chamber. He frowned. Where had the energy come from for such a showy display? Oh well, he was here now. He tucked his umbrella under his arm and approached the chamber, stopping at the threshold.

The room before him curved up in an elliptical white dome. Tiny cracks spiderwebbed the floor. There was no furniture. Within the frozen walls, an occasional shadow pulsed like a blue heart. 'A miracle of rare device,' the Doctor murmured. He walked in a few paces and examined the floor. The ice – he thought he might as well call it that – was reflective, like a shattered mirror.

'Very impressive,' he said. 'I once visited a tourist attraction like this on the Jungfrau.'

The emptiness in front of him thickened – like mist, if mist could be solid and was utterly white. It began to shift horizontally, like shuffling abacus beads. Putting itself together, the Doctor thought, calculating itself into a presence. He didn't see – probably couldn't have seen – the moment it manifested, only found himself looking up at a towering dead-white being with long hair and neutral eyes, wearing an equally dead-white garment that made the Doctor think of a winding sheet. It had taken humanoid form, masking its geometry so well that no trace of sharp angle was visible. The Doctor raised his hat. It inclined its head.

'Will this do?' Its voice was thin and toneless, and it spoke in unaccented Gallifreyan. 'I see you. Can you look on me?'

'You're quite clear, thank you,' said the Doctor. The being smiled. Though its slenderness was birdlike, the overall impression was of strength. 'I trust I am sufficiently numerical,' the Doctor said politely.

'Yes. Interesting equations. Many irrational and impossible numbers.'

'I should think so. Does that bother you? Possibly you find it a bit threatening.' The being didn't reply, nor did its expression change. 'Well, now that the introductions are over, I'd like to know what you think you're doing.'

'Becoming immortal, Doctor.'

'By draining the cosmos?'

'Is there another way?'

'Haven't you worked out the little flaw in your plan? Sooner or later, you'll run out of matter and energy to devour. You'll die in the end, anyway. So why not let everything else live?'

'We will continue for aeons. In that time, we will find a solution.'

'No you won't,' said the Doctor impatiently. 'You can't achieve a perfect non-entropic state without perfect stasis. And perfect stasis would be indistinguishable from death. Bodies at rest, as in eternal rest, as in rest in peace. You can only live forever by dying.'

'All paradoxes will be resolved on the quantum level.'

'It's exactly the quantum level you're going to have problems with.'

'That would be true, if we were matter.'

This stopped the Doctor. 'You must be either matter or energy.'

'We are concepts. The sapient races dream of our transcendent order and timeless perfection.'

'Don't pull Plato on me,' said the Doctor. 'If you were only conceptual, then you would already have eternal life. All this energy-robbery would be unnecessary. Where are you finding the energy for this conversation, by the way? You're fairly expressive.'

'I am expending only the tiniest amount of energy. We are so near to absolute zero that we encounter almost no resistivity.'

'That still doesn't answer my question. You've evolved into a purely mathematical, near-static form of being. You burn out planets and stars to maintain your anti-entropic state. But you must be drawing power from somewhere in your world, or you wouldn't be able to have this conversation, much less contact Brett and Unwin or make your attempts to pierce the barrier.'

'Some of us, pieces of us, sacrifice ourselves.'

'Then you're a hive mind.'

'Both hive mind and individual. At this level, we form what you know as a Bose–Einstein condensation. Many and one simultaneously.'

'And that one is weak as an infant.'

'Infants cannot gather their own food.' It broke into pixels and reappeared partly within the translucent wall, apparently its equivalent of sitting down. 'You have a great amount of energy, much more than a human.'

'Artron energy.'

'So much I suspect it is not all your own.'

'I'm connected to my TARDIS through transcendent biomechanics.'

Its mouth opened slightly, and a white tongue peeked in and out. 'That is power indeed.'

'Don't get your hopes up. I'm not such a fool as to come in here with any power you could access. The connection is based on irrational and imaginary equations; any contact would reduce you to zero or spiral you into infinity.'

It smiled. 'As to that, we do not need to go through you, Doctor. Already, we are in your TARDIS's computers, taking them over program by program.'

'A lie. You were stopped by the firewall. You haven't the code to go farther.'

'Haven't we? That brilliant boy is still on your ship. Perhaps you should have killed him.'

The Doctor's eyes darkened. 'I have no idea what you're talking about.'

'Who lies now? We were inside of him for an instant and found the memory. There's something wrong with him, you know.'

'Yes,' said the Doctor, 'I know.'

'But all of this is beside the point. We no longer need the code. Our worm slipped in as you came out.'

'Impossible. I calculated for that. You didn't have the power.'

'Ordinarily, no. But we happened to have use of the body of Mr Brett. Our one that died managed to access and transport the condensed energy of his decomposition. Interestingly, some of his personality came with it, I suppose because they had merged.'

'Brett,' said the Doctor scornfully. 'You really don't expect me to believe that, do you?' But he remembered the state of the corpse.

'Mr Brett is now a computer code: our worm. We are, of course, in contact with him. Fascinating information. At a certain point, possibly just about now, this construct of yours was to collapse. And a bolt of artron energy, with you as the medium, would then annihilate our world. Of course, you would die too, but still...' The Doctor was silent. It nodded. 'You're not quite as honourable as your reputation maintains, are you?'

'In a choice between the cosmos and my integrity, I'm happy to throw out my integrity.'

To the Doctor's dismay, the being emerged from the wall with its lower half transformed into a snake. Erect as a fakir's cobra, it rippled to him. 'You're very good at destroying others' civilisations.'

'Only when they try to consume every one but their own.'

'I see. You work out the numbers.' It smiled again. The Doctor wished it would stop. 'That's why it must have seemed to you quite reasonable to end one, small human life.'

'Only I didn't.'

'But you would have. If that girl hadn't come in, Ethan Amberglass would be dead. Even though, once you put your mind to it, another way presented itself. Your first instinct was to kill.'

'No,' said the Doctor, but he'd gone white as the walls around him.

'Did you really believe we were pulling you in? You were merely seeking your own.'

'No!'

'Morality has its equations too – they graph the curve of compassion between the quick and the dead. There are slivers of ice in your hearts.' It swayed up and bent over him. 'Little Doctor, you belong with us.'

CHAPTER TWENTY-FIVE

Brett stood by the screen examining the room with interest, to all appearances humanly solid. He wore an exquisitely tailored suit of grey wool.

'I feel rather like Rasputin,' he observed.

'You're only an equation,' said Ethan. He was on his feet, pressed back against the computer. Across the room, Molecross was frozen in place.

'If you break it down far enough, everything is. Though I suppose you mean that I'm non-corporeal. Well, not precisely.'

A blurry streak shot at and through Molecross, who cried out and nearly fell. Brett reformed on the other side of him. 'I actually find that unpleasant,' he confided. 'Organic matter is disgusting.' Moaning, Molecross backed away from him.

'So what's it like being dead?' said Ethan hoarsely.

'Oh, I much prefer it.'

'How, what… what, I mean,' Molecross babbled, 'where did you -'

A nightmarish idea was trying to occur to Ethan, but he fought it down. Brett flickered into pixels and rearranged next to him. Ethan would have stepped back, but the computer was in the way. 'That thing didn't die,' he said. 'It went home, and took you with it.'

'An oversimplification, but essentially yes.'

'W- Why are you here?' said Molecross.

Brett's eyes slid sideways at him, then back to Ethan. 'Who is that?'

'Molecross.'

The name meant nothing to Brett. He glanced incuriously at Molecross and returned to the huge screen. Molecross was almost shaking with fear. He shot a panicked look at Ethan, who shook his head – reassuringly, he hoped, though he couldn't find anything reassuring in the situation. Brett traced a finger over the screen surface.

'We're pure mathematics, you know,' he said. 'That lock wouldn't slow us down if it weren't continually shifting its code. And of course we can't use explosives from our side.' He blinked sleepily at Ethan. 'Do you have any more of those devices that very violent girl used?'

'Probably,' said Ethan, 'but I've no idea where.' Brett shrugged. His casualness gave Ethan a bad feeling. The nasty idea tried again to occur, and again Ethan swatted it down. 'What do you mean by "we"? What are you?'

'Just a code, like everything else,' Brett said, and the idea ripped through Ethan's defences and became a thought.

'You're the worm.'

'It's still a clever lad.'

'Worm?' said Molecross. 'What are you talking about?'

'Not *now*, Molecross.'

'Oh – a computer worm. Not a dragon.'

'Who *is* this person?' said Brett.

'No one. Harmless, believe me. Not too bright, as you can tell. You've got through the firewall.'

'No, I've bypassed the firewall. The Doctor created a door that goes both ways. He must have known that, but counted on our not having the power to push through it. And he was right, as far as that goes. But I –'

'But you were a source of power. That thing inside you fuelled up before it went back –'

'And gave us just enough energy to get me through as the Doctor went out. As a program, of course, so that I have a place to survive. This image is only a projection.'

'So the rest of you – the real you...'

'Is at work even as we speak.' Brett turned his head, as if listening. 'It's an enormous task. Might take years.'

'The Doctor will stop you.'

Brett turned an amused eye on him. 'What makes you think the Doctor is coming back?' Then he vanished.

'I don't understand,' said Molecross. 'Are they hacking the TARDIS?'

'They have hacked it.'

'What are we going to do?' Molecross's voice rose. 'How can we stop them?'

'I don't know!' Ethan booted up another computer and leaned over the keyboard, working frantically.

'What are you doing?'

'I'm trying to find the worm, or at least its trail. As I don't know what I'm doing, I'd say it's hopeless.'

Molecross watched him, feeling useless. Even with his pedestrian computer skills, he could see that what was happening on the screen was extraordinarily complex. He suspected it transcended full human comprehension. 'Perhaps you could try one of the console computers.'

'What?' Ethan mumbled, not really hearing.

'The console computers. They might have their own system, and separate data storage. Perhaps some sort of owner's manual.'

Ethan stood bolt upright. 'Yes,' he hissed. He grabbed Molecross and ran for the door.

'But we don't know how to get there,' Molecross objected as he was hauled down the corridor.

'Trust me, we'll get there.'

Ace charged up and down the hills. She hardly noticed their strangeness. She was so angry that she had to run or she'd explode. Damn the Doctor! Damn these whatever-they-weres!

Finally, she stopped, gasping for breath. How far had the Doctor gone? How far could you go in this place? She gazed down the hills to her right, seeing how they shrank and shrank and finally flattened to an endless plain. This was bloody maths: you could go on to infinity.

If this were actual snow and ice, there would be some tracks. But it wasn't, it was some naff construct. How could she find him? Use your head, idiot. He hadn't gone down to the plain – she could see it was empty. He might have gone up the peaks to her left, but why? The simplest thing would have been to continue on straight ahead, and there didn't seem to be any reason not to have done the simplest thing.

She started running again.

Molecross looked over Ethan's shoulder. 'What's that?'

'The directory of files and folders. This machine is ludicrously user friendly. The Doctor must have set it up for humans at some point. I wonder...' Ethan looked around the console board. 'Why don't you see if you can call up that user's manual? I'm guessing it's easy to access.'

'Here's a button that says "Manual".'

'Not funny, Molecross.'

'No, honestly, it says "Manual".'

'Then for God's sake, push it.' Ethan found the last previous version of the directory and began comparing the size of its files with the new ones. Please, he thought, let there be a difference. Let me find where the damned thing's hidden itself.

'This is in English,' Molecross said in amazement.

'Just read it, will you?!'

'What am I looking for?'

'A virus scan, if there is one.'

Molecross scrolled through the pages. 'I wonder if there's an index?'

'Why don't you bloody find out!' Ethan yelled. 'I swear, if I didn't have to stay with this I'd wring your neck.'

'All right, all right!' Molecross sulked for a moment, then said morosely, 'I wish Ace hadn't gone – she must know how to do some of this.'

Ethan wished she hadn't gone either.

'I can't survive with you,' the Doctor said. He stood held in the coils of the being – elliptical coils, part of his brain couldn't help noticing, not circular ones – his umbrella pressed to his chest. 'Your universe will turn me inside out and kick me into the void.'

'As you are now.'

'I am as I am now.'

'Yes,' it said. 'But also no. You are translatable.'

'I'm sorry?'

'You are reduceable to equations. We will take those in.'

'Impossible. My equations contain irrational numbers you can't process.'

'So little is impossible. I'm sure you've learned that.' The being pixelled and returned to its fully human appearance. 'We became what you referred to as a hive mind because our equations can meld. I lend x a letter, it becomes y. We form and unform among ourselves, solutions to problems no one has posed, our own form of social cohesion. It takes no energy; the laws of mathematics decree and execute our changes.'

'Powered by the abstract?'

'Nicely put.'

The Doctor almost said that he thought that was impossible too, but there didn't seem to be much point with the evidence otherwise standing in front of him.

'I only "see" you as equations,' it continued. 'By rearranging my own I will free some numbers and add them to you, changing your mathematical composition. Let me demonstrate by reconfiguring one of your equations as a square root.'

The Doctor's senses collapsed. He was only aware that he was being slit to pieces and rearranged, and that somewhere he was screaming. Then his vision returned in colourless kaleidoscope patterns.

'You look different now. I would describe the change to you, but my grasp of the vocabulary of the organic is limited.'

The Doctor heard himself make a moist, muffled sound. 'The situation is obviously damaging to you. I will reverse it.'

The Doctor returned to himself. He collapsed to a sitting position, then fell over and lay on the ice. The being looked down at him. 'Clearly we will have to perform the translation very delicately. I think that, for now, I must simply refocus you.'

'Here's something odd,' said Ethan.

'You mean the rest of it isn't odd?'

Ethan had made some sense of the manual and managed to call up a map of the TARDIS's systems, with links to explications of each operation. 'There's an indication that energy was timed to be released but wasn't. Something called Artron energy.'

'Does that do us any good?'

'Not directly. In fact,' Ethan admitted disconsolately, 'not at all.'

'I need some tea,' said Molecross. 'You're all right on your own. I'll make tea.'

'Fine.'

Ethan raced through the links. Many of the TARDIS functions weren't computerised – the best security system possible. The door lever, for example, was a completely mechanical device. Surely there were others. But where, and what did they do?

He had finally been able to locate Brett (he was unable to think of the program as merely a worm). The on-screen image resembled a defragging operation, only there was no way to turn it off. Ethan had tried to get ahead of the worm and block it and get behind it and repair its damage, but failed at both. The operation was, of course, impossible on an Earth computer, but he'd hoped it might be doable with a system this advanced. If it was, he wasn't the man to work out how.

As far as he could tell, Brett was going through the simplest operations first, working his way in deeper and deeper. He was going to make every single file accessible to his masters, or his other selves, or whoever they were. Oh God, Ethan thought, don't panic, don't panic.

Molecross put a cup of tea in his hand. Ethan drank without tasting it. It might indeed, as Brett had mused, take years to do the whole job, but at some point much earlier he was going to get to life support. And long before that, he'd get to things like lights – Ethan was surprised he hadn't already. There must be an equivalent of an emergency generator. 'Molecross, turn on one of those monitors. I'm going to send you some files to go through. See if you can find anything that might be a description of the off-line activities.'

'Like manual override?'

'No,' said Ethan between his teeth.

'That never worked anyway. I began to wonder why they even had it.'

'Because they were on the telly! Will you shut up and get to work?'

'I'm working. Only it helps me to talk.'

'Talk to yourself. Silently.'

The room went quiet except for the soft hum of the console. Ethan continued to chase the worm. He felt like a greyhound trying to bring down a mechanical rabbit. Admit it, he told himself, you don't know what you're doing. This is so far beyond you it might as well be on another pl– well, the TARDIS is on another planet, isn't it, or at least from one. No wonder th– Concentrate!

'Here's something,' said Molecross. Ethan jumped across to see the screen. 'It's like one of those find-your-route programs, a map of places and how to get to them. The emergency generator thingy is in the off-line room.'

'Oh, wonderful,' Ethan muttered. 'Who can make sense of it? It's a bloody maze.'

Molecross put a finger on the screen. 'Here's the way to go from here.'

'So what?'

'Well, perhaps the TARDIS will help. Like it helps us find our way through the corridors.'

Ethan hit Print. 'Ace was spot on,' he admitted. 'When you're right, you're really right.'

And in the event, Molecross was indeed right. For the first few turns, Ethan consulted the printed-out map, then he abandoned it. The TARDIS knew where they wanted to go and how to get them there. As it apparently shifted walls to help them, Ethan wondered whether all the rooms moved around now and then – if the map they had now was the same as the one they'd call up a week later: 'Isn't this the door?'

'I think so, but I don't know why I think so.'

'Looking Glass World,' said Ethan, and opened the door. They stared at the walls of machinery. 'This isn't good.'

'Perhaps the TARDIS will guide us to the right machine.'

Ethan took a few steps in. 'No, we're on our own.' He pushed back past Molecross. 'I need to find a computer – get a map of this room. Wait here.'

He ran down the hall. Molecross looked around confusedly. The machinery was almost absurdly old-fashioned, with buttons and lights and metres; not even digital. Because it was easier to fix if it broke down? Because the Doctor, incredible to think, didn't quite trust the superb technology that ran his ship? Or did he just like to play with machines when he had an excuse? Molecross understood that. He still mourned the changeover of pinball machines from manual to digital. Something tactile had been lost.

Most of the buttons were labelled; he was no longer surprised to see they were in English. Probably everyone saw them in their own language. Not that the labels meant anything to him. He certainly wasn't going to find one as simple as, 'Emergency Generator, On.' For example, this door with a small ruby-coloured window was called an 'Artron Energy Capacitor', whatever the hell that was. Molecross eyed the words thought-fully. Could it have anything to do with that mysterious energy Ethan had been talking about? He peered through the window. Something like an enormous metal coil rose up out of sight; he couldn't see it clearly through the tinted glass. How extraordinary. In spite of all the danger, how extraordinary. Aloud, he whispered sadly, 'I don't want to go home.'

'Molecross!'

'Here!'

Ethan ran up, print-out in hand. 'What's that?' Molecross pointed to the sign.

Ethan read it quickly, then again, more slowly. 'Interesting. But never mind that now. I think I've found what we need.'

He led Molecross to yet another panel of buttons and levers and lights. 'It's not even labelled,' Molecross complained.

'As if that would do us any good.' Ethan adjusted his glasses and went carefully over the print-out. 'The procedure appears straightforward enough.'

He began pushing and switching things. A little nervously, Molecross stepped back. This was the point at which, in a movie, something might accidentally blow up. He returned to the capacitor and realised that what he'd taken for a door had no handle. It was an observation window only – the actual entrance must be somewhere else. The capacitor wasn't part of the off-line system.

The room went black.

'Don't panic!' Ethan yelled 'It's all right!' With a hum, the lights came back on. 'Where are you?'

'I'm coming.' Molecross found Ethan leaning against the machine, grinning in relief. 'Everything all right, then?'

'Well, no. Brett's still infiltrating the TARDIS. But at least we won't suffocate in the near future.'

'That capacitor is in a different room. I think it may be on line.'

'Hm.' Ethan shuffled through his print-outs. 'On and off, apparently. The capacitor itself isn't on line, but the controls for the energy release are. I'd like to find those. If Brett turned something off, which seems likely, then I think we ought to turn it on again.'

CHAPTER TWENTY-SIX

There was blue in the hill Ace was climbing, deep down, like the blue she'd seen in ice. This was the first nuance in the dull sameness of the landscape, and she took it as... well, not a bad sign.

She wanted to call for the Doctor, but that didn't seem like a good idea. He'd come here to meet something after all, and probably the something was still around. Unless it wasn't. The Doctor wasn't fool enough to rely solely on diplomacy; he always had a trick in reserve. Which was just as well since, if she understood this whole business properly, he'd be trying to talk some civilisation out of continuing to exist. Naff, really. Who'd ever agree to that? The trouble with the Doctor was, he was naive. He really thought he could reason with psychopaths. It was touching, part of the reason she loved him, but he was damn lucky to have her as a backup.

Above her, she could see what looked like a dark gash in the whiteness. A cave? Here? She started to run and in a minute was peering into a wide crack. Looked like a cave. Sort of. At any rate, a few yards down, the passage opened out into a larger space. She crept towards this.

The first thing she noticed was the domed ceiling. The second was the machine.

Incredulously, Ace stepped into the room. At its centre rose an extraordinary structure of gears and levers and pendulums, all intricately fitted together and all of ice, or something that looked like ice. None of the elements was moving – perhaps it wasn't a machine at all, but a sculpture. As she watched, the Doctor trotted around from the back and paused to polish a bit of cog with his handkerchief.

'Professor!'

He looked up, smiled in happy surprise, and waved. Then he went back to fussing over the cog. Ace went towards him slowly – something was very, very wrong.

'Hello, Ace!' he said cheerfully, his Scots burr stronger than usual. 'Excellent to see you. How are you?'

'Better than you,' she muttered. Raising her voice, she said, 'What's this then?'

He clasped his hands in front of his chest, admiring the device. 'Beautiful, isn't it?'

'What's it do?'

'Do?' he said vaguely. 'What should it do?'

'It doesn't move, then?'

He shook his head violently. 'Movement,' he explained in a low voice, 'is to be discouraged.'

Round the twist. Well, nothing she couldn't handle. 'Very pretty. Let's go then.'

'Go!' he said in alarm.

'Yeah, go, Professor. Back to the TARDIS.' She took his arm. He knocked her hand away.

'Don't be silly. I'm not finished yet!'

'Right,' said Ace supportively, considering how best to proceed. 'Sorry. I forgot. So, when will you be finished?'

'Never,' said a toneless voice from across the room.

Ace stared at the tall, white, thin thing. A bloody worm, she thought. Only with hands and a head. 'What are you? One of those scumbags who's caused all the trouble?'

The Doctor climbed inside the machine and began smoothing bits with his pocket laser. She glanced at him worriedly. The thing crossed to her, stately, even dignified. She didn't like the way its colourless eyes blurred and cleared.

'Aren't you supposed to be numbers?'

'I am numbers. What you see is –'

'– an illusion. Right. Been there. What have you done to the Professor?'

'Simply released him to be himself.'

She snorted. 'That's not him.'

'No?'

'I mean, it's him, but it's not him. He's not some nutter building a useless machine.'

'It's not useless, Ace,' said the Doctor from within. 'Beauty is not useless.'

'It's not beautiful, either.'

He poked his head out between two gears. 'How dare you!' he screamed. Ace flinched. The Doctor's head vanished back inside.

'All right,' she said to the thing. 'What've you done to him?'

'You ought to go,' it said. 'This is no place for you.'

'Him neither.' Ace ducked under a lever and began to climb up to the Doctor. 'Professor...'

He was straddling some sort of axle and planing a gear edge just so. 'Leave me alone.'

'Look, something's happened to you.' The substance was certainly slick as ice, and gripping it chilled her ungloved hands. 'You need to get out of here.'

He turned a furious scowl on her and she stopped, shocked.

'Out of here? Out of *here*?!'

'You're only upsetting him,' said the thing.

'Shut up!' Ace screamed. 'Professor...' He was back at work. She climbed closer. 'Listen to me. It's all right. Only...'

She touched his arm. He spun and hit her, and she crashed down through the gears, landing in fragments of ice. 'Professor!' The Doctor ignored her. 'You've done this!' she yelled at the white thing. 'Put him back like he was!'

'This is how he was. It simply didn't show. Look how happy he is. Order, cleanliness, stasis. Everything in place. No grit in the timeline. No bumps in the universe. He has what he's always wanted.'

'You're lying!' she yelled. She felt stupid and helpless, like a tantrumy child. 'You're lying! Put him back!'

'Has he ever hit you before?'

'That wasn't him!' To her fury, she had begun to cry. 'That was you!'

It shook its head gently. 'Go home now.'

'Not without him.'

'He stays here. He knows so much that we need.'

'Then I'm staying too!'

'Without food or water?'

'*With* him!'

'If you wish, then. Everything is over anyway.'

'What d'you mean?'

'We are in the TARDIS.'

'Liar!' she spat.

'It is the truth. I hope there is no one there about whom you care.'

Ace actually hissed, like a cat, and would have leaped at it, if it hadn't pixelled and reformed several feet away. 'Bloody coward,' she snarled. 'If I got at you –'

'You couldn't harm me in the least. Any more than you can help him. He's lost to you, little girl.'

She jammed a hand in her pocket. '*You're* lost, you –' But whatever else she said was lost under the Nitro Nine's explosion.

Crouched with her arms over her head, ice pelting her back, Ace wondered if that had been the right move. She expected the Doctor to fall on her any minute – what if she'd hurt him? Glancing up cautiously, she saw that he was still perched unconcernedly, polishing something, oblivious to any disturbance. Ace looked around the room. The thing was gone, but she had no idea whether she'd destroyed it or simply driven it away.

'Professor?' she called softly. She started to climb again. Her jaw hurt like hell; the git had a punch on him. She'd never let him forget this. And if he didn't even know it had happened, she'd tell him and then never let him forget it. Under her bravado, a child's voice was wailing, 'He hit me, he hit me!' She wiped her tears on her sleeve. 'Surprised you've got any friends,' she mumbled. 'More trouble than you're bloody worth, you are.'

When she came level with him, he smiled at her as though she'd just arrived. 'Hello, Ace. How've you been?'

'Not so good, really.' She wedged herself into a space between two cogs and watched him. He was polishing and cutting and polishing again. She remembered a pet mouse she'd had that would pile all its cage shavings in one corner and, when finished, immediately shift them all to another corner, and so on, back and forth. It had always looked so purposeful. Her voice cracked: 'Professor...'

'Yes?' he said pleasantly.

'What've they *done* to you?'

'I beg your pardon?' He smiled at her brightly. Her stomach clenched.

'Er, look,' she said carefully, 'I'm just going to touch your arm now, all right?'

'Of course. Why shouldn't it be?'

No reason, she thought, fingering her bruised jaw. 'Right, then.' She reached over and laid a hand on his busy wrist. He smiled indulgently. His skin was shockingly cold. She took a deep breath. 'You know, there's bits broken down below. You might want to have a look at them.'

'In good time,' he said comfortably.

His skin was so cold she couldn't continue to touch it. It was stiff too. 'They're freezing you,' she said miserably.

'Hm?'

'What's wrong? There was something wrong back in the TARDIS too. Ethan knew what it was.' He had no reaction. 'Can't you tell me? Don't you know any more?'

He began to hum. Ace put her face in her hands and cried, her tears scalding on her cold palms. 'Oh, Professor...' He didn't look round. 'Professor... Oh God, Doctor...' She leaned forward and hugged him. He shifted, smiling in embarrassment, but didn't push her away. She was sobbing loudly now.

'Now really Ace,' he said, kindly but firmly. 'This is a bit much. I have work to do, and you're in the way.'

'No...' She buried her face in the side of his neck, bawling and sniffling. In a remote area of her mind, she hoped she wasn't dripping snot on him. Her tears burned. 'Professor... no...'

'Ace, you're getting –'

'No... please. This can't... you can't...'

'Can't what? Really, you're being...' He faltered. 'Being...' She cried helplessly against him. 'Ace, I...'

She pulled back, eyes streaming. He looked at her dazedly, touched her face, put his palm against her face. 'You're so hot. Are you all right? Are you feverish?'

Ace sniffed loudly. His eyes were dark with concern. 'What is it? Why are you –' He looked down, gave a little jump, and grabbed onto a lever. 'Where in heaven's name are we?'

'We're on... This is...' She sniffed again and rubbed her hand irritably across her eyes. 'You built this.'

'I never.'

'You did.'

'No, honestly, Ace, I never had any talent for sculpture. I was the despair of my art teach– Hang on.' He gazed up, then around. 'I remember,' he murmured, and gripped her arm. 'You shouldn't be here. It's dangerous. You –' He broke off. 'How did you get here anyway?'

'Later, OK? We should go now.'

'Go?'

'Don't get all strange again. Come on.'

'We can't go,' he said heavily.

'What are you talking about.'

'I had a plan...'

'One of those plans that doesn't work?'

'Yes. It was meant... I wasn't going to survive it.'

'You bastard!' She tried to hit him but he caught her wrist.

'So I didn't work out a way back. There isn't one. We're trapped.'

'You bastard!' She was sobbing again. 'Run off like that... Stupid, stupid... Well, bollocks.' She raised her head and wiped her nose. 'No we're not bloody trapped. Not while I still have some Nitro Nine.'

'Cor,' said Molecross.

'Yeah,' said Ethan.

They were staring through a large tinted window into the capacitor chamber.

'It's big,' said Molecross.

'Very.' Ethan crossed to the computer and began calling up information. Molecross remained at the window, transfixed.

'D'you suppose it's actually a good idea to release the energy?'

'The Doctor programmed it to happen, and I doubt he'd have done anything to harm the TARDIS.'

'Where's he gone, anyway?'

'God knows. He made it up. Hm.'

'What?'

'The energy was supposed to be focused through a medium into the Doctor's construct.'

'What medium?'

Ethan scrolled down more and more slowly. 'The Doctor.'

'Oh no, that's mad!'

'I don't disagree, but he was going to do it. He and the TARDIS share an artron field. He'd be the barrel for the energy bullet.'

'But Ace is in there with him!'

'He didn't plan on that. He was just going to blow up and take the aliens with him. Nice of him to let us know.'

'He was afraid we'd stop him.'

'Oh yes, that's bloody likely. Why not stop an electron or two while we're at it.' Ethan slammed a hand on the keyboard. 'This is so ballsed up only a genius could have done it.'

'We need to get him back.'

'Unfortunately, yes.'

'Oh, no, no, no, no,' said Brett. 'Bad idea.'

Molecross jumped. Ethan stiffened but didn't look around. 'Aren't you supposed to be screwing up the files?'

'This is much more interesting. Turn and face me, young Amberglass. I don't enjoy looking at your back.' Ethan turned. Brett nodded. 'That's better. Good manners are always in order.'

'What do you want?' said Molecross weakly. Brett squinted at him.

'Who are you again?'

'Adrian Molecross. I'm a journalist.'

Brett flinched delicately. 'Not the sort of company I usually keep.'

'Stop it with the upper-class snot thing,' said Ethan, 'and tell me what you want.'

Brett turned toward the door to the capacitor chamber. 'I want that.'

'Then why haven't you taken it?'

'I can't. Though the controls that modify and release it are on line, the energy itself isn't. We could take over the entire TARDIS system and not access it.'

'And if you connect with it now, that gives you plenty of power while you're waiting to harvest the rest of the ship.'

'I always said you were clever.' Brett looked through the window. 'Impressive. This whole place is astonishing. I'd never have dreamed there was such a thing.' He shimmered slightly and appeared denser. 'I'll need a bit of solidity for this.'

Ethan stared. 'Surely you don't think you can get the capacitor on line by touching it.'

'I have no interest in getting the capacitor on line. I also contain a code for transforming into a conduit. We will tap the energy directly, using it to power its own transfer.' He turned his head slightly, eyes distant. The door's computerised lock clicked. Brett opened it.

Ethan stood up, he had no idea why. He couldn't think of a

damned thing to do. 'It will kill you,' he said inadequately.

Brett snorted. 'You really haven't understood, have you? I'm not even alive,' – and he strolled into the chamber.

The door began to shut, but Molecross ran and blocked it with his body. Inside, Brett approached the capacitor thoughtfully, hands behind his back. In the red light, he was reduced to stark contrasts of light and shadow – a figure in a black-and-white film. Molecross knew he must be communicating with the others, receiving directions. With a grunt, he squeezed through the door. It slammed and locked behind him.

Ace ran over the hills, dragging the Doctor. He was disorientated and stumbling, but stayed on his feet until she slipped going downhill and he fell into her. They slid to the bottom, and when Ace sat up, the being was looming in front of them. Seeing it now, Ace realised there was something familiar about it, though she couldn't think what.

'No,' it said. 'The Doctor must stay.'

Ace grabbed for her Nitro Nine, but the Doctor put his hand on her wrist. 'That's no use.' He was lying on his stomach, his hat fallen over his eyes. Now he raised the brim and looked steadily at the being. It smiled, not quite believing.

'You would fight me on my own ground?'

'Ace,' said the Doctor. 'Don't watch this.'

'But I –'

'Don't watch!'

She turned away and covered her eyes. The being remained incredulous.

'Did you learn nothing before?'

'Before I wasn't ready.' The Doctor stood up. 'Shall we dance?'

Brett looked over at Molecross curiously. 'You can't stop me.'

'I know,' said Molecross. Behind him, Ethan hit the window and slammed it with his fists.

'Unbreakable,' Brett said.

'Well, it would be, wouldn't it?' Molecross approached the capacitor, craning his neck to see the top. 'All of this...' he said, 'I never thought I'd see it. I was certain it existed, but I'd never see it.'

'Then this is a touching moment.'

'I've experienced wonders now,' Molecross confided.

'Very nice for you.'

'So what's going to happen? Will a ray shoot through you?'

'Put crudely, yes.'

'Won't it destroy the TARDIS systems?'

'No. I've set all the infiltration programs in motion and disconnected.'

Molecross nodded seriously. 'Wonders,' he repeated.

'I'm sorry, but I won't be able to continue this fascinating conversation. I have work to do.'

Brett shut his eyes and his head fell back. His form shimmered. Connection established, thought Molecross. Absurdly happy, he stepped between Brett and the capacitor. As Brett jerked and glared, Molecross threw his arms joyfully around him.

Then the energy shattered them both to atoms.

This time, when he was sliced apart, the Doctor refused to be reassembled. He willed his spinning self to a still place, and began to translate his thought processes into mathematics. Dimly, he felt the being tugging, trying to get hold of his numbers and put them together logically. The Doctor thought not. He had no wish at all, in fact, to engage it on its own ground. That would be suicide. Perhaps this was suicide anyway. The thing had abruptly surged with power. The Doctor fought to stay scattered, but it was pulling him relentlessly, shaping him into a formula it could corrupt. He dodged and twisted, felt himself falling into order, set up to be disordered for good –

Then its grip loosened. The Doctor squirmed free. Immediately, he began to shift rapidly in and out of numerical combinations. He formed himself into equations that depended for solution on imaginary numbers – that should discourage his opponent. And indeed, he felt it reject him like poison. No, no: don't go away. Just let me get hold of one little equation, needn't even be a complicated one – his numbers shifted and regrouped, snatching at the being's equations. No. No. No. Ah! He trapped the string of numbers in parentheses and drew it close. This was simple. In fact, this was rather fun. He understood what Ethan saw in it. Although the task was hardly challenging. He simply moved a couple of numbers and changed a plus to a minus...

He snapped back to himself. Something had hit him very, very hard. Ace was yelling and shaking him. 'Stop that. I'm all right.' She stopped. The Doctor opened his eyes and sat up. The being was nowhere to be seen.

'It collapsed,' she gasped. 'Or something.'

The Doctor nodded, drawing deep breaths. 'Imploded. Computed to zero.'

'What?'

'It was made of equations. With a few tweaks and additions, you can rearrange any equation so that its answer is zero.'

She sat back, impressed. 'Well brilliant.'

'It was rather clever of me,' he agreed. 'It's one entity really, so now all of them/it are nothing. Not that they were much in the first place. They were as close to nil as anything that exists can be.'

CHAPTER TWENTY-SEVEN

The Doctor put up a stone to Molecross next to an ancient church not far from his cottage, then went through his files and distributed them among the subscribers to the *Miscellany*. Afterwards, he visited a certain London alley and regarded with satisfaction the lettering across a pair of junkyard doors: I M FOREMAN.

The spring thaw exposed Unwin's body. Animals had been at it. The village authorities buried him in their paupers' graveyard.

Briefed by the Doctor, the Brigadier wrote up his report and sealed it in his most secure file: a hidden safe in the UNIT basement.

Ace and Ethan said many intimate goodbyes. She promised to visit him often and she did, always the same while he grew older, always acting as if she'd seen him only yesterday, which was sometimes the case. Their friendship went on for one of her years and four of his, until the day he collapsed.

CHAPTER TWENTY-EIGHT

What little was left of Ethan's mind spent its time dozing. When awake, in the sense that word could be used, it did something that in a complete brain would have been called dreaming. From time to time, a spark of self-consciousness gleamed, but no tinder struck – Ethan vaguely noted his situation, was relieved there was no pain, occasionally wondered where his body was and how it was doing, and then went away. Needless to say, there were no visitors.

Which was why, he thought ironically, he should have expected the Doctor.

Ethan actually saw him. It was the first sharp, stable image he'd seen in... well, however long he'd been like this. The Doctor's appearance was – not unexpectedly – what Ethan remembered: the improbably spotless ivory suit, the elegant waistcoat, the absurd hat. No umbrella, which was actually a bit of a relief.

'I didn't think you'd like it,' said the Doctor. 'You always found it a bit ludicrous, didn't you?'

'Now that there are no secrets between us... Are you reading my mind?'

'In a way. I'm *in* your mind.'

'Oh.'

'I realise it's a bit of an intrusion.'

'No,' said Ethan – if this sort of conversation involved saying anything, which he doubted. 'I'm glad of the company.' The Doctor looked down. 'No sympathy necessary. Sometimes I hear music – you know, the way you can, full orchestra. A lot of Bach. Mostly, I'm just not here. It's no hardship – a bit like the place between wake and sleeping. Hypnapompia. Soon to be psychopompia.'

'Not that soon, I'm sorry to say.'

Had Ethan shoulders, he would have shrugged. 'It's not a hardship,' he repeated.

'Would you like...' The Doctor hesitated. 'I could arrange for you to experience something like corporeality. If you want.'

'Why not?' said Ethan, and found himself standing in front of the Doctor. He examined his hands, which looked as they always had, and his feet, which were wearing trainers. 'This is more for your convenience than mine, isn't it?'

'Now that there are no secrets between us... I confess, I find it difficult to talk to someone who lacks definition. Always have. It's a limitation in my line of work.'

'Yes,' Ethan acknowledged. The Doctor produced a pair of club chairs – Ethan couldn't recall if he'd seen something like them at Allen Road – and they sat down. 'Tea?' said the Doctor.

'Yes, thanks. It would be nice to taste something.'

'It doesn't have to be tea. Perhaps some nice cheese?'

'Tea's fine for a start.'

'Or chocolate?'

'Chocolate.'

The chocolate pot appeared, along with mugs and a little table. The Doctor poured. Ethan had to admit it was extraordinary to taste again. Tears pricked at the eyes he didn't have. 'This might be a mistake.'

'No,' said the Doctor, 'you'll remember, but you won't regret. Trust me.'

'No choice, is there?'

'No.' The Doctor sipped his own chocolate.

'Are you here – I mean, nearby – or is this some long-distance telepathic thing?'

'I'm in your hospital room.'

'Where is it?'

'I persuaded UNIT to take you in. All agreed you were owed it. You have a private room –'

'So I won't repel the neighbours.'

'– and the best medical care. You don't look repellent. A bit wasted, obviously, but otherwise as if you were asleep. The nurses shave you.'

'Hooked up to an IV?'

The Doctor nodded. 'Actually, your swallowing reflex still works. But there's a danger you might aspirate.'

'Can't have that.'

'They are trained *not* to kill people, you know. And it's not as if you're being kept alive by machine. The only way for you to go would be if they let you starve. They won't do that.'

Silence for a bit.

'How long...?'

'How long to go or how long has it been?'

'To go.'

'Hard to say. Possibly another year. Maybe longer.'

'And how long...?'

'Twenty months.'

More silence.

'Your brother's been to see you several times.'

'That's good of him. We weren't close. Has...' Ethan poured himself another cup of chocolate. 'Has Ace stopped by?'

'Often. She's here now. She's holding your hand.'

Ethan put a hand to his eyes and sat like that for a long time. At least it seemed to him a long time. Finally he said, 'Can she...'

'Come in? No. If she could, she'd be here.'

Just as well, thought Ethan, then realised he might as well have spoken. The Doctor nodded, agreeing.

'How long has it been for the two of you?'

'I'm not precisely certain. Longer than twenty months.'

'Had plenty of jolly adventures?'

'No,' said the Doctor. 'Interesting, though. This last one, I visited your moon. Also my own mind.'

'How'd you like it?'

'It wasn't as nice as yours.'

I dare say not, thought Ethan, then remembered that thinking was talking. But the Doctor only smiled sadly. 'You'd think after six previous lifetimes, I'd be better at...'

'What?'

'I don't know. Life. I wish...' Suddenly the Doctor's umbrella was there, and he rested his chin on it. 'Sometimes I wish I could have my memory wiped clean. Start fresh. I was very idealistic in the beginning, and often amusing. You'd have liked me.'

'I don't dislike you. It's difficult to have any attitude towards you, really. You're unknowable... How is Ace?'

'I will always take care of Ace,' the Doctor snapped. 'Always. She doesn't need protecting from me.'

'Of course she does. We all do. You bring the storm on your back.'

'Not always.'

'Always. You're like any force, sometimes benevolent, sometimes not. You destroy worlds. I was there.'

'They were as good as dead already.'

'You don't have to defend yourself to me. I'm alive because they're not. So are billions of others.'

'I'm not...' But the Doctor didn't finish. Ethan couldn't hear *his* thoughts, but they weren't hard to read. 'It recognised me, you know.'

'Knew you were the Doctor?'

'Knew me for one of it's own. Sensed the ice in my heart, hearts. I don't think ice was always there. Perhaps I'm fooling myself.'

'Ace said there was nothing to bringing you back, that as soon as she found you everything was fine. Is that true?'

'No.'

'How did she save you?'

'How?' The Doctor smiled. 'She was alive.'

'I'm sorry?' said Ethan. 'You weren't dead. Were you?'

'No. But she... She's strong.'

'I'm not following this,' said Ethan, a shade irritably. 'You're not strong? All you do is bang around facing danger. Monsters, aliens, monstrous aliens.'

The Doctor said nothing for a while, then he sighed. 'You know, a playwright of yours, Anton Chekhov, once said something along the lines of, "Any fool can handle a crisis, what takes strength is the ordinary day-to-day problems." I don't have any ordinary day-to-day problems. No family to take care of, no job to perform. No small futile tasks. I made sure I wouldn't have them. I travel from crisis to crisis. I drop in, I brilliantly fix things, and then I'm gone. I don't even clean up after myself. What happens to them, all those beings I've saved and left behind? Not my problem.'

Ethan thought about his beautiful numbers. Clean as bone. No messy, leaking, aging, hurting, dying flesh. Yes, he thought matter-of-factly, it's true. He'd sensed it all that time ago, when he heard Unwin rant against life, and now he saw it whole. He'd always been afraid. In his own way, he'd hated life. Just like poor Molecross chasing after the wondrous. Just like Unwin with *his* numbers, and Brett with his annihilating savagery. And like the Doctor as well. None of them could face the world. The only one of them truly alive was Ace.

'Yes,' said the Doctor. 'Without her, what would I be? What would I become?'

After a time, Ethan said, 'Well, I didn't want a life, and I didn't get one.'

The Doctor lowered his eyes. 'I'm sorry,' he said. 'I'm terribly sorry.'

'It's not down to you. I was going to die anyway. You'd sussed that, hadn't you?'

'It was a reasonable presumption. Hallucinations, headaches and a shift in the eye's processing speed can all be linked to a tumour; three of them in one place almost guaranteed it. And then when the alien fled you, that more or less proved the case. You were too damaged to provide a home.'

'Ah,' said Ethan. 'I'd wondered about that. So I was going to die, but not soon enough to thwart Brett.'

'Not nearly soon enough.'

'Still, you were only planning to lop off a few years.'

'That doesn't matter,' said the Doctor flatly. 'I'm not surprised you've never forgiven me.'

Ethan considered this. 'I haven't, have I?'

'No. And don't waste what time you have left trying.'

'It doesn't work like that. People always talk about forgiveness as if it's an act of will. But it either happens or it doesn't.'

'You're right, of course.'

'I know you believed it was for the best.'

The Doctor snorted. 'In the event, your death would have been a disaster. The TARDIS would even now be fuelling the destruction of the cosmos. I was so certain I knew what to do, so willing to sacrifice moral duty to the greater need. But I'd have both murdered you *and* defeated my purpose. A fine achievement.'

'But at the end of the day, you must always have to guess. An informed guess, but still...'

'Yes,' said the Doctor wearily. 'I make terrible choices, and I can't be sure of the ends. It's the road I've chosen.'

'Perhaps you should have stayed home.'

The Doctor had removed his hat and was rotating it in his hands. 'You may be right. I hope not. It's too late now.'

'You poor sod,' said Ethan quietly, 'I don't envy your life.' And he realised that at some unnoticed point in just the past few minutes, he had forgiven the Doctor.

'What about some cake?'

'Yes, thank you.'

A plate of cakes appeared. They munched on these for a while.

'You gave me the best part of my life, you and Ace.'

'That's kind of you to say,' the Doctor murmured. 'And in the case of Ace, undoubtedly true. I *would* like to give you something, though. That's why I came.'

'I had wondered.'

'I'd thought about it for a while, trying to work out what I could do. If anything. I wanted to... I know you say it's not bad for you, and I believe you. I believe you have peace. But I want to give you joy.'

'You really are an arrogant bastard,' said Ethan, almost admiringly. 'Give me joy? Now? In my condition?'

'Of course now and in your condition,' the Doctor said impatiently. 'It would hardly do you much good otherwise.' He stood up. 'Come with me,' he ordered, striding away. Ethan grabbed the last cake before following.

They walked in nothing. Actually, Ethan reminded himself, they weren't walking at all. This was the Doctor's willed dream. A door appeared and the Doctor opened it and stepped through. 'Come along,' he said, when Ethan hesitated.

'Why do we even need a door?'

'We don't. But I wanted a proper set-up.' The Doctor plucked Ethan's sleeve and brought him over the threshold. He found himself on a promontory overlooking a cloud-filled valley.

'Set-up for what?'

Like a conjuror, the Doctor swept his umbrella over the clouds. They fled in mist, and below him Ethan saw a landscape of peaks and valleys, not of earth and rock but of lines and curves, a graphed world of numbers. 'Follow it. Wander. Explore. I give it to you.'

'What is it?' Ethan whispered, his heart, his real heart, rising. He turned and looked into the alien, sky blue eyes. Fly into them. Fly free. Fly forever.

'Something no other human being will see for hundreds of years.' The Doctor clasped Ethan's shoulder, and his cold little hand felt warm. 'The proof of the Riemann hypothesis.'

ACKNOWLEDGEMENTS

Thanks to:

Todd Bethel, for listening, technical support and the suggestion
- unfortunately not usable - that the aliens are defeated because
they can only manifest in our reality as ducks.

Joe Adams, for his advice on music and maths.

Rita Kempley, for an extremely helpful suggestion.

Ed Schneider, for technical support.

Hans Christian Andersen.

And, finally, the authors of the New Adventures.

ABOUT THE AUTHOR

Lloyd Rose is the pen name of Sarah Tonyn, who lives with her sisters in the quaint village of Adverse Camber. Her solicitors are Hinchcliffe, Holmes and Baker.

Coming soon from
BBC *Doctor Who* books:

The Deadstone Memorial

by Trevor Baxendale
Published 4 October 2004
ISBN 0 563 48622 8

Featuring the Eighth Doctor

There is no such thing as a good night. You may think you
can hide away in dreams. Safely tucked up in bed, nothing
can touch you. But, as every child knows, there are bad dreams.
And bad dreams are where the monsters are.

The Doctor knows all about monsters. And he knows they
don't just live in your nightmares – sometimes, they can still be
there when you wake up. And when the horror is more than
just a memory, there is nowhere to hide.

Even here, today, tonight, in the most ordinary of homes,
and against the most ordinary people, the terror will strike. A
young boy will suffer terrifying visions.and his family will
encounter a deathless horror.

Only the Doctor can help – but first he must uncover the
fearsome secret of the Deadstone Memorial.

Recently published:

Halflife
by Mark Michalowski
ISBN 0 563 48613 9
Featuring the Eighth Doctor

'To lose one set of memories may be regarded as a misfortune.
To lose two smacks of carelessness.'

The Terran colony world of Espero seems the unlikely source of
a sophisticated distress call. And the Doctor, Fitz and Trix are not
the only ones responding to it.

While Fitz consorts with royalty, the Doctor's on the run
with a 16-year-old girl, and Trix meets a small
boy with a dark secret.

In a race for the minds and souls of an entire planet, the Doctor
and Trix are offered temptations that may
change them forever.

At least one of them will be unable to resist.

Recently published:

The Eleventh Tiger
by David McIntee
ISBN 0 563 48614 7
Featuring the First Doctor, Ian, Barbara
and Vicki

In interesting times, love can be a weakness, hatred an
illusion, order chaos, and ten Tigers not enough.

The TARDIS crew have seen many times. When they arrive in
China in 1865, they find banditry, rebellion and foreign
oppression rife. Trying to maintain order are the British Empire
and the Ten Tigers of Canton, the most respected martial
arts masters in the world.

There is more to chaos than mere human violence and
ambition. Can legends of ancient vengeance be coming true?
Why does everyone Ian meets already know who he is? The
Doctor has his suspicions, but he is occupied by challenges
of his own.

Sometimes the greatest danger is not from the enemy, but
from the heart.

Recently published:

The Tomorrow Windows
by Jonathan Morris
ISBN 0 563 48616 3
Featuring the Eighth Doctor

There is a gala opening for a new exhibition at Tate Modern,
'The Tomorrow Windows'. The concept is simple: anyone can
look through a Tomorrow Window and see into the future.
They can see what will happen next week, next year, or
next century.

Of course, the future is malleable and will change as you
formulate your plans. You can see the outcome of every
potential decision, and then decide on the optimum course
of action. According to the press pack, the Tomorrow Windows
will bring about world peace and save humanity from every
possible disaster.

So, of course, someone decides to blow it up. There's always
one, isn't there?

As the Doctor investigates and unravels the conspiracy, he
begins a Gulliver's Travels-esque quest, visiting bizarre worlds
and encountering many peculiar and surreal life forms...

Recently published:

Synthespians™
by Craig Hinton
ISBN 0 563 48617 1
Featuring the Sixth Doctor and Peri

In the 111th century, nostalgia is everything. TV from the
20th century is the new obsession, and Reef Station One is
receiving broadcasts from a distant Earth of the past. *Dixon
of Dock Green* and *Z-Cars* are ratings winners – and the
inhabitants of the New Earth Republic can't get enough.

But there are other forces that need Reef Station One. An
ancient-but-dying race sees this human outpost as a last hope
for survival, and millionaire Walter J. Matheson III sees it as a
marvellous business opportunity.

When the Doctor and Peri arrive they find a fractured
society dependent on film and TV. They also discover that the
Republic's greatest entrepreneur is in league with one of the
Doctor's oldest enemies.

The Doctor and Peri must unravel the link between Matheson's
business empire and the Nestenes. Because if they don't, they
could end up in the deadliest soap opera of all time...

Recently published:

The Sleep of Reason
by Martin Day
ISBN 0 563 48620 1
Featuring the Eighth Doctor

Caroline 'Laska' Darnell is a perfectly normal nineteen-year-old:
worried in equal measure about boyfriends, acne and exams. The
latest in a long line of suicide attempts sees her admitted to the
Retreat, a ground-breaking medical centre.

To her horror, she recognises the Retreat from her recent
nightmares. Laska knows that something is very wrong with the
institute. But who will believe her stories of an evil from the past
that has already made one attempt to destroy the building and all
its inhabitants? Laska inadvertently stumbles on the truth
surrounding her father's death – and realises that her family are
intimately connected with the history of the Retreat.

Laska discovers that the Retreat was once an asylum that almost
burnt to the ground in 1902. Her research brings her to the
attention of one of the Retreat's medical officers, the mysterious Dr
Smith, and his friends Fitz and Trix. Smith seems curiously aware of
the Retreat's past, and is utterly fascinated by Laska's waking dreams
and prophetic nightmares. But if Laska is unable to trust her own
perceptions, can she trust Dr Smith?

And, all the while, the long-dead hounds draw near…